BLACK DANCE

Also by Nancy Huston

Infrared

Fault Lines

An Adoration

Dolce Agonia

Prodigy

The Mark of the Angel

Instruments of Darkness

Slow Emergencies

The Goldberg Variations

Plainsong

The Story of Omaya

BLACK DANCE

NANCY HUSTON

Black Cat
New York

Originally published in French in 2013 by Editions Actes Sud, Paris.

Published simultaneously in Canada
Printed in the United States of America

FIRST EDITION

ISBN 978-0-8021-2271-1
eISBN 978-0-8021-9265-3

Black Cat
an imprint of Grove/Atlantic, Inc.
154 West 14th Street
New York, NY 10011

Distributed by Publishers Group West

www.groveatlantic.com

14 15 16 17   10 9 8 7 6 5 4 3 2 1

to Jean M.
and to Jennifer A.
and thanks to Joseph N.

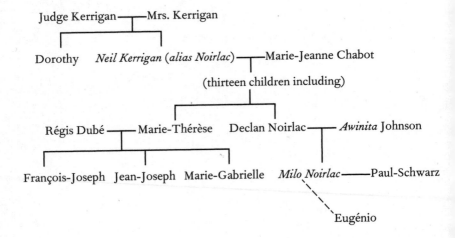

CONTENTS

I LADAINHA 1

Milo, 2010/1990
Neil, April 1910
Awinita, March 1951

II GINGA 21

Milo, 1952–56
Neil, May 1914
Awinita, April 1951

III MOLEQUE 43

Milo, 1956–58
Neil, 1916
Awinita, May 1951

IV MALÍCIA 65

Milo, 1958–62
Neil, September 1917
Awinita, June 1951

V TERREIRO 97

Milo, 1962–65
Neil, 1918
Awinita, July 1951

VI FLOREIO 125

Milo, 1965–67
Neil, 1919
Awinita, August 1951

VII MALANDRO 157

Milo, 1967–70
Neil, 1920
Awinita, September 1951

VIII SAUDADE 187

Milo, 1970–75
Neil, 1920–23
Awinita, October 1951

IX NEGAÇA 209

Milo, 1975–90
Neil, 1927
Awinita, January 1952

X BICHO FALSO 237

Milo, 1990–2005
Neil, 1939
Awinita, March 1952

I

LADAINHA

*Litany. Song that signals the beginning of a
capoeira* roda, *before the game begins.*

Milo, 2010/1990

DON'T WORRY, ASTUTO, I'll do the keyboard this time. I'll capture it—or seize it, as the French say. That was always your job, on pretext that you typed faster than me . . . yeah, but chances were you'd either get your computer ripped off in a train station or accidentally erase—*Oops, goddamn it!*—a whole month of our work including backup, so this time you can relax and let me handle it. Take advantage of the fact that you're flat on your back and hooked up to a drip to give your ten fingers a rest.

I love you, you bastard. Tell me your tale. Yeah, or at least a piece of it, ha-ha. Don't make me laugh, you'll make me cry. Come on, Milo, get serious. In all likelihood, this will be the last screenplay cowritten by Milo Noirlac and Paul Schwarz, directed by Paul Schwarz and produced by Blackout Films—so let's get it right, babe, let's get it really right. Kiss me. Come on, kiss me, you meshuga bastard, I won't catch anything. I love your ass off.

OKAY, THIS IS just a suggestion . . . INTERIOR—DAY. The camera finds Milo Noirlac—graying mahogany ponytail hanging halfway down his back, black cowboy hat, cowboy boots, white pants—and Paul Schwarz—wearing a new, unbleached linen suit that makes him look even svelter and more sensual than usual—in the crowded foyer of a tiny cultural center in Rio's Zona Norte. It's late morning, they've just screened their film for the men and women of the neighborhood who played bit parts in it, the response has been warm, people come up to hug, congratulate and thank them.

Given that the important producer/director of the film has a whole slew of important appointments with important distributors set up for the afternoon, he'll be driven to Centro by an important taxi. The more modest (though naturally no less handsome) screenwriter announces his intention of returning on foot to their hotel in Gloria. *Are you out of your mind? That's a five-mile walk and it's forty degrees Celsius out there!* says his gifted collaborator and favorite lay, who has never held much truck with high temperatures, as he mops his brow.

But Milo, giving his beloved a last touch on the arm, turns and saunters out into the street. As he moves away, close-up on that beautiful ass of his, charmingly molded by his white pants. Don't worry, baby—much as I'd like to, I won't overdo it . . . We'll be with you, inside of you, subjective camera: in your brain we hear the distinctive atabaque rhythm of capoeira—*ta, ta-da DA, ta, ta-da DA, ta, ta-da DA* . . . must be a *roda* going on nearby.

Upon emerging from the low white building, Milo turns left instead of right on Rua General Roca and heads for the hills. We follow him following the drumbeat beneath the hot sun. If there's a *roda* going on, he wants to join it, but he can't hear the twang of the berimbau, only the drumbeat, *ta, ta-da DA, ta, ta-da DA, ta, ta-da DA* . . . the one we listened to night after night as we lay in bed together in Arraial d'Ajuda—the one you *recognized* all those years ago on our first trip to Salvador, the one you think of as your heart call, your root call, the rhythm of your mother's voice. Important to establish that right from the start.

The drumbeat intensifies.

The minute General Roca starts up the hill, the Saens Peña area—a flat, dreary patch of urban sprawl with the sort of gray ten- and fifteen-story high-rises that can be found anywhere in the developing world—falls away and the neighborhood swiftly slides from moderate to abject poverty. No more whites or light browns, nothing but blacks. Milo's arms swing at his side, his hands are empty. Images of the Dublin slums, the Waswanipi Cree reserve, his father's rooming house in Montreal ricochet and reverberate in the scorching sunlight. Sweat pours down his brow and neck and back but he doesn't wipe it off. Men idling in doorways stare as he passes and he lets them stare . . .

(Oh, Milo! I once thought of it as rashness; your ex-wife Yolaine used to call it passivity . . . *If you leave me, you leave me,* you once told her, and today, were a crack addict to threaten you at gunpoint, you'd look him calmly in the eye and say, *If you kill me, you kill me* . . . But it's neither recklessness nor passivity, it's capoeira. Lack of fear and jealousy, openness, curiosity, indifference—all your character traits derive from the capoeira attitude, which you'd espoused long before you discovered the Brazilian fight-dance.)

As Milo advances the incline grows steeper, the drumbeat louder, the sun hotter. A bright green church looms up on the hill above him and again, because of the color green, he thinks of Ireland, a country he's never set foot in. *Ta, ta-da DA, ta, ta-da DA, ta, ta-da DA* . . . He sees dilapidated three- and four-story concrete blocks, their walls painted in peeling pastel colors and streaked with graffiti, and because of the corrugated tin roofs, he again thinks of the reserve, which he also doesn't know. Sunlight.

Black people staring at him. Tropical greenery. Tough dusty roots and grasses, leaves and vines. Gutted buildings. *Ta, ta-da DA, ta, ta-da DA, ta, ta-da DA.* Cement walls give onto gapingly empty ideas of rooms. The rise steepens again. He passes a staircase drowning in creepers and studded with broken glass, sees the remains of a candomblé altar, nothing left of it but an electric cross with all but one of its lightbulbs smashed, a few chipped statues of African gods and goddesses amidst dust and cigarette butts. The world reverberates, beats and glitters, summoning Milo with dreamlike intensity. *Ta, ta-da DA, ta, ta-da DA, ta, ta-da DA . . .*

Turning a corner, he finds himself face-to-face with a wild-haired, middle-aged black woman. His mother's age? No, his own, give or take a bit. The woman mutters something but he can't hear what she says because the atabaque beat now fills his head completely. *Come,* says the drum, *you're almost there.* From a terrace higher up the hill, a straggly group of teenage boys frown down at him, hostile, daring him to come up any farther. *What's with this crazy cowboy?*

He's directly below the green church now, and though the drumbeat is almost deafening, instead of a *roda* he sees only a series of overflowing dustbins. Then his eye catches the smallest of movements amidst the rubbish in the gutter—and he freezes. Abruptly the drumbeat softens into heartbeat. The camera becomes his eye. This was what had summoned him—a human heart beating from within a ripped-off, rolled-up tiny piece of cloth. A discarded newborn. Black. A useless, half-dead, famished, thrown-away boy. The madwoman's? No, she's beyond childbearing years. He approaches, his steps making no sound at all. When he reaches down to turn it over, the thing quivers.

Suddenly Milo's brain fills with a soft cascade of men and

women's voices from the past in French and English, German and Dutch, Cree and Gaelic. They gurgle and babble and blend as he stares at the unwanted infant. Is it breathing? Yes, it is. Milo sits down for a minute on the concrete steps that lead up to the church, in the thick shade of a rubber tree. Gets to his feet again, removes his black Stetson and sets it next to the baby's head so that its eyes will be protected from the sun, even once the sun has moved. Stands there. Moves a step away, a step back. Crosses the street, looks around, returns to the kid.

Finally, he turns and heads back down the hill. Watching, we sense an invisible rope stretched taut between the nearly quadragenarian gringo screenwriter and the tiny, dark-skinned, scarcely breathing bitty baby in the gutter.

CUT to Paul Schwarz, his new suit now clammy and wrinkled—isn't it infuriating how linen wrinkles?—and Milo Noirlac—as above, minus the Stetson—toiling back up the Saens Peña hill in the swift tropical sunset. Having smoked too many Cuban cigars today, Paul is panting.

"He won't be there anymore, Milo."

"Yes, he will."

"You'll see. Your hat's already been sold to tourists in Santa Teresa, and the kid has either been scooped up by the garbage trucks or devoured by a stray dog. He won't be there."

"Yes, he will."

"You're completely meshuga, Astuto. What was it, seven hours ago?"

"Yeah."

"He won't be there."

"Yes, he will."

"Jesus Christ. So what'll you do if he is, adopt him?"

"Find him a home."

"What's with the Good Samaritan shtick all of a sudden?"

CUT to the gutter across from the bright green church. The Stetson hasn't budged. The two men rush over to it . . .

WHAT DO YOU think, Astuto? Okay, I know you never think much of our first drafts, but still . . . Do you like the idea of starting off with the day you found Eugénio? Are you having fun, at least? Aw, don't go to sleep yet—we're just getting into it. You'll have plenty of time to sleep when you're dead. Come on, keep talkin', you indolent Quebecker. You know how films work: for the first ten minutes, the audience is infinitely tolerant and will accept whatever you choose to flash at them, but after that you'd better start making sense. Okay, so let's take advantage of that precious tolerance window to teach them the ropes of this film. The first two minutes are already in place. Stay with me. Hang in there, baby.

. . . . .

Neil, April 1910

IN VOICE-OVER, WE can hear the muddled mutterings of a gangly, well-dressed eighteen-year-old after his first night on the town.

Fog along the deep, dark Liffey this morning, or mist shall we call it, no, for soft not sticky in the air, feathery and floating, yes, but still, still, a bit thick and wet like sweat only coolish. It's six A.M., the haze is glazing and the eastern sky faintly tainting with the palest of lights and we're on our way home, jolly gentlemen, after one stupendous night with the bawds. Gulls wheeling overhead—have they any choice but to wheel? Must pen a poem about gulls and girls, directly after my morning nap. Yes, I've just done something that would shock my mother and annoy even my da, for everyone knows that a young man who plans to embark upon a career in the law should keep his personal reputation pristine—I've just wanked a wench, that's what I've just gone and done. What think you of that, Judge and Missus Kerrigan? Trussed up her petticoats and spun her round and lodged myself firmly between those alabaster thighs, then wanked her and spanked her. Strumpets don't mind a thump on the rump every now and then, 'tis all part of the fun. Must pen that poem the minute I get home.

Thus dithering and blathering, Neil Kerrigan stumbles from bridge to bridge, utterly delighted with himself.

Yes, at last I know what the jokes were all about, the innuendos, the suggestive raising of eyebrows and wiggling of hips, the priest's insistent prying during confession on the first Friday of each month—did you do this, did you do that, tell me how exactly, when, where and how many times—and often as I confessed his voice would change, his breathing grow labored, and I would wonder what was transpiring beneath his soutane. Yes, at last I know the convulsive shudder of one's being that comes in a woman's arms, as more powerful than self-pleasure as a bomb than a firecracker. Am I right, Willie Yeats? Sing to me!

> *O love is the crooked thing*
> *There is nobody wise enough*
> *To find out all that is in it,*
> *For he would be thinking of love*
> *Till the stars had run away*
> *And the shadows eaten the moon*
> *Ah, penny, brown penny, brown penny,*
> *One cannot begin it too soon . . .*

Sure and learning's a fine thing, Father Wolf, he goes on. *Singing in a bleeding choir as well. Yes, I know I used to be a good little altar boy with a fluty clear wavering voice that sang God's praises each Sunday morn, I know you believe the cant you pump into your flock about sin and sorrow, brimstone and hellfire, temptation and self-control, I'm not contesting your sincerity—but still, a man worth his oats deserves a bit of a rut on the weekend. Ha-ha! At last I've seen for myself the Monto brothels Cousin Thom told me about years ago, having himself heard of them from his raving classmate Jimmy Joyce. The madams, the girls one can pick and choose, the things one can say and do to them behind closed doors . . .* No, you must be shaggin' us, *said his comrades at University College,* can one really? *Precocious, cocky and unfazeable, Joyce was the most fascinating young prick Thom had ever met. The image of everything I longed to be and wasn't—yet. Rumor had it he'd already signed a publisher's contract for a book of tales about Dublin, and Thom and I wondered if tales like this would figure in it—tales about the underworld of the overworld, the dark side of the bright side, the hell side of the heaven side. Had Jimmy dared express himself in public as he did in private, holding forth about his priapic performances with the Monto Messalinas in a mind-boggling mix of English, Gaelic and Latin? . . .*

(Nice work, Milo! And then, through a series of ephemeral flashbacks, we'll discover the dissonance between the way Neil is describing the night's events to himself and the way they actually unfolded . . .)

Masses of girls and women roving the streets, standing or sitting on the front steps of houses—smoking and joking and yawning and scratching themselves, beckoning and clucking at the men who amble past. Puddles of piss and beer and rainwater on the ground. Neil follows Thom and the others into one of the Georgian houses.

Here we could use a close-up of his legs, his fine leather shoes, going up the steps in slow motion. *Yes,* we hear him mutter to himself, *one actually can do this. One's brain can order one's legs to mount a staircase to a brothel and the legs will obey . . .*

The Trinity boys cluster in the tacky foyer with limp lace curtains at the windows—but only at the *edges* of the windows—leaving the main pane brazenly naked. *Should I be seen, Good Lord, should I be seen! Should my father drive down Talbot Street in his carriage! Or Father Wolf, the roly-poly preacher who christened me at age six weeks and has kept tabs on me ever since!*

As if in a bad dream, Neil watches his friends select the pretty girls in swift succession and vanish, so that within thirty seconds he finds himself alone with the one remaining harlot—an old woman! Forty if she's a day, grinning up at him with tobacco-stained teeth, then grabbing his hand and pulling him after her down the hallway. He winces at the sight of her lumpy rump jouncing beneath her brightpink satin housecoat, gags at the thick mix of strangers' body emanations in the bedroom she draws him into . . .

"Tanks, luv."

Having divested him of half a pound, the woman slides her hand into his breeches and pulls at his member with ghastly efficient knowhow, then hikes up her petticoats and turns her back on him. Poor he, meanwhile—heart thumping in temples, eyes starting from head, sweat tingling on forehead, breath speeding malgré lui—loses sight of his own hands amidst the woman's flouncy mess of petticoats. He moans. *Good Lord, where are my hands? And is she not diseased, will she not have warts and sores, will I not* die, ta, ta-da DA, *will I not* die, ta, ta-da DA, *will I not* die—this in the capoeira rhythm as he pushes, a *die* with every push—*yes, for certain I will DIE.*

"Goodness, luv, you're scared stiff! You've just now left off wearing short pants, is it? A blushing virgin! Don't worry, darling, I won't keep it. You'll go home to mummy in one piece. Ha-ha-ha-ha-ha!"

The woman laughs at him even as she wiggles to hasten his spurt, force his body to express, in two dizzying breathless seconds, all it can express.

And now, as he stumbles home in the misty Liffey dawn a mere three hours and six Guinnesses later, Neil is energetically rewriting the night's script, carefully crafting the future tale of his erotic initiation. He needs to boast.

I'm as proud of having crossed the threshold of a Talbot Street brothel as that of Trinity Law School. Yes, dear Mother!

> *For man is made of cock and brain*
> *and never never never never again*
> *shall you lead me down the little rabbit hole*
> *with your insipid tales about the soul!*

. . . The soul God loveth, the soul God maketh and putteth into the flesh in order that we may resist temptation year after year and drudgingly trudge through this vale of tears to everlasting bliss or brimstone in the Beyond. No, Ma, no, Ma, no, Ma, no. Never met a soul in my life, Ma—never did run into a single soul. I do, on the other hand, have a cock and a brain, and beg to inform you that I intend to put both to good use. Never shall I set up a respectable household like your own, with a white-capped maid serving meals at appointed hours and dark-robed priests droning Mass of a Sunday morning. Done with all of that. It's the 29th of April, my first year at Trinity is drawing to a close and my future stretches ahead of me, green and lovely as a meadow. Oh, I shall cut capers in it, believe you me!

He dances on the bridge. Hop, skip, trip, delighting in the clack of his soles on the wood in the quiet dawn. *Yes*—he smirks, no doubt about it—*the sole exists.*

CUT to an hour later. Still running off at the mouth, Neil staggers up the shrubbery-bordered walkway to his parents' house in one of Dublin's wealthier surburbs.

Flagstones in the grass, grass wet with dew, don't mind if I dew. Mustn't wake them now—if I can simply, noiselessly jiggle the shaggin' key in the shaggin' lock, tiptoe into my room, slip between the sheets and lumber down to slumber without drawing maternal or paternal attention to the hour at which I returned to their fair abode . . . Ah, success. And so, though it be day, good night. The downy white pillows willn't tell on me, nor will the slut who got her wad. Ah, and a fine fuck she was, too, wrigglin' down below while gigglin' up above . . .

OKAY, ASTUTO, THAT brings us to . . . what, seven minutes or so, would you say? So we've got three minutes left of our precious ten to bring the final strand into existence, after which we can begin to braid. Over, under, in between, over, under, in between . . .

My mother once told me that the day she noticed how much I loved braiding her hair, as a kid back in Buenos Aires, was the day it first occurred to her I might be gay.

. . . . .

Awinita, March 1951

CLOSE-UP, MAYBE IN black and white, of ugly, cold, wet, gray, garbagey slush in the gutter of Saint Catherine Street, Montreal. A harsh sight. A woman's high-heeled boots walking in it—black and shiny, made not of leather but of some thin cheap leather substitute that lacks all of leather's essential qualities: suppleness, strength, especially impermeability.

Through the woman's eyes, we glance up at a streetlamp. It shivers whitely on as the gray daylight, after a halfhearted attempt at illuminating this March day for a few hours, gives up and dies. We go banging into a bar, where the light is even dimmer than outdoors. It's only four P.M. but Awinita, dressed in a shortish red dress and those high-heeled, shiny black boots, hikes herself up onto a red stool at the bar.

We are Awinita, we are the woman; always in her sequences we will be she. Now we catch sight of ourselves in a mirror above the bar. We are blond.

The barman (seen both in the flesh and reflected) serves us a Coke without greeting or even glancing at us. Our face being in shadow, he can't see it and neither can we. An indefinite amount of time elapses.

In the mirror, still from Awinita's point of view, we see a man enter the bar, tracking slush and depression. The door slams behind him. When he takes in the sight of a lone blond lady seated at the counter with her shimmering red back to him—young, from the curves of her—his eyes squint in surprise.

Emerging from the penumbra, the stranger resolves into a young man with red hair cut short and a face too gaunt for freckles. Our gaze flicks downward—the young redhead's cowboy boots are neither new nor clean—then back up to his face, now decked out with a smile.

"Mind if I siddown?"

"Free country."

"Free, my ass."

She laughs shortly. Pleasant surprise for him. Nice, low laugh the girl has.

He tries again, repeating, "Free, my ass," and succeeds; she laughs better.

"Happy to free your ass for you, sir," she mutters in a husky, jokey voice that shocks and excites him coming from such a young body or rather such a young face. He hasn't yet checked out either in much detail but he does so now and gets another couple of shocks in quick succession: this blonde is an Indian, and this child is with child.

Instead of doing a double take, he orders a double whisky. Oddly enough, the fact of the girl's pregnancy relaxes him, maybe because it implies she isn't underage (though of course you can knock up a twelve-year-old if you set your mind to it, or whatever that thing is called). The barman clunks his glass down into their silence just as, simultaneously, the girl and he decide to break it.

"What's your name?" says she, and "What you drinking?" says he.

"Declan," he answers, just as she says, "Rum and Coke."

Again they laugh and he can sense how, already, even before the liquor hits his brain, their laughter greases the cogs of their conversation, making it easy.

"Bring the lady another rum and Coke, if you please, sir," he calls out, lighting a cigarette and offering one to the girl, who takes it . . . and because of her instant acquiescence to drink and smoke he realizes she meant what she said earlier about his ass and that there could be other acceptances. A hard thrill rides through him from balls to toes and he wonders about the difference between the price of her body and the number of singles in his wallet. The second figure is probably higher than the first, though not by much. He'll need to sip his drink slowly and pray she's not a lush. Bad for the kid in her, too much rum. Quick, a sentence, anything . . . but all he can come up with, raising his glass, is a lame "And yours?"

just as Awinita thanks the barman for handing her what she knows to be a second glass of rumless Coke.

"My what?"

"Name."

"Nita."

"Nita. That's nice."

"Weird name, Declan. Hard to remember."

"That's okay. I'll say it to you again if you forget it."

"Huh."

"I can say it again right away, if you like: Declan."

"Didn't forget it yet."

"Yeah, but now if you do, you got an extra copy in storage."

"Funny man."

"Do my best."

"Declan. Sound like a brand name. Some cleanin' fluid or someting."

"Good old Irish name my dad gave me. Know about Ireland?"

"Whoa . . . Got anoder fag?"

"Sure."

"Got a dime for de jukebox?"

He fishes a dime out of his pocket, still doing subtractions in his head: he'll manage without his coffee tomorrow morning, and anyhow, no two ways about it, he'll have to swallow his pride and head back up to the farm later this week.

"What's your pleasure?" "Lady Day," says Awinita at the same time, and this time they really laugh.

She slips off the stool and struts over to join him at the box. Despite the curve of pregnancy, her whore-strut is touchingly child-like, so much so that he surmises she might be underage after all and his heart wrenches with wanting her. "Love it," says he, and as his left hand inserts the dime and punches in "Baby Get Lost," his right hand slides around the girl's thickened waist as though it were home. When, turning, she smiles up at him and murmurs, "Hey, baby, you're sweet," he pulls her close.

We can CUT here . . . find them together later, after the payment and the act, naked amidst a tumble of dirty bedsheets in a cruddy little bedroom above the bar? No . . . Be with Awinita in the thick of it, her eyes widening in surprise as Declan, having gotten things under way in the traditional galloping-stallion manner of human males under the age of twenty-five, slows down, withdraws and moves to do her good. We see his head bobbing just beyond her belly swell . . .

(Yeah, you're right, Milo, that could be tricky to get past the MPAA—don't want an R rating, to say nothing of an X—well, we'll cross that river when we get to it, hey? Dream first, cut later, you always used to tell me . . .)

We slip into Awinita's mind. *A huge bird flies across the sky with a great rushing noise. It touches the sun and bursts into flame. It tumbles over and over in the air, burning, dropping away, until it vanishes behind a distant hill* . . .

When we open our eyes, Declan has moved back inside of us, gently but passionately.

"You're so lovely," he murmurs. "You're so lovely . . ."

They are dressed again and sitting on the bed side by side. The spaces between their sentences are huge. Awinita strokes the back of Declan's neck with one finger.

"Never done it wit a Indian girl?"

"Nope. Specially not with a pregnant Indian girl . . . Who's the poppa, Nita?"

"A guy."

"A gone guy?"

"Yeah, gone."

"Well, how far along are you?"

"Ah . . . baby s'pose to be here like in May or June. Got a fag?"

"Sure . . . You're nice, Nita. You're amazing."

"You're not bad, too, Mister Irish Declan."

"Not everyone would agree with you on that."

"Some people tink you bad?"

He laughs. "Plenty of people. Guys up at Bordeaux, to start with."

"You been in de jug?"

"Just got out yesterday."

"Yeah? In for long?"

"Coupla weeks."

"What dey nail you for?"

"Said I stole a car."

"You didn't?"

"Nah. I just . . . you know . . . borrowed it."

"From who?"

"Sister of mine."

Awinita releases her low laugh.

"Nah . . ."

"I swear."

"You take your sister's car and she call de cops on you? Some broderly love!"

"I got a whole slew of brothers and sisters. Unfortunately Marie-Thérèse is the only one owns a car, and she's also the meanest."

"Marie-Thérèse? Don't sound Irish."

"Our ma's French and our pa's Irish, so in our family the girls got French names and speak French and the boys got Irish names and speak English."

"Why not Irish?"

"'Cause the British occupied Ireland for six hundred years and made us lose our language."

"Why not British, den?" mutters Awinita, but Declan doesn't hear her because the drink is making him voluble.

"Point is, the boys gotta work. Can't get a job worth shit if you're francophone."

"You got a good job den, Declan?"

"Nah, you kiddin'? I got a black-sheep reputation to live up to."

She barks a laugh; he pulls her to him and revels in the feel of her firm, round tummy pushed up against his rib cage. "Wouldn't be caught dead with a good job," he adds, and she laughs again, though not quite as loudly.

CUT to the bar, which has filled up with customers in the meantime.

Elated, Awinita purchases real drinks with one of the two five-dollar bills Declan gave her. The barman glowers at her when he sets their glasses on the bar but she turns her back on him saying, "Keep cool, Irwin," and spins her stool toward Declan.

"I don't get how you can call the cops on one o' your own family."

"Marie-Thérèse wants me *out* of the family. She'd kick me off the family property if she could. Says I'm a good-for-nothing."

"You good for *some*ting, man."

They laugh.

"Ah, but she doesn't know about that, eh? She's already married and a mom, goin' on for thirty. I'm twenty-four, how 'bout you, Nita?"

". . ."

"Hey . . . you're not underage, are you?"

". . ."

"Jesus."

"Jesus got notin' to do wid it. I been in de trade tree years already, help my moder out to feed de family. Your sister, she respectable and put her own broder in jail. How Jesus s'pose to figure dat out?"

Again they laugh, inebriated. Euphoria seeps into them. Declan knocks back his drink.

"Ever since she got her poor lumberjack of a fiancé to buy her a three-carat diamond, Marie-Thérèse thinks she's better than the rest of us. Poor Régis . . . He went into debt to pay for that ring . . ."

Billie Holiday sings "Tain't Nobody's Biz-ness if I Do" and the two of them dance close, Awinita leaning into Declan's shoulder with her eyes pressed shut.

A white woman, her face a blur, has fastened a sparkling diamond brooch to her throat. Bright red blood trickles down in two lines on either side of her jugular vein . . .

CUT.

. . . . .

II
GINGA

From gingare, *to lollop from side to side. The basic capoeira movement, which keeps the body in a perpetual state of swing.*

Milo, 1952–56

A BABY. In these scenes, we can alternate between objective and subjective camera, be now inside, now outside the baby's head, the baby's eyes. A screaming, skinny, jittery, seizure-prone baby, brought to this publicly-owned Catholic hospital at age three weeks and left there. Abandoned with relief by a man whose hands were shaking.

The world is fuzzy. Moving shapes, lots of white. Women's voices, shrill or harsh. Clipped syllables. Snippets of language—but that, too, is fuzzy, tone rather than words. The sisters all speak French.

"Garbage . . . A little piece of human garbage."

"Human? Are you sure?"

"Now, now, sister. Jesus loves us all."

"Hard to believe sometimes. Born in withdrawal . . ."

The kid's in a cot, surrounded by other kids in cots. Large, white female shapes move jerkily up and down the rows of cots. Close-ups on female hands. Reddish fingers emerging from starched white sleeves. Swiftly and unceremoniously, they change the infant's clothes and diapers, bathe it, feed it from a glass baby bottle, set it back in its cot.

Footsteps fading. Lights switched off.

In the half-darkness, the infant drifts into a brief sleep—then starts awake and clutches out wildly for contact. There is none. It's just spent nine months surrounded by total touch, liquid warmth, gentle rocking rhythm and suddenly—nothing. Dry air, echoing void. Heels clacking in the distance. The baby squirms and flails, wrings its hands, grabs at its face and at the air around it. Its diminutive arms and legs wave in the empty cosmos. Its high-pitched crying wakes other babies, who also start to cry. Neon lights flick on. Footsteps move in. Voices whisper annoyance: *It's that Indian whoreson.* Arms reach down, flip the baby onto its stomach. Tone of reprimand and threat. Footsteps fade. Lights flick off. Other cries fade.

Smothering, its nose and mouth jammed against the sheet, the child twists its head and gasps for air. Yelps. Wrinkles its forehead . . .

(Hmm. Excuse me, Milo, but . . . think we'll be able to find an *actor* for this role? Won't we get sued for cruelty to dumb animals? Maybe we should do these images numerically, you know? Cost a fortune, but . . . yeah, sure, sure, we need them, we absolutely need them. Okay. We'll see . . .)

Here we could accelerate to give the impression of endless repetition. Empty ceiling. Empty air. Darkness. A huge, fearful darkness. Other babies crying. Rustling sounds and footsteps in the dark. Lights flicking on, off. Neon flickering. A woman's clawlike hands snatching up the screaming, blue-faced baby, holding it high in the air and shaking it, then dropping it in its cot—*thawump.* Petrified with fear, it stops screaming. Footsteps move off.

Fade to a different quality of darkness—one that indicates time passing, a page being turned. A few months later . . . same white ceiling, same thrum and hum of French voices, but: exit the regulation hospital linen. The baby is being trussed and trundled, wrapped sausage-like in the cruddy blue blanket it first arrived in. New faces, not as blurry as the old ones—the boy's eyes are beginning to focus. Voices, not only in French now but also in German (even scrambled, the difference between the two languages is clear). Strong lights, long hallways. Shoulder camera to convey the jerks and jolts—he's being carried out of the hospital. Wham. Dazzling sunlight smack in the face. Whoosh. Blue skies, fresh air, high green waving branches. Slam of car door. Moved, held, jostled, slam slam, revving of motor.

Everything is a shock to Milo's system after six months in the humdrum hospital routine, but he no longer cries. Already he has learned that crying serves no purpose, learned to block out, black out, sink deep within himself, into the dark cave of silence that will be his refuge all his life long. From within his silence, beneath the impenetrable banter of his new German foster parents, we can hear the drumbeat of his mother's heart, his mother's people. *Ta, ta-da DA, ta, ta-da DA, ta, ta-da DA* . . . Milo's throbbing silence will be the background music for the entire film.

MILO IS TWO. These scenes will be shot from the vantage point of a two-year-old, amidst the feet and legs of giants. German is now more or less right-side up.

Lying flat on the kitchen floor, the little boy plays with a couple of potatoes that are fancy racing cars. Propels himself forward on his tummy with low vrooming noises. Is suddenly grabbed by the arm—*What are you doing? Milo! What are you doing?*—yanked up off the floor and into the air.

An angry woman has again taken hold of his entire being with one hand. Her other hand swats at his shirt and pants to dust him off, batting his penis on the way down. Still he doesn't cry, but his pedaling legs strike the woman's thigh—she cries out and releases him. He falls in a heap on the floor.

Milo is locked into a little closet under the staircase, in total blackness. We're in there with him—listening. Straining with all our might to hear sounds on the far side of the door. Hearing only our own breathing. We breathe in unevenly. Hold back our sobs. However long this lasts, it's an eternity.

Daily life in this household—quick flashes, not all bad: little Milo being spoon-fed . . . sung to in German at bedtime . . . dressed by his foster mother in a navy-blue snowsuit, boots, scarf and mittens, and taken out by his foster father to horse around in the snow . . . trying to pet the neighbor's cute little cocker spaniel through the slats of the fence between their yards and being reprimanded by his foster mother *No! No, Milo! Dogs are too dirty!* . . .

He's sitting alone on the pot, doing nothing. His foster mother checks, rechecks, finally gives up and roughly pulls up his pants. Later, furious to see he's shat himself, she disgustedly shakes out his underpants above the toilet, all the while berating him in German. Then she pins a diaper back onto his bottom, too tightly— the toddler's frown reflects his shame and discomfort—and shoves him back into the closet. Turn of the lock, *clack.* The blackness. Little Milo breathes in and out; a faint whine of fear is now audible in his breathing. His heart beats; time beats.

Suddenly the door swings open and Milo's world is flooded with light.

Who is this woman? Blond and young and beautiful, she drops to her knees so that her face is on a level with his, laughing in her low voice: *What ya doin' in de dark, little one?*

Question of your life, Milo. What ya doin' in de dark?

The kneeling woman holds her arms out to Milo as no one ever has. Tentatively he moves forward and is grasped and gently clasped to her welcoming flesh. She presses his face to her neck, not too tightly. Dizzy, he breathes in the commingling of perfume and sweat beneath her blouse. At last she draws back, smiles at the stunned child and murmurs, *Come wit me? Come wit your mom?*

Taking him by the hand, she leads him out of the closet, down the hallway, out the front door and down the steps . . .

Here we'll need music, Astuto, for it's a June day of insane felicity. The two of them go to a fair and ride on a merry-go-round together, laugh and lick ice cream cones as their horses go up, go down, yes, the laughter, the splendid music and the woman's flashing smile, her arms that lift him to set him on the high horse, the licking, the laughing, the going round, her dark eyes so tender gazing at him, her arms that lift him down to set him on the ground, in fact it was probably then that she bought him the ice cream cone, for he would have needed both hands to hang on to the pole, his impressions are all mixed in child chronology, the woman waving good-bye to him, sunlight dancing on his mother's blond hair, how could he know its real color was black, how could a three-year-old ever imagine that the most beautiful woman in the world would damage her own hair to make it blond? *Be good now, son, be strong, little one. You're gonna have to be strong, you know that? A resistant*—whispering into his ear the Cree name that means *resistant . . . Dat's your real name,* she said, and repeated it. *Don't forget it. It'll help you.* Opening the closet door . . . *Come wit me, come wit your mom! What ya doin' in de dark, little one?* Shutting the closet door . . .

Then *sccccrrrratch*—BLACKOUT.

. . . . .

Neil, May 1914

A MEETING OF the Irish Volunteers, somewhere in Dublin. Men's voices speaking in loud tones of urgency and anger. In the audience, Neil Kerrigan, at twenty-two, seems a different man. His features are graver, and he listens with all his might as gaunt, earnest poet and school director Padraic Pearse takes the floor.

"May I read you a poem I've just written?"

> *I have turned my face*
> *To this road before me*
> *To the deed that I see*
> *And the death I shall die . . .*

"Even the Daughters of Erin are arming themselves!" Thom McDonagh chimes in. "Arms, discipline and tactics, they say, should be the one thought, the one work, the one play of Irish men and women."

Never before has a revolution been led by poets, marvels Neil's inner voice. *All the brightest and most brilliant men—yes, and women, too.*

His cousin Thom had taken him to Monto and now he has brought him to Sinn Féin. Thom wants to make a man of him, and Neil is grateful: occasionally he even feels his blood stir with something akin to genuine indignation.

Thom has been drilling, Neil has not. Thom has been marching up and down, running, hiding, taking rifles apart and putting them back together, aiming, doing target practice . . . Neil has been reading for his final examinations.

"*Sinn Féin!*" Thom shouts, leaping to his feet along with the others (and this Gaelic expression will be translated as a subtitle: *Ourselves alone!*).

"Well, perhaps not quite entirely alone?" Neil whispers. "It does seem we've been seeking and receiving a fair amount of help from the Germans."

"Hasn't politics always been the art of intelligent compromise?"

"I s'pose so."

"No struggle is pure, Neil. The Germans have the same enemy as we do, and they've promised to argue for Irish independence at the peace conference after the war, if there is a war, and there will be a war. They have arms and ammunition and we do not, so we need and shall take their help. We shall do what must be done in order to win, conquer, establish and impose ourselves."

Neil's right foot bounces impatiently on his left knee. Again we hear his thoughts in voice-over . . .

I know as much, sweet cousin, about our people's moral strength as about their military weakness, and have no difficulty grasping that it is in Ireland's interest, if there is a war, and there will be a war, to aid and abet the German military in every way, generously sharing our coastline and coastal waters with German submarines and accepting German weapons in return . . . But none of this dying stuff, Pearse. Nor shall I follow in the diverging footsteps of poor Willie Yeats, torn between political activism and the inane theosophical ramblings of Madame Blavatsky! Yeats will get lost and I shall go on, for I have a job to do on this earth.

The bard now aspires, as he avows, to be Colder and dumber and deafer than a fish. *As for me, my soul is at white heat. I shall write of the fine determination in these meetings, the men and women in revolt from the mud and blood of their childhood, with official British history pounded into their brains at school but body memories of revolting injustice at the hands of the British occupier. Peasants dispossessed by the thousands, their land reclaimed, their villages burned, their cottages toppled with battering rams, their children screaming in the cold and rain—yes, Irish children trembling and dizzy at school, trying to think and to study on an empty stomach. I shall describe how today's young heroines and heroes of Erin scramble to find meaning in old tales, in the claim to roots, grunting as they snuffle like pigs in Celtic drivel, shoving their snouts into the soil of Ireland, seeking to unearth true meaning, old meaning, deep dark smelly truffle meaning. As if the Celts had not themselves invaded this island! They were invaders as much as the Brits were, merely a few centuries earlier! Our culture is not in the past; it is in the future! Our heroes are not the puffed-up Cúchulainns of yesteryore, but the amazing men and women who,* hic et nunc, *devote their lives to shaking off the shackles of the shite-eating Brits.*

"Yes, we are prepared to die," thunders Pearse, "but for *our* country, not for another! If war breaks out, my friends, you can be sure that the British will use us again as they have used us always. They'll turn us into cannon fodder, as they did in the Boer War fifteen years ago."

"I was there!" pipes up a haggard, gravelly-voiced man whose hair is streaked with gray. "Saw it with my own eyes, I did! Spent ten years o' my life fighting the Brits in South Africa. Raised the Irish Transvaal Brigade against them! Became a Boer citizen, I did!"

"That's MacBride," Thom murmurs.

Neil takes a closer look at the orator. Bad posture, bad complexion, red wine in his veins, Major John MacBride is an unpleasant man, whose bushy mustache no doubt conceals a weakness of the upper lip.

"There were five hundred of us battling the Brits down there, and *who* did we end up shooting, I ask you?" MacBride shouts. "Our own Irish brothers, our flesh and blood, the Dublin Fusiliers and the Inniskillings! It broke my heart, boys. The British prance about on tiptoe like sissy ballerinas, protected behind a great thick wall of Irish flesh. They wait till we've been mowed down, then take credit for the victory."

"He loves to tell the story," Thom whispers. "In Paris, he told it so often that he grew addicted to red wine."

Neil nods. John MacBride is a national hero, but he is also Willie Yeats's worst enemy, for it was he, a Catholic, a commoner, an adventurer, whom Maud Gonne, the great love and light of the poet's life, ultimately chose to marry. In 1903 Willie had been traumatized by Maud's telegram informing him of her plan to convert to Catholicism and become MacBride's bride. He'd written her letter after letter begging her not to make so grotesque an error . . . but to no avail. And oh, how it had tortured him to think of the two of them together. Maud, like himself, a person of upper-class Protestant and thus innately superior background, a higher type of person, in touch with life's most subtle, mystical, poetic, ecstatic, esoteric secrets—Willie's own brilliant, precious, unspeakably beautiful Maud—in bed, *naked*, her skin against the skin of this silly, noisy warrior, this callow, superficial, bragging, filthy, lower-class Catholic . . . No, the image was revolting, intolerable!

Like everyone else, Neil had followed the complex history of the love triangle in the newspapers. True to Yeats's predictions, within a year after the irons of holiness had been clamped round their bodies and wedlocked, John MacBride had disappointed his wife—and Maud, shortly after giving birth to the son they named Seagan (Gaelic for Seán), had sued him for divorce.

Oh, but it was ill thought of in Ireland, both to divorce and to cast aspersions upon Irish military heroes, especially if one happened to be a British-born Protestant female. Perhaps Mrs. Mac-Bride was *not*, as she claimed to be, a Volunteer committed to Irish freedom, but rather a filthy spy paid by the British to *infiltrate* the Volunteers! Meanwhile, poor Willie Yeats had continued to moon, sigh, long, pine and yearn for her, occasionally attempting to win her over by striking the stance of political commitment, but consistently reverting to his mistrust of the masses, the lower classes, the Catholics . . .

>*My dear is angry that of late*
>*I cry all base blood down*
>*As though she had not taught me hate*
>*By kisses to a clown.*

And so it was that as dramatic hours ticked by and her country suffered—that is to say, the country that, though born in England and raised primarily in France by French governesses after her mother died when she was five, Maud *felt* to be hers, given that her British soldier of a father, after having deserted the army and taken up the struggle of the Irish nation against his own and taught her to fight for justice always, had died in turn when she was eighteen and madly in love with him, thus making his political combat her raison d'être once and for all—as general strikes followed lockouts, which gave rise to demonstrations, riots, shootings and imprisonments, as Home Rule was denounced by Ulster as a thin disguise for Rome Rule and defeated and the tension rose . . . poor, gorgeous, frustrated, flaming-tongued, red-haired Mrs. MacBride was reduced to following Irish news from abroad, writing articles and raising money in Paris for the cause of Irish independence but no longer actually daring to set foot in Ireland for fear that, were she to leave France, she'd lose legal custody of young Seagan . . .

DAMMIT, ASTUTO—ARE YOU sure it's a good idea to bring this old love triangle into our movie? No, I haven't forgotten your theory about stories being trees with roots and trunks and branches, but this tree of ours keeps sprouting huge new branches we simply won't be able to afford . . . I mean, even apart from budget, we can't afford *storywise* to follow every little branch down to the smallest leaf and twig, you know what I mean? Our spectators are gonna get confused. First you make sure they know the Catholics of Southern Ireland are trying to rid themselves of the Protestant Brits, then you tell them Yeats and Gonne are pro-independence Protestants—about as typical as pro-Hamas Israelis, right? What's *with* this Maud Gonne anyhow? You'd think you yourself—and not poor shortsighted Willie Yeats—were desperately, endlessly, hopelessly in love with the woman. Hey, man! I mean, she died sixty years ago!

Yeah, I know, Milo. Dead people are as real as we are. And characters are as real as we are, too. Bringing them alive is our job. In fact, it's the only thing that justifies *our* being alive (for those of us who are). I agree, I agree, it's just that—look—listen to me, there's an *information* problem here, because we know stuff *no one* at that 1914 meeting of the Irish Volunteers could possibly have known. Right? To protect his reputation, John MacBride sued a Dublin newspaper for libel, and from then on the Irish public was kept in the dark about the details of Gonne's case against him. No one ever learned that one night in Paris, when she was off at a political meeting, MacBride had come home blind drunk and attempted to rape every female in the household, including Françoise (the maid), Elaine (Maud's father's illegitimate daughter), and Iseult (Maud's *own* illegitimate daughter). I mean, the facts get really complicated here. Okay, don't get all het up, we can leave it in for now. We'll figure something out.

NEXT SCENE: A solemn procession of students, scores of them, some taller, some smaller, but all male, bodies draped in black

gowns and heads topped with flat caps, filing down the Trinity
College walkway, up the monumental staircase and through into
the grand auditorium. Judge and Mrs. Kerrigan, Neil's parents, are
in the audience.

(If we want to recognize them, we'll need to establish them
in the first scene—maybe, creeping home at dawn from his disastrous night on Talbot Street, the young man will *not* have
been able to slip into bed unnoticed, maybe his mum will have
been standing sternly waiting for him at the top of the staircase,
maybe she will have called out sharply to his dad to interrupt his
shaving and come take a look at this cur cringing down there in
the entryway, its clothes disheveled and liquor on its breath . . .
Or maybe his younger sister, Dorothy, passing him on the front
steps that morning as she strutted off to school, will have snitched
on him . . .)

Neil, his right foot bouncing with impatience on his left knee,
is back at last night's rally. Over and above the drone of official
commencement ceremony speeches: *In the great tradition of our
forefathers . . . Outstanding institution founded by Queen Elizabeth in 1592 . . .* —he hears the rebels' voices rising, hot with
desperation.

"Our strikes have failed! Our men have gone back to work with
no rise in wages! And now, with our young'uns dying of hunger and
tuberculosis, half the city jobless, living in the dark off bread and tea,
hundreds of pure, virtuous young Irish women reduced to chattel at
Curragh for the fun and games of the British soldiers, those arrogant
bastards still riding up and down our city, occupying our castle and
our customhouse, running our lives and humiliating our quiet citi-
zens with their shouted orders—now, as if that weren't enough, they
want to draft us yet again! *We shall resist, we shall resist.*" (Chanted in
Neil's brain, the phrase rises and becomes a slogan.)

"Dear, dirty Dublin is starving! How many are we? Seventy thousand. Seventy thousand Cúchulainns! Seventy thousand heroes! Sure, up in Ulster they are more, and better armed. The buggars are talking about secession. Unionist buggars. Creeping, cruddy traitor coward bugs. They may be more, but justice is on our side. This cannot go on. Up with free Ireland!"

"*Neil Kerrigan.*"

Hearing his name called, Neil mounts the steps to the stage and strides forward, as practiced earlier in the day, to shake the rector's right hand and receive the paper cylinder of the LLB diploma from his left. The rector's assistant sneaks up from behind to drape the ermine ribbon around his neck and Neil starts in surprise; the man accidentally knocks off his cap, he bends over to pick it up and his own falls off. Neil picks that one up and they bang heads straightening up, then sheepishly trade caps as the audience titters loudly for at last something has happened, at last they are no longer bored, and when Neil moves back to his seat grasping his diploma their applause is as wild as Victorian applause can be, i.e., audible. Neil's sister Dorothy leans over and simpers into his ear, "You're red as a beet, you know."

CUT to the well-heeled crowd milling about in the great chandeliered reception hall after the ceremony. False smiles glued to their faces, Neil's parents shake hands and accept congratulations left and right; Neil is repeatedly asked to reenact the little incident with the caps, to show how it went. We hear him seethe. *Do they not know? Is it* possible *they do not know that Irish babies are dying of hunger a mere stone's throw from here? That hundreds of our country's best men are rotting in the jails of Britain for having dared to defend our dream of independence? That their world is about to go up in smoke?*

A horse-drawn carriage takes the four Kerrigans home in silence. As they move through the front door, the maid calls out from the kitchen.

"A parcel came in the mail for you this morning, Mr. Neil, sir. Postmarked in London."

"London?"

Neil's hands tear at the package: a book. A book of stories. Joyce's *Dubliners*!

"Oh my God, then it actually has happened, Jimmy actually has managed to publish his tales."

Envy and admiration vie in Neil as he quickly flips to the title page . . .

(No, Milo. I'm sorry, but we can*not* go into the history of the publication of *Dubliners* at this point. No. Out of the question. You know too much. Shut up. Maybe Neil can tell his grandson about it years later, in Quebec. We'll cross that bridge when we come to it . . .)

The camera moves in close to read the words inscribed above and below the title in Joyce's surprisingly graceful, legible hand:

Here at long last, fully seven years after my pregnant brain gave birth to them, are my Dubliners—a greedy, hypocritical, weak, silly, pusillanimous people who love to lie through their teeth and of whom, because of the vise of virtue in which our country is currently imprisoned, the truth can only be told from afar. I take the greatest pleasure in offering them to my friend Neil Kerrigan.

And in parentheses beneath the scribbled signature:

(Are you a man yet?)

"So he managed to get around the law after all," says Judge Kerrigan, "by publishing them abroad."

"What would that man know about Dubliners, I wonder?" scoffs Mrs. Kerrigan. "He's been in Europe for a decade!"

"And why would he send them to *you?*" Dorothy pipes up. "It'll be a bad influence, won't it, Mother?"

Neil's hand moves in wonder on the page of a genuine published book in which his name has been inscribed by the author . . . CUT.

Neil in a pool of warm lamplight in his bedroom that evening—
deeply, utterly absorbed in the tales.

A few hours later: Neil talking to himself as he walks along the
Liffey in the depths of night.

*I shall someday write as well as or better than Jimmy Joyce or Willie
Yeats. I think, oh no, I know I can. Practice law, yes, fine, no problem,
for a few years—just to get myself established. But in the dark, in secret, I'll soon start spinning magical webs of words to enchant the masses.
I'm only twenty-two. No writer is world famous at twenty-two—with the
possible exception of Rimbaud, but he doesn't count because he retired
from literature at age nineteen to smuggle weapons to Abyssinia. I'm
only twenty-two, and though Jimmy Joyce is fully ten years older than
I, his first real book (apart from slim volumes of student poetry) has just
now come out, and is not an extraordinarily fat one, either. Besides, he's
not serious competition. He's gone off to Italy or Yugoslavia or wherever
and will probably, now that he's got* Dubliners *out of his system, forget
all about his native land. I've been training since the day I was born.
The pablum of priests my mother fed me was spiked by my teachers with
the heady brandy of Irish lore, I guzzled down Shakespeare, Milton and
Browning on my own, and now I feel ripe and ready. The fruit of my
imagination is fairly exploding with seed. Semen and sense! A billion
teeming, bubbling words in the cerebellum like a billion sperms in the bal-
locks—fertile, gusty, gutsy, true. I'm merely waiting for the event that
will jerk my brain into gear so it can start spewing out lengthy chapters
filled with violence and beauty, philosophy and pain.*

*I, I, I! Not shy, sweet, bespectacled William Butler Yeats, losing
himself in Ouija boards and reincarnation for the love of Maud Gonne;
not distant, bad-boy, scoffing, scabrous, scatalogical James Joyce, fid-
dling with twaddle, but diffident in face of battle—neither Willie nor
Jimmy but I, Neil Kerrigan and no other, shall father the great literary
opus of the new Ireland! I shall be both true poet and true fighter, my*

name greater, higher and louder than anyone else's—Neil Kerrigan!
Have you read the latest Kerrigan? Louder, higher, greater, the full
male thrust of my loins surging into my poems and tales . . . Pen is
sword. Penis is word. PENISWORD . . .

YOU OKAY, MILO? You all right, man? You want me to call the nurse or
anything? Yes, I know the tubes are supposed to be bringing you everything you need to stay alive—Irish whisky, beef stew with plenty
of potatoes, late Emily Carr paintings, early Wim Wenders films,
the return flight of Canadian geese in May, Pierre Elliott Trudeau
(sorry, just wanted to make sure you were still alive), ah, heroin,
capoeira ceremonies in Salvador de Bahia, endless nights of fucking
with Paul Schwarz . . . hey. What else could you want, right?

Sure, Astuto. I'll let you take a five-minute nap, and then we'll
get back to work . . .

. . . . .

Awinita, April 1951

RAIN AND DARKNESS, seen through the window of the cruddy little
bedroom above the bar.

Awinita's stomach is rounder than before, and she wears a floaty
blue shirt to make this less apparent. We're in her eyes again, currently looking down. A man's hands come in under the shirt. Gently, she pushes him away.

"Aren't you forgettin sometin', sweetheart?"

We see the man's hands dig a wad of bills from his jeans pocket.
A heavyset man in his forties. Unpleasant body: rigid, rilled with

fat. Turning, he licks his thumb and counts ten singles onto the little Formica table near the window.

"Would you mind maybe," says Awinita in a husky whisper as he comes at her undoing his belt (close loud sound of the belt buckle, one of the Pavlovian signals that warns the woman's brain it will soon be time to waft her elsewhere), "from de side or from behind?"

"Yeah, I'd mind," the man says, pushing her toward the bed and grabbing at her blue shirt to tear it off (but, being inside of it, we'll never see her body in these scenes). "Damn right I'd mind. I pay good money to fuck you and I'll fuck you however I bloody well feel like fucking you, ain't no squaw gonna tell me what position I gotta fuck her in, for the luva Christ! No skin off my back if you lose your bastard! Make one less Injun on welfare, guzzlin' down my tax money!"

A spot of pink. It grows, shivers and shimmers into a carnation . . . The flower grows a long green stem and dances gaily for a couple of seconds . . . Then the stem splits in two and its ends rise up to meet above its head. Meanwhile it goes on dancing. Watching it is painful— like watching a ballerina dancing on her crotch.

The rain hurls itself against the windowpanes. Fleetingly, in the shadows, we see the man heaving with his full weight on top of us.

"Don't you know what condoms are for?" he says. "Don't they teach you that up on the res? They sure should! Only useful education for Injuns. Well, no point in usin' one now, eh? Can't get pregnant twice, can you? No matter how two-faced you Injuns are, not even you can conceive two bastards on top of the other. Huh . . . uh! Uh!"

In slow motion, in black and white, pelted by unrelenting rain, Awinita lets herself into a tin-roofed shack. One room. No electricity, only candlelight. Packed dirt floor. Fireplace made of clay or mud and willow sticks. Her floaty blue shirt is the only touch of color in the scene. Gathered in silence around the table are her mother and several siblings, their faces drawn and still with hunger. Smiling, Awinita sets her purse on the table, opens it and proudly withdraws a huge roll of dollar bills. But far from lighting up, her family's faces only grow sadder. Tears roll down their cheeks. Awinita stands there, money in hand, not knowing what to do. The dim light grows dimmer.

Back on Saint Catherine Street, we hear the door slam as the john departs.

CUT to Awinita seated at the bar. People milling around her, music. When the barman brings her a Coke, we see that the stool next to hers is empty.

"Thanks, Irwin."

Awinita sips her Coke. A blond man in his thirties (glasses, attaché case, suit and tie) perches his straight businessman's ass on the stool next to hers. Close-up on his face: close-shaven, thin-lipped, a faint air of nastiness around the mouth . . .

(Yeah, you're right, Milo—it's important to get the johns' faces, show how frighteningly diverse they are. All, though, are weighed down by their stories, and desperate to shake off some of the weight . . .)

Irwin brings Awinita a Coke, takes a banknote from the blond man, rings up two rum and Cokes . . .

"Tanks," says Awinita, nodding vaguely at the drink. "Pleasure. What's your name?" "Nita." "Hey, Nita, I'm John." "Good to meet you, John." "Good to meet *you*, Nita. Had no idea I'd be meeting somethin' so good when I ducked in here." "You jus' wanted in out of de rain, eh?" "Right." "Well. Cheers, John." "Cheers, Nita . . ." (Problem, Milo. Familiar problem: what to do with boring dialogue . . . Nah, skip it. Maybe shoot the scene from the far side of the room, over by the jukebox, now playing Nat King Cole's "Too Young." Just their lips moving . . .)

The blond man looks at Awinita and she looks back at him. His eyes say, "Are you . . . ?," and hers, "Long as you're not a cop, baby," and his, "Here, upstairs?," and hers, "You got it all figured out, smart boy." Leaning forward, his lips form the words, "How much for the back entrance?: and hers, "Fifteen." The business-man winces. "Hey, that's steep," he says, making as if to bolt, but already Awinita's hand is on his thigh, already his blood is racing and they both know the moment for mind-changing has been left behind.

Three five-dollar bills on the Formica table.

He hadn't noticed. Only when he puts his arms around her from behind does the fact of Awinita's pregnancy register on his brain. His hands freeze on her belly.

"Jesus," he says.

"Kinda doubt it," says she. This makes him laugh, which re-laxes him.

Awinita's eyes are closed. On the pale pink screen of her eyelids . . .

A whole forest of cartoon trees shoots up at once. Multicolored birds flit swiftly in and out of their branches—their singing, too, is sped up. Shrill trills and twitters, jerky flutters. In the space of a few seconds, the sun rises and sets several times. The seasons rush past: the trees shed their leaves, look dark and wintry for a moment, then sprout new leaves again.

Meanwhile, we hear the sound of a belt buckle—a different belt buckle. A zipper being undone. Clothes rustling. The sound of a key turning in a lock. A mattress creaking. A door being pulled to. A key turning in a lock. A door being slammed. *Ta, ta-da DA . . .* Yes, we can bring in the capoeira beat here—but faintly, as a hint, a way of breathing, a vestige. *Ta, ta-da DA . . .* A key turning in a lock. Pants being zipped up. A belt buckle. Pants being zipped down. A man pissing into a toilet. Loose change jingling. *Ta, ta-da DA* . . . A man guzzling beer, then burping. Key in lock. Snore. Door slam. Fart. Quarrel in next room. Doors. Mattress creaks. Zippers. Buckles. A man groaning as he reaches climax. This sound track gradually dies out. FADE TO BLACK. Howling wind . . . CUT.

Awinita sits smoking at the bar, looking tired.

"Want a coffee?" the barman asks her.

"Sure. Tanks, Irwin."

Another man comes to sit on the stool next to her. Tall and youngish, with filthy long black hair and a phony leather cap. He has a lisp.

"You alone, mith?"

"Not anymore!"

"Mind if I thit with you for a while?"

"Make yourself at home."

Just then the door to the bar opens and Declan walks in, hatless. Though wet, his red hair is longer than when we saw him last; he hasn't returned to jail. Close-up on his green eyes as, catching sight of Awinita, they light up in a hazel blaze.

We move toward him: Awinita has left her lisper in the lurch.

"Well, if it ain't Mister Cleaning-Fluid."

They're in each other's arms.

"I missed you, Nita."

"I missed you, too, baby."

CUT.

. . . . .

III

MOLEQUE

Kid, urchin. Originally simply meant child. Today designates street kids, juvenile delinquents.

Milo, 1956–58

AT FOUR, MILO is a nervous, bristling hedgehog of a child who speaks mostly German with a smattering of French and English, but he especially speaks silence. Silence is the tongue he shares with dogs and cats and trees and flowers, stones and lakes and rivers and skies, turtles and fish, birds and beds, tables and chairs and ceilings and curtains. When you think about it, most things in the world don't talk and would never do anything to hurt you. Telephones are in between. They look like objects, but in fact they're nearly people. They talk. His foster mother listened to the telephone talking, then came and told him he'd be leaving. The telephone told her he had to. He doesn't know why, that's just the way it is. If you take it as your starting point that everything is unfathomable, and stick to it, you'll never be disappointed.

Strangers came and took him to a building he'd never seen before. For three days he lived there in a large dorm room with other little children; then other strangers came to fetch him and now he's living in their house.

He's not really *living* there, he's just pretending. His plan is to string them along for a while, let them believe he's settled in with them in this house in the suburbs, take a few days to get his bearings, then run away. Though these people call him Milo, he knows he has another name—the one the blond woman gave him after they rode on the merry-go-round together. A cocoon-like name he felt safe inside. For the time being he's forgotten it, because he was so small when she told it to him—but it's in his memory somewhere and will come back to him someday, he's sure of it.

The new family are the Manderses. There's the father, Jan, handsome and bald with glasses; the mother, Sara, with big, soft breasts and a lilting voice; a boy, ten, Norbert, with spiky blond hair; and a girl, seven, Ana, whose nose is covered in freckles. The parents are Dutch, which sounds like *Deutsch*, which means German, only they don't speak German, they speak Dutch, but since they now live in Canada they've resolved to speak nothing but English, only sometimes they forget and lapse into Dutch which sounds like Deutsch which means German.

As Norbert can't help boasting to Milo right off the bat, Jan built the swing set in the backyard with his own two hands . . .

(Don't cry, Astuto. I know, your eyes are as dry as ever but you can't fool me, I can tell you're crying, so c'mon, stop it. Don't forget that snippet of wisdom we gleaned after years of talking and drinking and fucking together—to grow up is to admit that pretty much everything you believed as a child is false. You believed that the sun rose and set, that your soul was immortal, that adults were strong. Wisdom is rough . . .)

Jan Manders takes Milo over to the swing set, plunks him into the huge black tire that dangles there, and starts pushing . . . Gently at first, until the boy gets used to it, then *Want to go a little higher?*

Milo nods. *A little higher?* Milo nods, excited. *A little higher?* Milo nods. *Okay, that's high enough . . .*

He feels safe, surrounded on all sides by the hard warm ring of black rubber, watching the trees swing back and forth above his head, his whole self given up to sheer, pleasurable sensation.

Sara Manders is rolling out dough for a piecrust. A radio is playing in the background (what year are we? '57—yeah, okay, Ella Fitzgerald, Sara could be humming along with Ella) . . . Milo comes over to watch her and she hoists him onto a chair and helps him help her, tying an apron on him, dusting the rolling pin with flour, then gently guiding his hands on the pin to flatten out the ball of dough.

At bath time she splashes warm water on his back and neck and rubs him gently everywhere with a sudsy washcloth.

At bedtime she reads to the two older children on the living room couch and he creeps up in his pajamas, presses his back to the back of the couch, sticks his thumb in his mouth, closes his eyes and listens. At first, because there are so many words he doesn't know, it's just the lilting, the rhythm and melody of her voice that hypnotize him, but after a while the images of the stories start to crystallize and he looks forward to the moment when, picking up where she left off the night before, Sara will thrill them again with her imitations of the sulky donkey and the Queen of Hearts and the parrot that squawks *Pieces of eight! Pieces of eight!*

"What does that mean, Mama?" Ana asks, and Sara admits she doesn't know, her English isn't good enough . . . but her imitation of the squawking parrot has them in stitches.

(Was it your grandfather, Milo, who finally told you about pieces of eight? Helping you think it through. *Why do we call a quarter two bits, my boy? Because British pounds were divided into eight pieces or bits . . .*)

When she comes to kiss him good night, Sara runs her fingers through Milo's hair. Her own children's hair, like the little that remains of Jan's, is thin and blond; hers is light brown but Milo's is thick wavy brown with auburn glints in it. *What beautiful hair you have, Milo!*

It had never occurred to the boy that something about him could be beautiful.

SWING SWIFTLY THROUGH the cycle of a year.

Autumn: little Ana teaching him the rudiments of reading as she learns them at school.

Winter: the skating rink. Milo inherits Ana's pink-and-white skates from the year before and is relieved when no one teases him for wearing pink. By afternoon's end, cheeks red, eyes flashing in silent pride, he skates around the rink all by himself and the Manders family applauds him. At the drink stand where Jan buys them hot chocolate afterward, they get jostled by a noisy group of preteens yelling at one another in French. Though he can't quite understand the language, it stirs memories in his brain (transient images of neon lights and white-clad arms) that make him want to die.

Spring: Norbert shows him that if you cut an earthworm in two, both halves of it will wiggle on miserably for a while. On the front porch, Jan takes Milo in his arms and points up to the sky—hugely white and alive, vibrating, screaming, with the return of the Canadian geese.

Summer: a barbecue in the backyard. The five of them gobble down spareribs, fingers and lips scarlet with sauce. Point at one another and laugh. Tell jokes. Play pranks. Ana pours a glass of water down her father's back, provoking a roar. When night falls, they go out hunting for fireflies in the grass.

And then . . . at some point during the second fall . . . a strange young woman in the kitchen, making dinner. Jan standing by the closed door to his and Sara's bedroom, talking to a doctor. Another day, a glimpse into that room—Jan emerging from it in tears—reveals a motionless mound barely visible among the bedclothes.

A hearse parked in front of the house. Taking his little sister in his arms to comfort her, Norbert himself bursts into sobs. Jan helps Milo pack. Hugs him long and hard. Stacks his luggage in the trunk of a strange car. Sitting up straight and stiff in the backseat, Milo doesn't respond when the Manderses, gathered in the driveway, wave him good-bye.

He's furious with Sara for dying. But it's taught him an important lesson—people can't belong to each other. Never again will he wholly entrust himself to anyone.

CLOSETS. BROOMS. BELTS. Blows raining down on the child's head. Shouts. Voices calling his name, "*Milo . . . Milo . . . Milo . . . Where is that boy? Milo . . . Milo . . . Milo . . . Where are you? I'll teach you to hide when it's time to go to school!*" Women's legs banging up around him. Women's arms thrashing out at him. He's rolled up in a ball, not crying, not sobbing. His body limp and passive, his mind a blank.

Sometimes, from the dark and secret heart of the blackout, images well up (perhaps use animation here?). A cat without a smile . . . a smile without a cat . . . Tinker Bell touching something with her magic wand and turning it into something else . . . John, Michael and Wendy Darling soaring through the air . . . *I can fly, I can fly, I can fly!* . . . Canadian geese screaming as they cross the sky . . . Legs without bodies, bodies without legs . . . Captain Hook screaming as the crocodile bites off his leg . . . Long John Silver also losing a leg . . . both pirates limping about on wooden legs . . . wooden arms, wooden noses . . . Pinocchio's nose lengthening with every lie . . . Alice growing so tall she fills the whole room, her head scrunched up against the ceiling . . . then shrinking swiftly until she can drown in a bottle of ink . . . We dive into the ink bottle with her.

BLACKOUT.

．　．　．　．　．

Neil, 1916

A BUCOLIC SHOT: the front steps of the Kerrigan house in Dublin's genteel suburbs, early on a lovely April morning. Briefcase in hand, Neil plants a perfunctory kiss on his mother's cheek. The way they embrace indicates that the balance of power in the household has shifted over the past two years. Mrs. Kerrigan now clearly respects her son, admires him, even. And he, having matured, can contemplate her fears and foibles with something approaching benevolence. As he turns to go, she protests mildly.

"I can't understand what work there is to be done on a holiday! Surely none of your colleagues will be in the office today."

"I've told you before, Mother. A lawyer's work, like a woman's, is never done. I always have numerous cases to prepare, and since I'm the youngest partner in the firm I need to be sure that every file is watertight. What happened on Easter Monday, anyway? Was Jesus so exhausted by the Resurrection that he needed a day off?"

"Neil!"

"Joking, Mother. Joking."

CUT to Neil meeting up with his cousin Thom (also carrying a briefcase) on the docks at Victoria Quay. Fast camera work translates their excitement. Ducking into an abandoned warehouse next to Saint James's Gate Brewery, they swiftly exchange their suits and ties for Volunteer garb. Thom assembles a rifle, Neil pockets a revolver and they join other young Sinn Féiners converging in combat gear on the Sackville Street General Post Office. Among them are a surprising number of women. Close-up on beautiful Countess Constance Markiewicz, her arms crossed, her features calm and determined.

Padraic Pearse and James Connolly begin to harangue the rebels.

"Again our boys are dying in droves," Pearse thunders. "Right at the present moment, *a quarter of a million* Irishmen are risking their lives for the sake of the Union Jack. And why do they sign up? We all know the answer: because they're hungry!"

"The submarine *Aud* was due to land at Tralee on Good Friday," Connolly goes on, "bringing us arms and ammunition from Europe. Well, the Brits scuttled it! All our precious weapons are at the bottom of the sea! Men, the time is ripe, we must seize the day! Wrench our city of Dublin and our land of Eire back from the hands of the enemy!"

Thom is ready. Proud. Bursting with impatience to prove himself. As for Neil, he's scared. Never has he known hunger, misery, or loss; he hasn't the *body* for courageous revolt. Gradually, the voice in his head effaces the loud voices of the rebel leaders.

Though the rhetoric repels me, though I regret that we should need to appeal to the masses through their guts instead of their brains, though I wish we could kick the Brits out without clinging like Padraic Pearse to ridiculous propaganda about the Celts, or like John MacBride to reactionary Catholicism, or like James Connolly to dogmatic Marxist theory—I'm willing to do battle on the rebels' side. But in my brief-case, in that briefcase now stashed away in the abandoned brewery, is a weapon far more powerful than the gun in my pocket: the manuscript of my first book of poems. Well, prose poems, actually. A revolutionary form—a joyous mixture of English and Gaelic which, by its accurate reflection of our mongrel history, will shock all. The new Ireland will need new writers, and I shall be first among them. As soon as I find a publisher, my words will set fire to my countrymen's hearts.

Maps are being perused, lists of names handed out. Of the six-teen thousand rebels nominally available in Dublin, only a thou-sand have shown up.

What happened to the others? our hero wonders. *Are they cow-ards? Or is their reasoning more logical than ours? . . .*

SUBJECTIVE CAMERA: FLASH images of Neil's perceptions over the ensuing days and nights. The tricolor, then the green flag with its golden harp are run up onto the roof of the General Post Office and the Volunteers burst into cheers. Pearse, his voice shaking with emotion, reads out the Proclamation of the Irish Republic. Hailed and heckled, jostled and shoved by overexcited young men, passersby respond with dismay and anger. The gates of Trinity College swing to, clang shut, are locked.

Neil's inner voice: *This is what I must write about. Scrap those Anglo-Gaelic poems and write the great novel of the Easter Rising in Dublin. Find language, the rhythm of words, that will plunge the reader into the state we're in right now—make him feel the erratic beating of our hearts, Ta, ta-da DA, ta, ta-da DA . . . the thrill of fear in our balls, the simultaneous tension and suppleness of our muscles. Never have we been more alive than we are now, so close to death.*

The next day, as they take up their assigned post at the entrance to Saint Stephen's Green, Neil and Thom speak together in whispers.

"The Brits will have a hard time finding men to send over today, Neil." "Why's that?" "Krauts just made a zeppelin raid on East Anglia." "I see . . . Quite the coincidence, hey?" "Problem with that, Neil?" "Don't know how to fit it into my novel." "Good novels should be full of contradictions, shouldn't they?"

Hearing a cascade of bullet reports from close by, they drop to the ground. Just then, who should come strolling down Grafton Street in their direction, clad in civilian dress, nose in the air, but Major John MacBride? He brings up short upon reaching the entrance to Saint Stephen's Green.

"What the hell are you young'uns doing on the ground?"

"We're taking back our country, sir," explains Thom, hastily getting to his feet and dusting off his pants.

"Yes?"

Glancing around, the major gathers that something is amiss. The cousins bring him up to date in a few low-spoken words.

"How is it I was not kept informed of these plans?"

"Ah . . . well, Major MacBride, sir, your being so famous an enemy of the British, it was feared you might be under surveillance. We felt we couldn't take the risk."

"But you're welcome to join us now, sir," Neil puts in politely. "If you've nothing better to do, that is."

John MacBride hesitates; the winey red of his cheeks deepens and we divine that his military pulse has begun to race.

"Well, I was on my way to my brother's wedding, but . . . first things first, eh? I'm certain my brother will understand if I change my plans. Though unprepared and unarmed, I have no choice but to throw in my fate with that of Ireland once again . . ."

(Milo, this is terrible dialogue. Just terrible. In three decades of working together, I don't think we've ever written anything this bad. Yeah, sure, you're just kidding, but meanwhile crucial events are unfolding and we need to convey them somehow . . .)

"Where can I make myself useful?" MacBride says eagerly.

"At Jacob's," says Thom at once. "They need more men over at Jacob's Biscuit Factory. Only fourteen of the forty who were supposed to be stationed there showed up, all young and sorely lacking in experience. Perhaps you can take charge of the situation there."

"I most certainly can," replies MacBride.

Saluting, he turns on his heel and vanishes (thus putting an end to this very weak scene we'll definitely need to rewrite . . .).

AS DAYLIGHT WANES, confusion and uproar in the city of Dublin. Sandbags. Barricades. Dark shadows dashing this way and that. The sound of panting. *Ta, ta-da DA, ta, ta-da DA* . . . Thuds that might be bodies or sandbags. Night falls. The next morning, stationed on the Liffey at the exact spot where Neil cut his post-Monto capers in the opening scene, the British gunboat *Helga* starts shelling the city. Gulls wheel and scream overhead. The General Post Office is in flames. All Sackville Street is burning. Smoke rises from ruined buildings in the city center. *Ta, ta-da DA, ta, ta-da DA* . . . British soldiers swarm through the streets, overwhelming the rebels by their sheer number. A Sinn Féiner is shot to death by a British sniper crouched on the roof of Trinity. By Tuesday night, the sky over Dublin is a deep red.

Tenement buildings along the Liffey burning. Poor people scurrying out of them, the women clasping bawling babies in their arms, the men in a state of black fury, shaking their fists at the insurgents, screaming till they're hoarse: *We've lost everything . . .*

Neil's inner voice: *How write this? How explain it? What rhythm of syllables printed on the page could convey their* We've lost everything*? No more proof than this is needed of the absence of God. None of the priests of my childhood ever spoke a word of truth. Darwin alone has told the truth, Darwin alone! Animals, the lot of us, scurrying to survive. From time immemorial, the strong annihilate the weak and the weak do their utmost to grow strong and take over. I myself have just played a role in destroying the lives of the weak, and never will I be punished for it. The evil are no more punished than the good are rewarded, either in this life or in the hereafter, since there is no hereafter. Sorry, Ma. Ah, will you ever be disappointed, all you multitudes of bigotty priggish ladies, whether Catholic or Protestant! I can just see you waking up after death, looking around and saying,* Bloody hell, what is this void? You mean there's no Heaven after all? Are you telling me that for seventy-five years I put up with all those truckloads of shite, for nothing? *Afraid so, Ma. Afraid so, O ye prissy ladies who kept your thighs squeezed tight, saving yourselves up for eternal bliss with Jesus after death—no Heaven after all, no just deserts. Even in my father's law courts people don't get their just deserts. Justice is no more nor less than a diabolical power game. The truth is the last thing that interests people in a law court! I'll write this, yes, I shall! Write the novel of the Easter Rising, its leaders aspiring to be great and famous men, its followers aspiring to be men at least, at last, to feel strong, escape from their mothers and sisters, impress their girlfriends and pass on their genes. That's what politics are about—survival and nothing else . . .*

(Yeah, well, maybe we could make Neil's spiel a *bit* less long-winded. But don't forget that at this point in his life he's still green and arrogant, not yet the grandfather you'd one day come to know . . .)

A couple of days later. Dark rings under their eyes, Neil and Thom are again posted at the entrance to Saint Stephen's. Scattered here and there throughout the park are other Sinn Féiners (we recognize Constance Markiewicz in the background). All are discouraged, exhausted, overwhelmed. They haven't slept for days. In the bushes just behind the cousins, the camera reveals a waif of a rebel, blond and barely pubescent, asleep on the job . . .

"Neil! The Brits now outnumber us thirty to one."

"That's not the worst of it. The Dubliners themselves are against us. How can we free Dublin against its will?"

"Ah, passivity! The greatest force in human history."

"People need to eat, Thom. They care about sitting down to meals together. Did you hear them scream at us? Never shall I forget the despair in their eyes. Thom, I've been thinking . . . *Aargh . . . !*"

They've just been grabbed from behind by a group of British soldiers. Their weapons are torn away from them. Starting out of sleep, the blond adolescent freezes in fear and glues his stomach to the ground. As one soldier holds each of the cousins, bending his right arm forcibly at the elbow and twisting it up behind his back, another rummages through their pockets and under their clothes. Incongruously, Neil's brain flashes to that dreadful moment in the Talbot Street brothel when he'd lost sight of his own hands. The blond kid watches from his hidden vantage point as Thom puts up a struggle, swearing at the soldiers and taunting them with Joycean rhyme and humor, calling them *twitbrits* and *clitwits*. The man holding him shoots him at point-blank and he collapses on the sidewalk, his corpse partly on Neil's feet.

Stop sound track. White silence in Neil's brain. Face white, too.

The muzzle of a gun in *his* back, too.

"What's your name, you little bugger?"

He stutters his name in a white whisper and adds: "I'm a lawyer and my father's a magistrate, you can't . . ."

"Feck the law," the soldier interrupts him. "You're next on the sidewalk unless you give us a good reason not to put you there. Where are your leaders, baby boy? Where are your feckin' leaders, you little knock-kneed patriot? Give us the names and whereabouts of your leaders. A nice, big name to make us happy."

Numbness and strangeness. Paralysis of Neil Kerrigan's facial muscles. Sense of unreality, of theater. Time slows, seems to stop. Neil stares stupidly into the face of the soldier shouting at him, a man his age. Sees his fear. Shares the man's fear and tension, his rage at being tense and fearful. Weirdly, it's as if this British soldier were his cousin—as if, at the instant of his death, Thom's soul had slithered up into the enemy's body and were now staring out at him through the enemy's eyes and trying to warn him: *Careful, Neil. Take it easy, man. Careful, now. Everything's critical here.*

The name slips out: "MacBride."

Synapses are exploding like slow fireworks in his brain. *Mac-Bride out of the way . . . Maud Gonne would be free . . . I'd be doing Yeats a favor . . . eliminating the last impediment to their marriage . . . He'd be grateful . . . and want to do me a favor in turn . . . help me find a publisher for my novel . . .*

"What?"

"Major John MacBride," Neil repeats, his voice white.

The blond kid in the bushes is still there. Listening. Quaking with fear and listening.

"Come off it."

"Yes. Himself."

"Where?"

"At Jacob's."

"We'll take you with us. Oh, for the luva Christ, the kid's be-shat himself. We'll take you with us anyway, you pile of stinking shite. If you're lying, you're dead. You know that, eh?"

"I'm not lying, so help me . . ."

Simultaneously shoved forward and firmly held from behind, he stumbles off and we follow the clumsy group into the dark.

· · · · ·

Awinita, May 1951

"I DUNNO WHY I like you so goddamn much, Mister Cleaning-Fluid."

"Must be 'cause I'm cute."

"Not 'cause you're rich, anyhow."

They laugh. They finished making love a few minutes ago and Declan is still inside of Awinita, body spooned against her back, arm draped round her enormous tummy.

"Maybe I make you happy in bed," he whispers.

"Hmm. Don't let it go to your head."

"That's not where it goes, Nita."

They laugh. Neighborhood sounds come sifting through the open window: traffic, the yells of construction workers, the clatter of dishes from a nearby restaurant kitchen, even a couple of gulls screaming overhead. The clock on the bedside table shows eleven. Declan arrived at the end of Awinita's shift at five or six A.M. and they've spent what they call the night together.

"Sure you never get me mixed up with one of your johns?"

"How could I? You ain't paid me since de first time we came up here. *I* buy *your* drinks now."

They laugh and cuddle.

"Seriously. You can tell the difference?"

"Yeah. Never saw a guy had such a big . . . head o' red hair."

They laugh. His right hand gently brushes her neck, her face. Stopping it with her own hand, she takes his fingers into her mouth.

"And from behind?"

"Hmm?"

"When I'm behind you, you can't see my hair . . . *Then* what's the diff?"

Silence.

"Hey, Nita? Tell me. Me or a john: same diff?"

Long silence. Finally: "Johns don't bring me flowers."

On the Formica table in the background, we notice a single wilted rose in a too-large chipped blue vase.

"Dey don't hold me tight when we dance. And dey don't ask so many questions."

"That why you love me?"

"I say I love you?"

"Yeah!"

"Okay, den shut up."

They laugh. Declan gets out of bed and, pulling a flask of whisky from the inside pocket of his leather jacket (draped over a chair), takes a couple of serious swigs. Lights a cigarette, moves to the window and stands there smoking, naked. We're in Awinita's eyes, looking at his body . . .

(Okay, Milo, I'll keep it simple. We won't make a lingering inventory of Declan's physical beauty, moving slowly from the nape of his neck where his red-blond hair curls and furls, down the curve of his lower back over his buttocks and thighs . . . It'd be easy to fall in love with your father at age twenty-four, but all right, we'll leave the spectators free to notice his charms or not, as they see fit . . .)

"What do the johns talk to you about?" asks Declan, smoking, his tone curious rather than aggressive.

"Whatever."

"No, really."

"Why?"

"Just . . . you know . . . to know what kinda stuff you go through here."

In black and white in Awinita's mind, a chaotic cascade of stills. Men in blurry close-up, contorted and sweating, shouting into the void; other men sitting on the edge of the bed talking to her, at her, in urgent self-absorption; still others drawing snapshots from their wallets to show her their houses, horses, cars, kids and wives. FADE TO SHADOW: and, in the shadow, imperceptible shift to animated images . . .

A woman's hand grasps a dark purple snake that writhes and twists, struggling to get away. She maintains her grip and finally it goes limp; the snake's head drops and its forked tongue hangs out.

"Lotta dem boast," she sums up. "Dey wanna be admired."

"Do they ask you your name?"

"Sure. Some o' dem ask it tree, four times."

"Do they come back? The same ones?"

"Happens."

"And you don't get attached to them?"

"Happens."

"But differently from me?"

"Everybody different."

"Nita!"

He laughs, she doesn't.

"You got Indian clients?"

"Indians are broke, Mister Cleaning-Fluid."

"So'm I."

"Well, maybe you part Indian! Now shut up and lemme get some sleep."

"Naw, don't go back to sleep, Nita . . . Let's go down to the river."

CUT. Quick shot of Awinita in the tiny bathroom, tipping pills into her hand and gulping them down with tap water.

On Saint Helen's Island, passersby gape at the two of them walking hand in hand: the small, conspicuously pregnant Indian girl with bleached-blond hair and the gangly, flame-headed youth in cowboy boots. Declan takes her to a spot he knows, a tiny cove amidst rocks, its water a still pool. Beyond, the rushing river. Sitting on the minute, pebbly idea of a beach, her bulk between his skinny bent legs, his arms protectively circling her belly; they stare out at the water, boats and birds. Declan takes a swig of whisky.

"I love it here."

"Yeah, 'sokay."

"Want some?"

"Tanks . . ."

"I really only feel at home in nature, you know? I'm a country boy at heart."

"So what ya doin' in de city?"

"No jobs in the country."

"You got a job now?"

"Nah. Prefer to live offa you."

He laughs, she doesn't.

"Awinita . . ."

"Yeah."

"Since . . . I mean, since you're planning to give the kid up for adoption anyhow . . . why don't we . . . like, go someplace together? I mean . . . why don't we just leave Montreal and go live out in the forest someplace, make a life for ourselves? Awinita, come away with me! We're both young, we can start over."

"Start what over?"

"Whatever! We could buy a stand of maple trees and learn how to make maple syrup . . ."

"Buy it how?"

"You ain't got any savings?"

She says nothing. We remember the tin-roofed shack, the packed dirt floor, the weeping family.

"Your dad didn't leave you any money when he died?"

Again she says nothing.

In front of them, an Indian man of forty or forty-five, his body transparent, is bent over the water's edge. He's holding something in his hands, but we can't see what. Suddenly he smashes it on a rock and tosses the pieces into the air. They fall—heavily at first, like gold nuggets, then gently, like raindrops. The drops disturb the still pool. The man gradually dissolves.

"*Your* dad's de one who got money," she says at last.

"Only hitch is, he disowned me."

"How come?"

"Third jail sentence, he got fed up. I disappoint him, Nita. Seems like none of his sons turned out the way he hoped. He wanted us all to go to university. Workin' on the land is beneath us, he says. Back in Ireland he was a lawyer, his dad was a judge, his friends were a buncha famous writers . . ."

"So how come he left?"

"Somethin' happened during the First World War, I don't know what. Maybe he refused to be drafted by the British, somethin' like that."

"Dey drafted Indians from here, too," Awinita murmurs, but Declan doesn't hear her.

"He came to Canada, found himself a nice plump Québécoise to marry. Then she started churning out babies and he worked his ass off on her father's land. If I heard it once I heard it a thousand times: twenty years of backbreaking labor in Pierre-Joseph Chabot's foresting industry . . . all the while clutching at his dream of getting a novel published. After a long day's work on the property, he'd sit up reading and writing in his library late into the night. When his folks died, he had *eighteen boxes of books* shipped over from Dublin. And that still wasn't enough. Every time he went to Montreal or Ottawa he'd come home with a fresh armload of books. Plays, poetry, first editions . . . *But Neil, darling, what good will all these books do us?* I remember my mother saying. *We can't feed our children with poetry!* Truth is my mom was slightly pissed off 'cause she'd grown up in the sticks and wanted *out* of them. Ran away to Montreal at age eighteen to become an actress, landed up waiting tables instead, in a coffee shop on Notre-Dame. That's where they met. So she was none too thrilled when he insisted they head back to the sticks. She figured if she had to wade through cow and baby dung from morning to night, least *he* could do was shut up about Shakespeare. He used to corral all his sons into his study every Sunday morning, read out loud to us in English from these ancient books, stuff about Greek wars, British kings, whatever. I learned to hate that library of his. The girls meanwhile, being francophones, would be off at Mass with our mom . . . She died giving birth to her thirteenth baby and, being the oldest girl, Marie-Thérèse took over. She raised us with an iron hand, that's for sure, but she couldn't change our father's ways."

We gently leave the ground and go wafting up in the air to join the gulls wheeling above the Saint Lawrence. We fly through our own long, undulating hair . . . But as we move through it, it begins to wrap around us—more and more tightly—until finally we're nothing but a hard little ball of hair. We bounce.

"When I was twelve or so," Declan plunges on, "my da got a package in the mail, a signed copy of a book by some Irish writer with a woman's name . . . Janice or some such, I forget. The book was a mishmash of foreign words and hard words and nonwords, as if the guy'd taken a big stack of books from all over the world and tossed them into a pot and made a stew of them, then ladled the stew onto the pages . . . After about an hour of listening to that horridge-porridge, I got mad. How dare my father waste my time with this when I had stuff to do, buddies to see . . . That day, I swore I'd never be caught dead with a book in my hands. My brothers musta done the same 'cause none of us ever made it past junior high."

"Not so different," Awinita murmurs in her husky voice.

"What's not so different?"

"You."

"From what?"

"My johns."

"Thanks!"

"'Sokay. You're a guy, and guys like de sound of deir own voice. Hey, gotta get back to work."

. . . . .

IV
MALÍCIA

The very essence of capoeira, malícia *allows you to see the darkest sides of human beings and society without losing your joie de vivre.*

Milo, 1958–62

THE CHILD OF absence is in the closet again—or rather in *a* closet again, not the same one as before. There've been a number of closets already in his short life and he's found a way to survive in there—he makes an even darker closet for himself inside his head, enters it of his own volition and firmly closes the door behind him. Calling out to no one, needing no one, finding what he needs within himself.

Once he's in there, in the dark of the dark, he's filled with anticipation because, closing his eyes, he can summon images and voices and they will come to him. He can elicit the cocker spaniel at the house next door to the German family when he was little and play with it as he was never allowed to at the time, since there was a picket fence between them and only two of the pickets were broken. Now he can throw a stick and the dog will bark excitedly, scamper to fetch the stick and bring it back to him, growling in pride—a game to be endlessly repeated. Then Milo can pet the dog's head, say *Good boy*, reward it with a biscuit and feel its small wet scrapy tongue lick his palm because they love each other more than anything in the world. In the dark of the dark he can also meet up with his best friend, an imaginary boygirl named Ness like the Loch Ness monster, and the two of them can take off for wild adventures on the moon or Mars or under the sea or in the jungle or the desert or on the tundra, or exploring glaciers at the North Pole or volcanoes in South America or the topmost tips of the Himalayas . . .

(The self-created closet gradually became your carapace, Milo. It would protect you forever. Your concentration was so extreme in there that you could accept literally anything—blows, rape, verbal attacks—and keep a hot star burning in your brain . . .)

Other times, in the closet, little Milo hears his mother's voice singing to him and whispering his secret name, or the voice of Sara Manders reading him a bedtime story. He feels Sara's ample bosoms against his back as she holds him on her lap and cuddles him, strokes his head and marvels at the beauty of his hair . . . Curled on the closet floor, he hugs his own body and sometimes, listening to these beautiful women's voices or feeling their breasts, his hand slips into his pants and he strokes himself and whines and pants until a blaze of light happens in his brain, after which he can relax and sometimes fall asleep. One day he's doing this and suddenly the blaze of light turns into a real light, pale and appalling—his foster mother has opened the closet door and flicked on the switch and found him there with his hand inside his pants and his head thrown back, drinking in the slow deep joy of a woman's flesh moving softly on his skin. She yells, catapulting him out of his reverie, then grabs the weapon nearest to hand—the long metal tube of the vacuum cleaner—and clobbers him over the head with it: *God forgive me, but if I don't beat this evil out of you there'll be no hope left, you'll grow up to be a criminal just like your parents! Bad seed on bad ground!* As her blows rain down on Milo's head and back and

shoulders—his arms protect his face—the woman also kicks him
with her pointed shoes wherever she can fit a kick in . . .

YOU'RE RIGHT, MILO—MOVIEGOERS enjoy blood and gore of all
sorts; they'll watch in mesmerized delight as people cut each other's head off, stab each other in the back, or bomb whole cities to
oblivion; many of them also revel in seeing adult males rape little
girls; but for some reason, though it's one of the most widespread
forms of violence on the planet, grown women hitting little boys
makes them squirm . . . Go figure, eh?

(Hear that, Milo? You've even taught me to say *eh?* like a Canadian. Hey. Are you doing all right? Are *we* doing all right? Can
we go on, my love? I love you, Astuto. Let's go on. Yes, yes, we'll
change the name, no problem—do it in a single click, soon as we
finish the first draft . . .)

THE LITTLE BASTARD knows how to read now, in English. He
learned to read with a vengeance. Having completed the first two
grades of school in a single year, he reads everything he can get his
hands on, even if it's only the dreary *Reader's Digest* in the bathroom or the newspaper called the *Gazette* or the Bible his current
foster mother keeps on her bedside table for daily inspiration. The
printed words waft him away to freedom, set his mind spinning
with stories. The main thing is to be out of this world, out, out . . .

Though we can also toss in a few images of Milo's so-called
real life during those years (Milo in the classroom, his attention
riveted on the teacher, on the blackboard, oblivious to the children
around him . . . Milo in the school courtyard, bullied by older boys
and unexpectedly fighting back so that within three seconds the
leader's nose is gushing with blood . . . Milo walking home alone
in the four o'clock December dark . . . Milo shoveling snow . . .

mowing the lawn . . . sitting stiff and straight on the pew of a Protestant church between two stiff and straight adults, one male, one
female, whose heads we'll never see), it's clear that his *real* real life
now unfolds inside the closet, in the dark of the dark. Ecstasy of
images, voices drifting through silence . . . He's become addicted
to solitude.

And then—brutally—he gets weaned of it. Cold turkey.

He comes home from school one warm June day, opens the
screen door and brings up short. His foster parents (still headless
torsos) are seated in the front room with a gray-bearded stranger;
packed and waiting in the hallway is Milo's suitcase. At lightning
speed, his eyes shift from grown-up to suitcase to grown-up, but
no matter how often he changes the order of his perusal, he still
can't fathom what's going on.

CUT to the enormous, dimly lit hall of Windsor Station in
Montreal. Chaos. Hordes of people rushing every which way
amidst the hiss of steam engines and the strident sigh of whistles,
shouting, smoking, waving, embracing and calling out to each
other, dragging bags and trunks in their wake. Spiffy, red-hatted,
chocolate-skinned porters shoving luggage carts. Arrival and departure announcements that sound like threats, reverberating over
the loudspeaker in French. After scanning the crowd, the camera
zooms in from behind on the old man, who is pulling Milo's heavy
suitcase with one hand and Milo with the other.

The boy balks, in shock. The gray-bearded stranger turns to
him and at last we see his face. It may take us a moment to recognize Neil.

"Come on," he says. "We'll miss the train."

"I don't want to go."

"What?"

"I don't want to go."

"They beat the bejesus out of you and you want to stay with them?"

"I don't want to go."

"I didn't ask you if you wanted to go. I'm your grandpa and I'm taking you out of that Protestant hellhole."

"You're not my grandpa."

"So I am, bless you. Look." He draws an Irish passport from his breast pocket. "Know how to read? Neil Noirlac. You see, it's written there. And what's your name?"

"..."

"What's your name, young'un?"

"Milo."

"Milo what?"

The boy can't help muttering Noirlac under his breath.

"Right. And where would you have gotten a name like Noirlac?"

"I don't want to go."

"Do you know its meaning?"

"I don't want to go."

"*Black lake*, it means. Did you know your name was *black lake*, my boy? Do you speak French?"

"I don't want to go."

"Come on, now, Milo, or we'll be missing our train! Way they've been treating you, those Protestants are lucky I came without my gun."

"You got a gun?"

"Naturally, for hunting rabbit and lynx and moose."

"Will you teach me how to hunt?"

Neil gathers the child in his arms and pretends for a moment that he is strong enough to carry him. He isn't, though, and, sensing this, Milo gives in.

"I'll come wit you," he says, "if you teach me to hunt."

"You've got a deal."

CUT to the two of them in a train, hurtling northeastward through the province of Quebec. Around them, other passengers are chattering in French. Neil takes out a paper bag and hands a sandwich to Milo, who accepts and devours it without a word, staring out the window at flash-by forest as he chews. Never before has he set foot outside of Montreal.

CUT to a Dubé family meal, the noonday meal they call dinner, in the kitchen of a large farmhouse in Mauricie. Seated on benches on either side of a long maple wood table are Neil's oldest daughter, a brittly pretty woman named Marie-Thérèse; her husband, Régis Dubé, his cheeks mottled with smallpox scars; and their two strapping teenagers, François-Joseph and Jean-Joseph, all slurping soup and shouting in French at the same time.

Milo is lost. Even were he able to revive the dormant rudiments of French he once possessed, this clipped, slanted, rural version of the tongue would be opaque to him. Occasionally Neil leans down to translate for him, but every time she catches him at it Marie-Thérèse slams her hand on the table.

"Papa! Stop that at once! This is a French-speaking house, he might as well get used to it from the start. I don't want you running off at the mouth again with your bullshit bilingual notions, do you hear me?"

"How can he be expected to learn?" Neil protests, stroking his beard. "The poor kid doesn't understand a word we're saying."

"He'll learn as he goes along, like everybody else."

"Gotta be patient," Régis suggests, his mouth three or four centimeters away from his bowl of soup. (Régis is a cowed man who seems perpetually to be ducking, even when not bent over to eat.) "Rome wasn't built in a day," he adds, so softly as to be inaudible to all but us.

"So where did this Anglo cousin come from?" queries François-Joseph.

"Yeah, Grandad, where'd you dig him up? 'S not every day you get to meet a cousin who's already eight years old!"

"He's Declan's boy . . ."

"Who else?" grumbles Marie-Thérèse.

"But where's he kept him all these years? We never saw Uncle Declan with a kid . . ."

"I had no idea, either," says Neil. "Declan came over last week to try to wangle some money out of me . . ."

"Nothin' new about that," observes Marie-Thérèse.

"Just as you say! I told him he'd exhausted my patience, to say nothing of his credit . . . So to force me to give in, he wound up telling me the fifty bucks weren't for him. Claimed he needed the money for his son's pension . . ."

"Doesn't it just break your heart?" says Marie-Thérèse, shaking her head.

"I didn't believe him myself. Come on, I told him, you can't pull the wool over my eyes with tall tales like that! Where is this so-called son of yours?"

"A miracle he could even remember, after so many whiskys . . ."

"Well it turned out to be a miracle indeed! He fished out the child's birth certificate and a whole slew of official papers . . . Believe it or not, Milo had been in five different foster families and Declan had never lost track of him . . ."

"Good heavens!"

"You were in five different families?"

Milo shrugs, gaze trained on his plate. He can tell the conversation revolves around him, but the gist of it escapes him.

"Why'd they move him around so much?"

"Beats me. But the idea that a grandson of mine had been living in Montreal all this time without my knowing about it . . . well, I just couldn't stand it. I had to go get him."

"I understand," Régis mutters. "You did the right thing."

"Just makes one more mouth for us to feed!" Marie-Thérèse sighs.

"Oh, one mouth more or less," says Neil.

"Easy to say, for people who have their noses in books all day long," says Marie-Thérèse. "The rest of us work hard to make ends meet!"

"Come on, now, Marie-Thérèse!" says Neil. "I couldn't leave him in a Protestant household!"

This is his last card, but it's a joker and he knows it. Of all the tales of his youth in Ireland with which Neil had regaled the family when Marie-Thérèse was little, the one about the stolen children had made the deepest impression on her. During the endless merciless strike that had paralyzed and famished the entire city of Dublin in 1913, British soldiers had gone stomping into strikers' homes, kidnapped their children and shipped them off to Great Britain to be taken in by Protestant families. And what honest Catholic worker could bear the prospect of finding himself with a stubborn, glitter-eyed little Protestant at his own kitchen table? They'd returned to the factories . . .

After dinner, Milo's cousins take him on a guided tour of the farm. Close-up on their great rubber boots squelching in the mud as he follows them across the barnyard. In the barn, he recoils at first from the clouds of bottle flies and the pungent smell of manure, but is soon irresistibly drawn to the cows. He feels more empathy with these big kind warm brown tail-swishing dumb beasts than with Jean-Joseph and François-Joseph, fourteen and thirteen respectively, who belch and fart, smoke and swear and swagger to make sure he knows who's boss.

"Cat got your tongue?" they ask him.

He says not a word in the course of the visit . . . CUT.

A SERIES OF ephemeral, floating scenes to sketch out the following year. Milo at school, Milo in the stable . . . lingering a moment over Milo at church. We recognize him squeezed into one of the front pews along with his young schoolmates . . . His cousin's classes are farther back; the rows for parents and grandparents start in the middle of the church. We notice that Marie-Thérèse and Régis are among them, but not Neil . . .

Dissolve to a winter evening on the farm. Marie-Thérèse has summoned Milo to help her with the job of pickling cucumbers. The kitchen air is opaque with steam.

(The telephone plays a role in this scene, so we'll have to go back and establish its presence during Milo's first dinner at the farm: a black Bakelite contraption on the wall above the table. Maybe Marie-Thérèse could mention it, proud of having a telephone at last. Or maybe it could ring during the meal, causing everyone to jump because they're not used to it yet . . . We'll see . . .)

Seated next to the wall, at the farthest end of the long maple wood table, Milo carefully pours vinegar into jars as his aunt peels and chops garlic across from him. Suddenly she looks up at him.

"You're a little infidel, aren't you?"

"Sorry?"

"You lived with a Protestant family and they put a bunch of lies in your head?"

"I dunno."

"Do you believe, at least?"

"Believe what?"

"In everything the preacher says at Sunday Mass. In God the Father and the Holy Virgin and Our Lord who died on the Cross for our sins, and all the rest, and that if you don't believe you'll go to Hell?"

". . ."

"You don't listen at all in church, do you?"

". . ."

"Don't think I don't notice it. I watch you and I can tell you're not paying attention. You don't sing with the rest of us and you don't pray with the rest of us, you just sit there. You go off somwhere else in your head."

". . ."

"That's what you do, isn't it, Milo? I've seen you, there's no point in denyng it."

"I don't deny it."

"Well, believe me, Milo, this won't do at all. Because in two or three years you'll have to go to catechism classes, and prepare for your confirmation, and prove that you've grasped the essence of the True Religion!"

". . ."

"That you're not a heretic Protestant like the family your grandad found you in!"

"I'm not anything."

Marie-Thérèse's voice begins to rise.

"What do you mean, you're not anything? You live with the rest of us, don't you? Your name's Noirlac, isn't it? Like it or not, you're part of this family, and I'm gonna teach you to be a good Catholic!"

The child's stubborn silence makes her see red.

"You hear me, Milo? Otherwise you'll land up at Bordeaux like your good-for-nothing of a father . . . A lazybones delinquent! A parasite! Hey, are you listening to me? Hey, I'm talking to you! All right . . .".

Taking the receiver off its hook on the wall, she clobbers him over the head with it. *Bong!*

Involuntary tears start to Milo's eyes but he turns his head, looks out the window and concentrates on the falling snow. Joins up with the lion, the witch and the wardrobe, the little match girl, the ruby-eyed nightingale, the ugly duckling. Will not give his aunt the pleasure of making him cry . . . (I can just see you, Milo, sitting way at the end of that table, scrunched up against the wall. I can *see* you . . .) She hits him again. *Bong!* She's acquiring a taste for that *Bong!*

"You're proud, aren't you? A boy from the big city, hey? Too good for us country bumpkins, hey? Is that it? Is that it, hey, you whore-son?" *(Bong!)* "Hey! Answer when you're spoken to!" *(Bong!)* "Do you at least know you're a whoreson? Well, if you didn't know it before, you know it now. Oh, the bitch and the boozer, your parents were made for each other! Two losers! Two nothings! Son of nothing, son of less than nothing, that's what you are—you hear me?" *(Bong, bong!)* "Son of absence!"

Milo's head is on the table amidst the pickle jars. Since his arms are crossed over it for protection, Marie-Thérèse sometimes smashes his hands with the receiver. She's out of control.

"Your slut of a mother didn't want you. Minute you came out, she tossed you into the trash bin!" *(Bong!)* "That's the way savages behave: mothers flick their babies away like gobs of snot." *(Bong!)* "They don't give a hoot in hell about their children's souls!" *(Bong!)*

Just then the door bursts open and Régis stomps into the house, his boots covered in snow. A freezing gust of wind enters the room with him.

"Christ it's cold out there! . . . Hey! What's going on?"

Seeing herself as he must see her, sweating, shouting and disheveled, towering over the cowering child, Marie-Thérèse freezes.

"Gotta teach him a lesson," she mutters, hanging up the phone. "He's bad seed. I gotta knock some sense into him."

"Well, stop clobbering him over the head!" says Régis in an uncharacteristic display of marital authority. "Whip his ass, if you gotta whip something!"

"Yeah, a lot of good your discipline has done our boys. You never wanted to hit them, and look how they turned out! Two big brutes with no ambition. All they care about is getting drunk and chasing skirts. Those two'll never be able to take over the farm."

"At least find something else to hit him with. That phone's brand new! You'll damage it."

"So . . . I won't let you spoil Milo the way you spoiled the other two, you hear me? I'll take care of Milo. Listen, Régis" (she lowers her voice), "that boy is smart."

"Okay, do as you please. I could care less about Milo, anyway. He's your nephew, not mine. Do as you please."

"You bet I will!"

Régis treads out of the room, exhausted, and Marie-Thérèse sits down next to Milo on the bench.

"Come on, little one," she says, cajoling and kissing him. "Let's make up. I like you a lot, you know. The two of us are going to get along just fine, you'll see. Come on, relax, sit down beside me . . . I'm your mom now. You know that, don't you? Your other mom's probably no longer of this world . . . The gutter kills . . . She prob'ly shot up, too . . . Hey, come on, Milo, darling, give Auntie Thérèse a little kiss . . ."

She pulls him close, but he goes so rag-doll limp that all she can do with his body is release it.

"Okay, well . . . It's getting late. Go ahead, run off to bed. I'll finish up the job by myself, as usual. No hard feelings, hey? No hard feelings, Milo?"

BLACKOUT . . .

I REALLY SHOULD write a book about passivity someday. I hope you'll forgive me for having put my own words in Thom's mouth, in the scene at Saint Stephen's Green: *Passivity! The greatest force in human history!* Also one of the most cruelly underestimated, since people prefer to see themselves as courageous, in charge of their own lives . . . and, especially, free! Freedom is described in contemporary novels and newspapers as that without which human beings cannot survive—oh, but we can, we can, and we do! Freedom is anything but an irresistible impulse, an overwhelming urge, the smallest common denominator of humankind. On the contrary, it's a rarity. A luxury, like gilt hummingbirds' eggs. The vast majority of human beings don't give a hoot in hell about freedom. They care about two *other* things— doubtless wired together in our reptilian brains—survival and group acceptance.

No, love, I'm not talking about you—I know you're no more passive than a possum. But you're the one who got me interested in the subject, and . . . Okay, Astuto, okay, I'll stop speechifying. No need to rub it in. I know I'm in no state to write a book.

. . . . .

Neil, September 1917

WE COME UPON our young hero hunched over his desk in a corner of his bedroom. Sun streams through the frilly white curtains to his left, making the blankness of his pages painfully bright. Behind him, the maid is loudly plumping up the pillows on the bed.

"Shall I make you a cup of tea, sir?"

"No. Please. Please, Daisy, how often must I ask you not to speak to me when I'm writing? Can you see that I'm writing, yes or no?"

"No, sir."

"Oh! Even when his pen isn't dashing madly across the page and being dipped into fresh ink every few seconds, a man seated at a writing desk in front of a sheet of paper is writing, Daisy."

"Yes, sir."

"An important part of writing, indeed the *most important* part, takes place before the pen gets set to paper, inside the brain. The mysterious, burning furnace of the brain, wherein spiritual metals are molten and smolten. Through a series of chemical reactions, these cause floating, inchoate forms to appear, then thrust them into reality, where they miraculously crystallize into works of art that seem to us as immutable and inevitable as if they had always existed."

"Yes, sir," repeats Daisy. And she beats a retreat with a false obsequiousness that verges on insolence, moving backward, curtsying and waving her feather duster, finally pulling the door to behind her.

"How *dare she?*" fumes Neil, swerving angrily back to the blank page on the table in front of him.

He scrawls a sentence on it, and we hear him think it as he writes: *There were numerous truths of the Easter Rising, depending upon one's vantage point.* He crosses out *one's vantage point* and writes, instead, *who and where one was.* Crosses out *was* and replaces it with *happened to be.* Crosses out everything, crumples the page and tosses it into the wastebasket.

No, no, no, no, we hear him say to himself. *Though a thousand things were indeed occurring simultaneously in different parts of the city, we have no choice but to recount them successively. No blah blah, no holding forth. We must be in the action. In, for instance, the body of the young Sinn Féiner shot to death by the sniper on the roof of Trinity College. No, that's no good . . . He died on Tuesday; his chapter would be far too short. Well, how about a seagull, then, watching events unfold from above? No, ridiculous. Gulls cannot fathom human behavior, let alone human speech. Thom, I want to do this for you. You lost your life and I did not, so it's serious now. I need to do it. All right, let's just start somewhere, anywhere, it doesn't matter where; we can correct it later.*

Bright-eyed and bushy-tailed, his sister pops her head through the door.

"So you're staying at home again today, are you?"

Neil doesn't deign to turn toward her.

"You're not going out to look for work today then, Neil?"

"I *am* working, Dorothy."

"Are you, then? Sure and it looks like hard labor you're doing, too! And a great lot of money I'm sure it will bring in to help with the family finances, justifying the lengthy and expensive education you were given. Don't wear yourself out too much, now, will you? When your fingers tire of holding the pen, be sure to take a nice long bath to relax them."

"Dorothy, have I not ordered you on several occasions to refrain from bursting into my room without knocking?"

"Oh, sorry. Simply wanted to wish you a good day, brother. You've grown more and more irritable since you decided art was your true calling in life—d'you know that, Neil Kerrigan?"

"Might I prevail upon you to leave my room at once?"

"I liked you little enough as a lawyer, but as a novelist you're insufferable. Ta, then. I hope you'll at least make yourself useful by helping Daisy peel the potatoes for our supper!"

And, with a peal of laughter as intolerably bright as the sunlight, Dorothy vanishes.

His nerves at snapping point, Neil grips his pen tightly and we hear his inner voice . . .

The question is not only how to be in different places at the same time, but how to be in the same place at different times. The place, assuredly, is Dublin City. But we cannot talk about the Easter Rising of 1916 if we do not understand the strikes of 1913–1914 . . . the rise and fall of Parnell in the 1890s . . . or the six-hundred-year history of the British occupation. And we must go not only backward but forward in time as well. Show how the people of Dublin, though not supportive of the rebellion during Easter Week itself, gradually came to espouse the rebels' cause as, day after day, early in May, their leaders were cruelly and systematically executed by British firing squads. Pearse, Plunkett, MacDonagh, Connolly . . . sixteen in all, including the one whom I personally denounced, Major John MacBride. A swaggerer to the end: boasting that he'd faced British fire before, he met his death without the customary blindfold. And then I was denounced. By whom? Must have been that blond kid in the bushes. To whom? I'm still not sure—both ways? To the government and the rebels? A two-way traitor, I became. Traitor to my class—the bar defrocked me. Traitor to my cause—the Sinn Féin cast me out. But it's not my own tale I want to tell, it's the tale of my city. The upheaval of Easter 1916 left dear dark Dublin ruined and ravished but renewed. Ripe for revolution.

Neil's knuckles are white from squeezing the pen too tightly.

Three loud, swift knocks at the door.

"What now? Who is it?" he shouts, leaping to his feet.

"Your mother," comes the icy answer.

Yanking the door open, he sees fear in his mother's eyes and realizes he must be a sight: hair on end, rumpled shirttails, wrinkled trousers, suspenders awry; he hasn't slept a wink.

"Your father would like to have a word with you," says Mrs. Kerrigan stiffly, advancing not so much as the pointed toe of her pink velvet mule beyond his threshhold.

CUT to Judge Kerrigan's den, replete with all the symbols of virile wealth and power: leather-bound books serried on bookshelves, framed diplomas, green lampshades, polished oak desk, gilt leather blotters and paperweights . . . you get the picture. The man's success is ostentatious not to say ferocious, and any one of our potential spectators could probably write the ensuing dialogue as well as we can, Milo.

"You wished to see me, Father?"

"I did."

"Well, here I am."

"I've been thinking about your future, Neil. Things cannot go on like this. It's been eighteen months since we learned of your involvement with the rabble rebels, a year since the bar defrocked you . . ."

"My dream, as you know, Father, is not to be refrocked. Not as long as every court of law in Dublin is run by the occupying forces."

The judge's voice booms out, covering his son's.

"Neil, I'm convinced it is not completely hopeless. There might be a way for you to regain access to your profession."

Neil waits, and knows he won't have long to wait. Turning his back on his son, Judge Kerrigan moves to the window and lights his pipe.

"You must volunteer to join the army."

"Impossible."

"I've made preliminary inquiries at the Castle. Because of their respect for me, two or three individuals are willing to put in a good word for you. You could start out directly with officer rank."

"Despite my *besmirching of the family name*?"

"Yes, that could be overlooked. Give it some thought. I advise you to seize the opportunity. It is unlikely that a second chance for saving your reputation will come along."

"Father, I am twenty-five years old. You are aware of both my political convictions and my artistic aspirations, and yet you find it natural to ask me to betray both, simply for the sake of restoring the name Kerrigan to its virginal purity . . ."

"You will not address your father in such terms, young man. I am not a blank page to be sullied by the smutty mutterings of scribblers such as yourself and Jimmy Joyce. *Portrait of the Young Man as an Artist*, indeed! How gumptious can you get?"

"It's the other way around, Father. *Portrait of the Artist as a Young Man*."

"Traitors, the lot of you! Your country is in need? Joyce runs off to hide in Switzerland, and *you* can think of nothing better to do than take up with a crowd of rag-a-tag outlaws! Well, now that your mates have all been shot, why don't you go help the Bolsheviks who are currently laying waste to Russia? Perhaps they have a better chance of winning!"

"I'm a *writer*, Father."

"Neil, I am *most* weary of awaiting evidence of that claim's validity."

"What does that mean?"

"It means that unless you either accept the generous offer I've just made you or give me some tangible proof that you've become a respectable member of the Irish literary establishment, you will no longer be welcome in my household. Writers are known to enjoy starving in miserable garrets at the outset of their careers, are they not? Find yourself a miserable garret in which to starve. Kindly remove your belongings from the premises by next Sunday."

"I'll give you the proof."

"That will be all, Neil."

"I'll give you the proof!" says Neil in a slightly louder voice.

Ignoring him, Judge Kerrigan sits down at his desk and violently opens a ledger.

CUT to Neil dragging a box of old papers from under his bed and rummaging through it. Finding his old manuscript of poems. Slipping it into a black folder.

CUT to County Galway: a cab deposits Neil in front of Thoor Ballylee. Black folder under left arm, he walks toward the tower. Close-up on his face. His expression is part awe, part amazement at his own audacity. Weeds and wildflowers grow rampant at the tower's base; no glass graces its windows . . .

(Think we can do this, Milo? Think we can get permission to shoot inside Yeats' Tower itself? Wouldn't that be fantastic? With . . . uh, say, Lambert Wilson in the role of Willie Yeats? Yeah . . . Fantastic.)

Neil is let into the tower by a portly, gray-haired maid, complete with white cap and apron. After leading him up a winding flight of rickety stairs, she ushers him into the poet's drawing room. The place being as yet unfurnished, the echoes of their footsteps ricochet on stone walls . . . Yeats seems in a bit of a dither. Spectacles askew, gray jersey misbuttoned, he paces up and down the room and runs his hands through his hair.

"So you're the young poet who wrote to me last week."

"I am, sir."

"Did you see the wild swans?"

"The . . ."

"Did you see them, the wild swans, as you were brought here?"

"I'm afraid I didn't notice them, sir. Was it today they flew south, then?"

"How . . . how . . . how are they the *same* swans every year? The *same* uplifting passion, the *same* fierce beating of wings against the sky? Flinging themselves multitudinously southward in the *same* breathtaking flight, while we humans . . . age, change, hesitate, lose our certainties and our teeth . . ."

"Uh . . . that's true, sir."

"Why have you come to me?"

"I need help, sir."

Yeats glances discreetly at the envelope on his desk.

"Your letter said as much, Mr . . . ah . . . Kerrigan, but why have you come to *me*?"

"Only because . . . er . . . I once tried to help *you*, sir."

"Kindly explain yourself. I'm certain I never set eyes on you before today."

"Well, sir . . . though myself the son of a Dublin magistrate, in 1914 I became involved with the Irish Volunteer movement . . . and . . . um . . . er . . . being aware of the . . . ah, unfortunate impediments in the way of . . . er . . . Mrs. MacBride's obtaining a divorce, I . . ."

Suddenly attentive, Yeats turns to him.

CUT to half an hour later. Yeats is serving them each a brandy and laughing uproariously.

"I don't believe it . . . *You* denounced Major John MacBride! You!"

"I did, sir."

"And now, in return for this favor you did me, unsolicited and indeed unbeknownst to me, you wish for *me* to do *you* a favor and help you find a publisher! Oh it's a *marvelous* tale, Neil Kerrigan! A marvelous tale indeed. Unfortunately, your hopes will be dashed. At twenty-five, it's time you learned that one's fondest hopes and dreams in life are generally dashed. D'you see this thoor?"

"I do, sir."

"I purchased it six months ago, in March . . . Here is the deed. I own it now. Well. What do you say to that?"

"It is . . . ah . . . very . . . spacious, sir."

"Too spacious for a man who lives on his own, is that what you mean?"

"Perhaps, sir."

Yeats downs a second glass of brandy.

"More fitting for a family man . . . am I correct, Kerrigan? I should bring a wife here, is that what you mean? But what wife? Ay, that's where the shoe pinches! *What wife?* You're right: since 1889, my body has cried out with the need to love Maud Gonne, and my poetic imagination has depended on her! A decade ago, after torturing me with her elegance and eloquence for fifteen long years, she finally deigned to open her robe and her thighs to me . . . but doused my passion by praying daily that we be released from earthly desire."

"I understand your . . . frustration, sir."

"The woman has a terror and a horror of physical love, Kerrigan. Is it not a crying shame, given her spectacular shape, skin and allure? How are you fixed in this area, by the by?"

"Well, sir, though I've made a few forays into Talbot Street like everyone else, I mostly please myself."

"And confess it afterward?"

"Oh, no, sir. I've not set foot in a church since the Easter Rising. The priests' unconscionable behavior during the events cured me of my faith for good . . . So if I understand correctly, Mr. Yeats . . .

er . . . despite the fact that Major MacBride has now gone on to a better world, Maud Gonne MacBride has once again declined to be your wife?"

Willie tips back his head and sips.

"*Once again*, this time, was once too often. Having *once again* gone down to Normandy last summer, having *once again* found her surrounded by a squawking growling twittering menagerie, I *once again* threw myself on my knees before Maud, pressed her hand to my lips and begged her to be mine. *(Singing)*

> *Oh my lovely, be thou not hard*
> *Look thou kindly upon me*
> *Wilt thou not come with an aging bard*
> *All the way to Ballylee?*

". . . Though she spoke warmly to me and played tarot with me and assisted me in interpreting my dreams, she scoffed at my advances. No, Mr. Kerrigan, Mrs. Gonne MacBride will never have me, and at last I have understood why: she is married to her dead father, and to the cause of Ireland he espoused. But did you know that in addition to her young son sired by the rustic major, Mrs. MacBride has an older, illegitimate daughter by a French journalist?"

"Yes, I have heard as much."

"A girl by the name of Iseult, now twenty-two. As heartbreakingly beautiful as her mother at that age. I've known and loved Iseult since she was born."

"I see."

"So last month, with Maud's I must say insultingly skeptical permission, I threw myself on my knees before Iseult, pressed her hand to my lips, and begged her to be mine." *(Singing)*

Oh my lovely, be thou not hard
Look thou kindly upon me
Wilt thou not come with an aging bard
All the way to Ballylee?

"And she?"

"Said no."

Yeats falls into a prolonged silence.

"And so?" Neil prods him gently after a while, seeing that the daylight is waning in the sky.

"Well, I recently made the acquaintance of *another* young woman, a certain Georgina Hyde-Lees, also three decades my junior . . . So last week I threw myself on my knees before sweet Georgie, pressed her hand to my lips, and begged her to be mine. *(Singing)*

Oh my lovely, be thou not hard
Look thou kindly upon me
Wilt thou not come with an aging bard
All the way to Ballylee?

"And she?"

"Said yes. The banns were published yesterday and our wedding is scheduled for a fortnight from today. Children *must* play at the foot of my thoor, do you understand?"

Not knowing what to answer, Neil remains silent.

"But let us come back to you, Neil Kerrigan. You want to write, so?"

"I do."

"Then leave Ireland."

"I beg your pardon?"

"No one can write here. Go away. Your father's advice is excellent. He's doing you a favor by kicking you out. Desert his home."

"But surely not for the British army?"

"No. For literature."

"He says I've besmirched the family name."

"Change names. Change countries. Change selves."

Yeats leafs rapidly through Neil's manuscript of poems.

"Forget these. They were written before the Rising, by a bright young lad all puffed up with ambition but empty of wisdom. Then the British savaged our city and shot our sixteen leaders; your cousin Thom was killed before your eyes; Dublin's finest buildings burned to the ground; the poor came wailing out of their houses . . . and

> *all changed, changed utterly.*
> *A terrible beauty was born.*

. . . I believe you now have an inkling of what wisdom might be, or at least where to look for it. Am I correct?"

"I hope so, sir."

"Then go. Go to England. Or, better still, to the Americas."

"But our cause? The national cause of Ireland and Irish freedom, for which Thom and so many others gave their lives?"

"Don't worry. Events will follow their course. You won't forget the cause. May I read you a few lines from one of my recent poems? I have it in manuscript only; it may be years before Ireland is ready to read it. It's called 'The Leaders of the Crowd.'"

(Jaysus, I don't know, Milo. Are you sure? The whole feckin' poem, as the Irish would say? That's the schmaltzy side of your personality, nice in real life, but disastrous in art . . . Whoa, okay, don't have a conniption fit . . . you've got your poem! As Lambert Wilson reads it out loud, we can go wafting out the open window and hurtle through the sky of County Galway with the wild swans . . .)

> They must to keep their certainty accuse
> All that are different of a base intent;
> Pull down established honour; hawk for news
> Whatever their loose phantasy invent
> And murmur it with bated breath, as though
> The abounding gutter had been Helicon
> Or calumny a song. How can they know
> Truth flourishes where the student's lamp has shone,
> And there alone, that have no solitude?
> So the crowd come they care not what may come.
> They have loud music, hope every day renewed
> And heartier loves; that lamp is from the tomb.

. . . Do you understand, Kerrigan?"

"It's not easy to grasp at first hearing, but I think I get the gist of it, sir."

"The most important lines are these:

> How can they know
> Truth flourishes where the student's lamp has shone,
> And there alone, that have no solitude?

. . . Remain a student, Neil. Protect thy solitude. And keep thy lamp shining."

"Why is the lamp said to be *from the tomb*?"

"Where will you find wisdom, Kerrigan, if not in the words of dead men?"

"In the arms of living women?"

William Yeats bursts out laughing.

"Ah, you're a lad after my own heart! Here . . . Allow me to give you one of my books."

He picks up a copy of *The Wind Among the Reeds* and writes in it.

For Neil Kerrigan. May he not follow in the faltering footsteps of this aging bard, but blaze his own young virile path with words, carving momentary meaning out of the rich dark nothing that surrounds us all. W. B. Yeats, 16 September 1917.

BLACKOUT.

. . . . .

Awinita, June 1951

RADIO MUSIC . . . A vague gurgle of babbling, squabbling girls . . . The camera explores the home Awinita shares with a dozen other prostitutes in their late teens and early twenties, some native, some not—a run-down ground-floor apartment somewhere on the Plateau Mont-Royal. Burlap curtains on the windows are permanently drawn to discourage neighborly curiosity.

Arriving in the kitchen, the camera discovers Liz, a buxom, fortyish brunette dressed in a yellow pantsuit, sitting smoking at the table. She runs the place, and all the girls who work for her know that Friday is accounts day. Before her are a ledger and a cashbox; coffee percolates on the stove nearby. In various states of dress and undress, the girls file in one by one, sit down across from her and hand her their weekly earnings. Licking a finger, Liz carefully counts the bills into her cashbox, inscribes the amount in the ledger, deducts what the girls owe her for rent, clothing and drugs, and hands them back the difference.

Awinita wanders woozily into the kitchen dressed in a cheap black satin kimono, her pregnant tummy now at full ripeness. The world wobbles and blurs before her eyes. The envelope she hands Liz seems almost weightless. The procuress peers into it and frowns.

"What's this supposed to be? I hope this isn't supposed to be your rent money, Nita . . . You already owe me . . . ah . . . seventy-four bucks in back rent, to say nothing of the advances I've made you . . . Ten for clothing . . . twenty for medication . . . that brings us to a grand total of one hundred and four. I've told you before, Nita, this isn't a charity operation."

"De guys," Nita says in a low voice, ". . . dey scared to go up with me. Dey scared sometin' could happen while dey up dere."

"When are you due?"

"Any day."

"Okay . . . And your plan is to give up the baby?"

"Yeah."

"At once?" "Yeah." "So you think you could be back at work when?"

"Like a week or two."

"Okay, listen. You know, I don't mean to be hard on you, Nita, but I've got my books to balance. One more week of credit is all I can give you. Either you catch up on your debts or you find someplace else to live."

"Sure."

"All right. One more week's delay for the rent. Think you can do without your pills this week?"

"I need 'em."

"At least try to cut down, for your baby's sake. Let me give you half the usual amount, that way you won't be tempted."

"Gimme the pills . . . I'll try and cut down myself."

"Price of diazepam went up to twelve bucks last week."

As Liz inscribes her new debt in the ledger, Awinita virtually wrenches the tube from her hand.

CUT to the bathroom, where she gulps down a pill and stands waiting for it to take effect.

We find her on her mattress in a corner, snoring softly, as Deena, Cheryl and Lorraine paint their fingernails and chatter up a storm.

CUT to a few hours later. The quality of the light has changed. The other girls have left. The bedroom floor is strewn with underwear, balled-up tissue papers, candy wrappers, twisted nylon stockings and half-spilled ashtrays . . . Alone on her mattress, Awinita has her first contraction. She calls out to her mother in Cree.

Subjective camera: we stare up at the roof of the ambulance beyond the mountainside of our stomach. In our peripheral vision, city lights flash by unevenly. Sound track: siren wail, muttered exchange between two male orderlies in the front seat and, occasionally, our own deep, wrenching groans.

CUT to the emergency room of a large Montreal hospital. We're giving birth. The world is rendered blurry and fantastic by our pain. Flustered nurses cluster around us. (All or nearly all of them would be nuns—right, Milo, in Montreal in 1951?) Their hands on and in our body are ungentle, and their words no less wounding for being prudishly spelled out.

"Another Injun *b-a-s-t-a-r-d*."

"I've seen a dozen this past month, if I've seen one!"

"They've got no future, God bless 'em. You almost feel like putting them out of their misery before it begins."

"The ways of the Lord are unfathomable, Sister Anne."

"She's giving it up for adoption?"

"Yes. Doesn't even want to see it."

"How hypocritical can you get? Doesn't make what she did any less of a sin."

"Maybe she was *r-a-p-e-d*?"

"How would I know?"

"Can a *s-l-u-t* be *r-a-p-e-d*?"

Soft feminine gales of laughter. "God only knows!"

We close our eyes beneath the blindingly bright lights.

Tall trees crash headlong to the ground, crushing bushes and undergrowth. Forest animals bolt away with terror in their eyes. A fire starts, spreads and rises, leaping into the air to meet the sun. Then the sun vanishes and thunderclouds make war upon the fire, hurling their rain-bullets at its ecstatic, dangerously rearing body.

A gigantic grunt of relief issues from our guts and lungs and we hear, severally:

"Ah! Here it comes!" "Here it comes at last!" "It's a girl!" "It's a little girl!" "Don't you want to see your daughter, miss?"

The pink light on the screen moves slowly from left to right and back again: we're shaking our head no.

Soft, thin pink material, pink cloth, floats and sways in the air, curves and dances until it becomes a butterfly. Moving slowly and gracefully, the pink butterfly approaches the burning forest. Its wings evaporate in the scorching heat before the flames touch them. Its narrow dark body bakes to a crisp, freezes with the extreme heat, then crumbles into ash like a cone of incense.

The baby is gone. A male voice suddenly resonates above the women's: the obstetrician has arrived.

"You should have done an episiotomy, she's all torn up. What did she have?"

"A girl."

"Normal?"

"Oh, yes, Doctor. Everything's A-OK."

"All right. I'll go fill out the adoption forms, then."

A swinging door goes *thuck* as he passes through it.

"A-OK, Doctor," one of the nurses whispers sarcastically. "Apart from the fact that it's an Injun bastard, of course . . ."

The others huff with laughter.

"Shall I sew her up, or shall you?"

"You go ahead. I'll make you a cup of tea for the nausea afterward. Deal?"

"Deal . . . Maybe I should just sew it up completely so she'd stop corrupting our poor vulnerable men. Eh, Sister Anne? What do you think? Maybe we should just sew up the whole yawning mess?"

"Now, now, Sister Claire. Don't forget, sinning in word is as bad as sinning in deed."

Back to the sweltering shadows of Awinita's mind.

Terrified kittens hunching in withdrawal, puffed-up with hostility, their saucer-eyes sizzling with resentment.

Finally the stitching is done and we sink gratefully into oblivion . . .

DOES THE GIRL get a name, Milo? No, not in our film. There she is, barely born and we're gonna have to push her out of the story. Let's at least take a good look at her before she disappears.

Hey . . . you doing all right? We can stop talking for a while if you like. I could even come back tomorrow . . . Okay, no sweat. I'll stay. Must be weird, to say the least, to think you have a half sister walking around somewhere on the planet and you'll never know who she is, where she is or what kind of life she lived . . .

Hang in there, Astuto. This is no time to give up. The Good Lord will be coming by with your daily tritherapy a mere few hours from now.

．　．　．　．　．

V

TERREIRO

A place or house of worship: terreiro de candomblé. *More generally, any location or site.*

Milo, 1962–65

SUNDAY MORNING MASS in the tiny village church we've seen before. Now ten, Milo is seated in the third row next to his best friend, a boy named Normand. Heftier and quite a bit older than Milo, Normand has clearly been kept back in school a number of times. (A motley crowd, your crowd of friends, Astuto. All your life long, nothing but misfits and artists and outcasts, fat girls and queers.)

Bored, the two boys are playing with fire and the name of that fire is laughter. They pass the Sunday service schedule back and forth, each trying to make the other snicker with his doodles in the margin. Normand's drawing shows a plumply pregnant young woman being peed on by a boy, and bears the title *Hail Mary, what a disgrace*. Milo manages to choke down his amusement. Now it's his turn; he bends his head and scribbles. A moment later he hands his friend a drawing of apples, pears and cherries tumbling from between a woman's legs, captioned *Blessed be the fruit of thy womb*. Normand snorts, causing heads to swivel.

Jean-Joseph Dubé leans over from the pew behind them. In a matter of seconds, he has lifted the program from Normand's hand, looked at it, and passed it back to their teacher. Glancing at the paper in turn, Mrs. Morisette lets out a low cry of shock. As the congregation rises for the next hymn, she squeezes past everyone in her pew, strides up the aisle, grabs the two boys by the hair (though Normand is taller than she), and marches them back to the middle pews where the parents are seated.

Close-up on Milo's face, shutting down.

CUT to the farmhouse kitchen: Marie-Thérèse screaming at him as she whips him on the back with Régis's leather shaving strop:

"How dare you embarrass me like that in front of everybody! Stupid little pagan! Whore-son! Evil seed! I'll scrub your soul clean if it's the last thing I do on this earth!"

Beyond the windows in the backyard, using a saw as a guitar and an empty oil barrel as a drum, François-Joseph and Jean-Joseph are mock yodeling Roger Miron's country-western hit at the tops of their lungs:

> *À qui le p'tit cœur après neuf heures?*
> *Est-ce à moi, rien qu'à moi?*
> *Quand je suis parti loin de toi, chérie*
> *À qui le p'tit cœur après neuf heures?*[1]

CUT to the sky. A piercing sapphire-blue summer sky on a hot day. Crows flap across it, cawing blackly. Ominous, shimmering heat. The camera swoops down to a clump of poplar trees in a corner of the property, where Milo is sitting hunched on a tree stump.

---

1. *Who gets your heart, baby, after nine?*
   Is it mine, is it really all mine?
   When I'm away, do you toe the line?
   Who gets your heart, baby, after nine?

We approach him gently from behind, then swing round to find his hands busy whittling.

A few seconds later, the statuette is completed. Though less than three inches high, it is expressive: two deer's legs topped by a two-faced human head, one of the faces grimacing in fury, the other in fear. Milo holds it up and blows on it, scattering wood chips. Kneels at the foot of a tree, digs a hole in the ground with his penknife and deftly slips the statuette into it. Fills in the hole, pats down the dirt, smooths over the surface, pulls the grasses together above it until there is no trace of a disturbance. The Dubé property is being given an invisible but potent underground population: scattered here, there and everywhere, dozens of these figurines are in the ground already. They are Milo's allies. Like his, their lives unfold in the darkness. Like him, they have to learn to find their freedom there.

Sound track: organ music . . .

CUT TO NEIL's library, a Sunday morning in January. Afflicted with a head cold, Milo has been allowed to miss Mass. Neil has settled him onto his lap and is reading out loud to him from Oscar Wilde's *The Importance of Being Earnest*. Milo reads along, exulting in the correspondence between the written and spoken words. Suddenly we see him laugh. The music fades.

"Is it not a marvel?" says Neil, gently covering the child's small hand with his large, age-speckled one. "That this Irishman, Oscar Fingal O'Flahertie Wills, by himself rebaptized Wilde, born on the far side of the Atlantic Ocean in 1854, can make a Canadian boy laugh a hundred years later?"

"A hundred and eight," says Milo.

"Wha? . . . Yes, you're right, a hundred and eight. And this is only the beginning, Milo. These shelves contain countless treasures. I'll introduce them to you one by one. My library will be your school away from school and your church away from church. We must just keep it a secret from Marie-Thérèse; that's not a problem, is it?" (Milo shakes his head.) "Books from all centuries and continents. Poems, tragedies, comedies, histories, war and adventure, nonsense and fairy tales . . . All of humanity's multitudinous joys and sorrows at your fingertips, my boy! Some of these volumes are worth a pretty penny. Look at this one, Milo . . . and this one . . . In my youth, the greatest writers of Ireland were my friends. James Joyce and William Butler Yeats . . ."

"But they both say *To Neil Kerrigan*, not *To Neil Noirlac*."

"Wha? Oh. Yes, well, you see, I changed names when I came over to Quebec."

"You mean took your wife's name?"

"No, no, she took mine, only it was . . . a pseudonym, if you like. That means a false name. Writers often prefer to publish their books under a pen name, you see . . . just as Oscar Wilde did."

"And your children all took your false name?"

"Yes."

"So my name is false, too? I should really be Milo Kerrigan?"

"Oh, no, don't worry about that, Milo. By the third generation it becomes true. Now, listen, I have something important to tell you . . . I've already made arrangements . . . When I die, everything in this library will go to you . . . But that, too, is our secret for the time being, yes?"

CUT to the living room downstairs. A Saturday afternoon in February. Fire in the fireplace, slow snow falling outdoors.

Now sixteen and fifteen, Jean-Joseph and François-Joseph are sprawled flat on the living room rug. Spectacular battles between cowboys and Indians unfold before their eyes in black and white, accompanied by bombastic music. The two boys gorge on fried potato peels, guzzle home-brewed beer, belch loudly. Every few minutes, testing the decibel potential of their newly matured male vocal cords, they roar with laughter. In the laundry room across the hall, Marie-Thérèse sighs in exasperation as she feeds clothes from the washer through the mangle.

CUT to Milo, who is hunting in the woods with his uncle Régis. He shoots a rabbit and the two of them rush up to it. The animal is large. Blood gushes from its nostrils into the white snow. Not wounded, dead on the spot. Milo's bullet entered the brain just above the eye, leaving the body perfect and intact. Régis is proud of him.

"How come Grandad never comes hunting with us?" Milo asks his uncle as they head back to the house.

"Hah! The day Neil Noirlac starts hunting . . ."

"But he told me he hunted moose, lynx and rabbit."

"Oh, is that all?" Régis laughs. "Your grandpa tracks a different kind of prey."

"But he told me he had a gun!"

"I've never seen it, but yeah, I've heard tell he's got one. Brought it over from Ireland with him. A German revolver from the First World War, for the luva God!"

"Maybe he hunts at night?" Milo ventures hopefully.

"Right. And he eats the moose he kills at night, too, so he won't have to share them."

They bundle into the shed next to the house. As Milo looks on, Régis skins and guts the rabbit, using a sharp knife with consummate skill to make incisions, peel back the fur, slit open the stomach. Then he cups out the animal's innards with his bare hands.

"Next time around, you skin what you kill. Okay?"

"Okay, okay."

CUT.

When grace has been said, Marie-Thérèse lifts the lid of the pot: "Know who shot this rabbit? Milo did!"

"Smells heavenly," says Neil.

"What?" says Marie-Thérèse. "Only God is heavenly, Papa. Stop your blasphemy . . . And stop teaching Milo to blaspheme, you're setting a bad example! You filled my brothers' heads full of atheist writers, and look how they turned out: the only thing they're good at is shoveling clouds. Do you hear me, Milo? Literature isn't a job, it's hot air. A lot of hot air, that's what it is!"

"Can we eat the goddamn stew?" says Régis.

CUT.

Scenes from Milo's nightmares. Lights glare, telephones ring, shrill voices vituperate . . . Cars come to a halt in a screech of brakes . . . *Ta, ta-da DA, ta, ta-da DA* . . . Car doors slam . . . Milo, in an enormous train station, is grabbed, shoved, handled, dragged, manipulated by strange hands . . . His head bangs into the legs of strangers . . . a forest of legs . . . Several superimposed speeds and rhythms of footsteps—heavy boots, ladies' high heels, men's city shoes . . . Trains bang and clang, their steam hissing fiercely. . . Telephones ring with insistence . . . then leap off the wall and come to clobber him over the head all by themselves . . . Ambulance and police sirens wail . . . *Ta, ta-da DA, ta, ta-da DA* . . . Doors slam . . . Women's voices natter . . . Bright lights come closer and closer . . . WHITEOUT.

Sitting bolt upright, Milo chokes back a cry of fear.

"That goddamn Milo can't let us get a good night's sleep," François-Joseph grumbles in his half-sleep. "Shut up, you little flea! Shut up! Will you shut the fuck up, for Christ's sake?"

Heaving himself out of bed, Jean-Joseph lurches across the room and swats Milo on the side of the head. To scare him, he clamps both huge thumbs on Milo's gullet and makes as if to throttle him.

"Will you shut your goddamn trap?" he says, speaking in an enraged whisper so as not to wake the rest of the household. "It's not enough we gotta hear about your good marks at school from dawn to dusk, no, you gotta ruin our nights, too, with your stupid squealing. You're ten years old, for Chrissake! You're not a baby anymore! If you don't feel like sleeping, least you can do is piss off and leave us in peace, you little prick!"

Milo's pulse flutters madly under Jean-Joseph's thumbs. His arms and legs flail.

"Little prick thinks he's better'n the rest of us," mumbles François-Joseph, still in bed. "His mom's a fuckin' slut and he thinks he's better'n the rest of us!"

Turning toward the wall he releases a long, loud fart. Jean-Joseph laughs. Releases the flailing boy and staggers back to his own bed.

"Your slut of a mother shoulda strangled you at birth. Woulda been good riddance, frankly."

During breakfast, the phone rings and Milo jumps out of his skin. His cousins point at him and guffaw.

As Milo milks a cow in the barn, eyes closed, cheek dreamily pressed up against the animal's flat brown flank, François-Joseph and Jean-Joseph sneak up behind him and set off an alarm clock— *Drring! Drring!*—then go into stitches when, leaping to his feet, stiff with fear, Milo upsets the milk pail.

Close-up on the frothy warm white milk, flowing all over Milo's shoes.

Milo in bed at night, eyes on ceiling, afraid to go to sleep. Close-up on his face as he hears François-Joseph pad across the room and crawl into Jean-Joseph's bed . . . A series of rough, muffled sounds coming from that bed . . . He sticks his fingers in his ears until it's over . . . but now he's unbearably wide-awake. When the brothers start snoring again he rises, slips out into the hallway and tiptoes downstairs. In the living room, before turning on the TV set, he makes sure the sound button is turned all the way down. We watch him watching a 1930s movie—*Hôtel du Nord*, say, starring Louis Jouvet—with the sound off. His lips move. Approaching, we realize he's inventing dialogue for the film . . .

(That's when your vocation was born, my darling. I owe a great deal to your horrible cousins and your abominable aunt. Had they not tormented you, you'd never have become a screenwriter and I'd never have met you. Paul Schwarz's life without Milo Noirlac—inconceivable! . . .)

In his class at school, a girl starts smiling at Milo and casting him sidelong glances. Though only twelve, she already has generous bosoms and knows how to flaunt them, purposely making them bounce when she walks. At recess, she finds a way of slipping Milo a snapshot of herself. Turning it over, he reads: *Je t'aime beaucoup! Edith*. He looks up and flashes her the loveliest of grins. (You never had to pursue women, Milo, they always pursued you. That, too, must have contributed to your rare gift for inertia . . .)

Now a double series of scenes in rapid alternation. No dialogue, only music; maybe early Beatles songs . . . We're in 1964.

Marie-Thérèse standing over Milo as he does his homework at the kitchen table and drilling him relentlessly, forcing him to take dictation. She has become his dictator.

Milo walking Edith home. When they reach her place, she leads him by the hand back to the woodshed and smilingly pushes him against the wall there. Then she presses up against him and glues her lips to his. Feeling what this does to him, his hands rise to her breasts of their own accord. He kneads them slowly and thoroughly, in a dizzy daze. Edith makes not the slightest move to stop him.

Marie-Thérèse shouts at him, testing his knowledge of French and berating him for every mistake he makes.

Edith puts her hands on either side of his face and shows him what a French kiss is. Pulls his head down and strokes his hair as he kisses her large, soft breasts through her thick sweater, first the left one, then the right.

Marie-Thérèse clobbers him over the head with the telephone.

Up in the hayloft with Edith's picture, Milo pants and swoons in silence, coming divinely in the straw as the cows low quietly beneath him.

Walking home from school, Milo nearly gets hit by a car because he didn't hear it coming. He lies awake at night with his hand over his left ear, testing—no, he can hear nothing in that ear.

SOUND IN: MILO and his aunt in the doctor's office after his ear examination.

"This will help some," says the doctor as he hands Marie-Thérèse a prescription, "but he'll never fully recover his hearing in that ear. Make sure he avoids ear infections like the plague, or it'll be total deafness."

Marie-Thérèse is fairly bursting with pride: Milo has just skipped another grade at school.

"See? You're top of the class! We'll show them, won't we, you and I?"

"I want a dog," says Milo in a low voice.

"What?"

"I want a dog," he says more clearly, staring out the window.

"You want a dog! Okay, listen. If you're still top of the class on your next report card, if you get an average of more than ninety-five percent, I'll buy you a pedigree dog. Is that a deal?"

CUT to a pet shop in a nearby town: Milo and his aunt choosing a dog together. Marie-Thérèse's face glows with pride. She's beginning to think her dreams for the boy's future might actually come true.

"Whichever one you want, Milo. Choose whichever one you want."

"Look . . ."

Soft, fuzzy, furry, head like a bear's head. Long, thick tail that drags or wags.

"Is that the one you like?"

"Yeah. You see? It's mine. It recognizes me."

Marie-Thérèse motions to the saleslady.

"What kind is this?"

"It's a mongrel. Half German shepherd, half coyote. Not expensive; I can let you have it for ten bucks."

"It costs what it costs. I made a promise and I intend to keep it!"

"Your little boy sure looks happy, anyway."

Marie-Thérèse doesn't correct the saleslady.

As they drive back to the house together, Milo ecstatic in the backseat with the dog, Marie-Thérèse glances at him in the rearview mirror and says,

"You're more of a son to me than my sons are anyhow. What're you gonna call it?"

"Oscar."

"What?"

"Oscar."

"Ridiculous. Oscar's no name for a dog! Well, whatever. It's up to you."

"That's right."

Neil understands better.

"Oscar . . . because he's half Wilde?"

"Yeah," says Milo.
". . . Like you?"
"Maybe. Only my wild half isn't de one people tink it is."
Neil chuckles.
"You know, you're right."

A KALEIDOSCOPE OF scenes from the next few months: Oscar running after Milo when he leaves for school at seven in the morning, running to meet him when he returns at four . . . following Milo as he gallops through the forest on horseback . . . swimming with him in the nearby Lac des Piles . . . waiting between his feet at mealtimes, swallowing the tidbits Milo slips him under the table— soundlessly, as both know it's forbidden (one day Oscar forgets and his tail thumps the floor) . . . sleeping at the foot of his young master's bed, front paws crossed, protecting Milo from the monsters in his room and in his dreams.

The kaleidoscope slows down, then zeroes in on . . . boy and dog staring into each other's eyes. We circle the pair. A lingeringly beautiful shot.

EARLY OF A summer evening. Milo sits on the porch next to Marie-Thérèse, helping her shell peas. They're alone in the house. Suddenly she turns to him and says, so softly that he's disconcerted:

"You know where the hunchback lives, Milo? About halfway into town . . . You go past his house on your way to school."

(Okay, Astuto, we can try to write this episode if you insist . . . but I warn you, there's a better than even chance we'll need to excise it later . . .)

"Yeah, I know it."
"Could you deliver a message to him?"
"To the hunchback?"

"Yeah, look. I've got the envelope all ready. Just give him this and wait for his answer. And on your way home, here, take this. Buy yourself some bubble gum at the grocery store; you know, the kind with Beatles cards in it. But it's just between the two of us, all right? I don't want you blabbing about it."

We follow Milo from a distance as, Oscar at his side, he jogs through the endless summer dusk, his red T-shirt a dancing splotch of color in the gathering shadows. Now twelve, his shoulders have broadened and his chest is growing muscular . . . but still he is light on his feet, alert and supple. In his mind he replaces Marie-Thérèse's droning, dictating voice with his mother's soft, hoarse voice from long ago. *You gonna have to resist, little one,* she says. *Be strong, be tough, don't forget me.* Other snippets of wisdom gleaned over the years he repeats to himself in her voice. *Fear noting, son. You got de right to walk on dis eart', just like de animals. Trust de animals—dey'll never betray you—but beware of humans. Don worry 'bout God or de Devil or what happen after deat'. Heaven and Hell are man-made and here on eart'. What will be will be. Respect nature. Respect your body, it's a part of nature. Respect de ground you walk on. De sacred isn't above you or below you, it's inside of you and all around you. You're a part of it, son. Praying's a waste of time. Everyting you do, good or bad, is a prayer, so don't let dem make you pray. When dey tell you to pray . . . dream, little one. Dream.* He goes up the porch steps and knocks on the door. On the mailbox is the name *Bernstein* . . .

(No offense, Milo, but I'm afraid the spectators will simply refuse to believe that your aunt's lover, out in the sticks of rural Quebec in the early 1960s, was not only a hunchback but a Jew. Yeah, I know it's true, but that's not enough of a reason. Sometimes reality just isn't plausible . . .)

The man who comes to the door is in his midfifties and crowlike: black-haired, black-garbed, beady-eyed, hunchbacked, hook-nosed, yellow-toothed. He must be rather sweaty, too, for Milo wipes his hand discreetly on the seat of his shorts after their handshake. Mr. Bernstein motions to the boy to sit down as he reads Marie-Thérèse's letter, then brings him a glass of water to drink while he writes an answer. Milo is simultaneously curious and indifferent, attentive and uninvolved. (Your life philosophy was now firmly in place: you want to know, but . . . whatever.)

Love letter in hand, he trots home in the dark with Oscar, stopping off at the general store to purchase, not a packet of bubble gum with Beatles cards in it, but a pack of cigarettes. He lights up as he walks. Practices being nonchalant about smoking.

Marie-Thérèse grabs him by the shoulders and sniffs at his breath. "Is that cigarette smoke? Don't tell me you've started smoking . . ."

Milo stares at her coldly. Her eyes drop to the ground.

Several such trajectories. Back. Forth. Back. Forth. One day, as he's burying yet another statuette behind the house, he sees Jacob Bernstein, shoes in hand, climbing out of Marie-Thérèse's bedroom window. The man heads for the road, tiptoeing absurdly through the high grasses in his sock feet and glancing about to make sure no one is watching him. His hunchback somehow makes his stealthiness even more ridiculous. CUT.

OVER THE COURSE of the next few years, Milo, you would piece together the implausible tale of your aunt's love life. Long ago, at age sixteen, she'd gone to Quebec City to try to make a life for herself. She'd been hired as a servant by the writer and recluse Jacob Bernstein and the two of them had fallen head over heels in love. Horrified, Marie-Thérèse's mother, Marie-Jeanne, had put her foot down. *Are you out of your mind? A man twice your age? A hunchback? A Jew? You can't be serious!*

Eventually, reluctantly, the girl had obeyed her mother's order to come home. She was devastated. Far from healing, her heartbreak had festered within her, making her tense, miserable and pragmatic. The following year, she had married Régis Dubé, the only one of her local suitors whose marriage proposal had included a diamond ring. They'd taken over the property and started a family together. And then, a mere few months after the wedding, Jacob Bernstein had bought a house in the area and the love affair had resumed. It had thrived—before, after and even during Marie-Thérèse's pregnancies. With a rare gift for secrecy, the lovers had now been carrying on for nigh on thirty years.

Though you resented your aunt, Milo, you also respected her—for knowing about love.

. . . . .

Neil, *1918*

ON ITS WAY to Liverpool, Neil's ferryboat passes another, crossing the Irish channel in the opposite direction. On that boat, though he has no way of knowing it, disguised as a Red Cross nurse, is the formerly fiery, now aged and gaunt Maud Gonne.

She'd attempted to come back to Dublin back in February but had been promptly arrested, along with seventy-odd other nationalists including Countess Constance Markiewicz, and deported to England. Nine harrowing months at Holloway Prison have done considerable damage to Gonne's health. She is emaciated and chastised, her splendid red hair has grayed—but today at last, after so many long years of exile, frustration and furor, Maud is coming home to Ireland! Her plan, naturally, is to head straight for her beloved apartment on Saint Stephen's Green—loaned free of charge during her absence to her wonderful old friend, the poet William Butler Yeats. She has no way of knowing that Willie's young wife, Georgie, is currently pregnant with their first child, and that Willie will refuse the returned exile entrance to her own home, for fear that she might infect the mother-to-be with cholera, curiosity, or politics. An unhappy ending indeed to the thirty-year friendship between gentleman poet and lady politician.

Neil, using his father's money and connections for what he hopes is the last time, has papers forged for himself in Liverpool.

"Neil Noirlac," he tells the man who runs the clandestine printing press.

"A French name you want, is it? For living in French Canada?"

"That's right. I simply took the name of my hometown and exaggerated it a bit. Dublin means *dark pool* in Gaelic, Noirlac means *black lake* in French."

"I see. Sumpin' as if we were to take Liverpool, swell it up and turn it into Cirrhoselac?"

Neil gratifies the man with a laugh.

"Do you not want to change your Christian name while you're about it, so's they fit together?"

"No, Neil Noirlac is fine. I like the alliteration."

"The what's that?"

"Never mind. Another way of fitting."

"'Tis as you please. Speaking of fitting, you've heard the one about the two Irish fairies, haven't you? Gerald Fitzpatrick and Patrick Fitzgerald?"

(Of course we'll cut that, Milo. Sorry. Terrible taste.)

*   *   *

. . . And now he is on the steamer.

For nine endless days and nights, in the near-darkness of his cramped cabin beneath the deck, as the late-November storms buffet it from Liverpool to Quebec City, Neil empties the contents of his stomach. He brings up Trinity College, Queen Elizabeth, Queen Victoria, King Edward VII, King George V and Archbishop Billy Walsh of Dublin. He pukes up Saint Stephen's Green and the death of his cousin Thom. He rids himself of Daisy, Dorothy, his mother, his father, his former life, his former self and the very name *Kerrigan*—good word to say while vomiting—has a certain spitting-out quality to it.

YOU WANT THIS sequence to make us claustrophobic, Milo. Come to think of it, Neil must have accepted at least *one* more favor from his father. Who but that powerful magistrate could have secured him passage on this steamer from Liverpool to Quebec City . . . or from Southampton to Montreal?

You don't know much about this time in your grandfather's life, Astuto, but it doesn't much matter; the main thing is to have the camera show him, in his cramped quarters on the ship, sitting on the trunk that contains all his belongings, including the invaluable signed copies of *Dubliners* and *The Wind Among the Reeds*, and puking his guts up for three minutes straight. We don't need to actually see or hear him doing this; we can guess at it from the heaves and tremors of his body. Meanwhile, in voice-over, we'll hear him telling you the tale of his crossing thirty-five years later . . .

ARMISTICE HAD BEEN signed a mere fortnight ago, and I'd managed to hitch a ride, as it were, on one of the first vessels bringing Canadian soldiers home. The troops were seriously thinned out: as they will teach you someday in school, Canada had left sixty-two thousand of her young men in the soil at Ypres and Verdun! As for my shipmates the survivors—exhausted, wounded, mutilated, mad—they were mere stumps of their former selves. But I wasn't thinking about the soldiers, Milo. I was vomiting.

Though I grew up in the Bay of Dublin facing the sea, I'd never set foot on a real boat before. The Irish, you see, unlike the British, French, Spanish, Portuguese, or Italians, are not seafarers. Over the centuries, the ocean has generally brought them bad news in the form of conquerors and marauders, so they prefer to turn their backs to it. Apart from digging up cockles and mussels along its edges, they have not tended to think of it as a source of amusement, discovery, or food. This is why, unbelievable as it may seem, when the Irish potato crop was wiped out by mildew in the mid-1840s, it did not occur to them to eat fish and a million of them starved to death. But I was not thinking of the potato famine as I crossed the Atlantic, Milo, I was too busy vomiting.

For more than a century already, Ireland had been degurgitating its own population. Puking up the poor. Heaving up the destitute. Splattering its ill and hopeless, ragged and starving masses all over the planet. Oh, Milo, the misery of my country is beyond belief! In a single century, that tiny island spewed eight million desperate human beings off its surface. How could there be any left? you might ask, and a good question it would be! The answer can be summed up in a single word: Catholicism.

Big families. Personally, I'd always suffered from having only one sibling, and an unpleasant one at that. I envied the James Joyces of the world, who grew up in the rough-and-tumble company of a large family. Ten young'uns there were in the Joyce clan—ten who survived, that is—of a dozen born! Only later did it occur to me that my mum must have had everything removed after Dorothy's birth: in those days, Catholic families with only two children were unheard of.

Yes, British landlords were bleeding the country dry, but frustrated celibate priests tirelessly incited their overworked and undernourished parishioners to indulge in constant copulation so as to go forth and multiply. They painted hair-raising verbal pictures of what awaited married couples in Hell if ever it occurred to them to slough off on their conjugal duty and stop churning out kids: fallow wombs ripped open, lazy penises transpierced with pitchforks, unborn babes flung into cauldrons of boiling oil for all eternity . . . Don't forget, Milo—horror movies hadn't yet been invented and neither had TV; people back then weren't accustomed to digesting war footage with their evening meal. These images of Hell were very real to them. They stuck in their brains, tormenting their consciences by day and giving them bad dreams by night.

The Irish multiplied like rabbits and died like flies. Their country couldn't feed them! They were packed half dead onto boats; droves of them died on the boats and got flipped into the sea; other droves made it to Sydney, New York, or Toronto and died there of starvation; those who made it to La Grosse Île, just upriver from Quebec City, turned out to be good at dying of cholera. This they did at the rate of five thousand a year for so many years that the island came to be known as Île de la Quarantaine. But still the Irish kept going forth and multiplying, hoping against hope that the next life might be better than this one, sure an' nothing could be worse.

Oh, the poor Irish, Milo! An undereducated, gullible people, forever kowtowing to teachers and preachers, kings and popes, following their orders, fearing what they were told to fear, praying to the God they were told to pray to, abdicating their wills, allowing themselves to be downtrodden, endlessly cooperating in their own destruction. How I longed to help them! To write a book that would turn their resignation into some unprecedented form of intelligence! But now Ireland had spewed me up in turn. I was persona non grata in my own country, disowned by both the pro-British establishment and the nationalist independence movement.

So why did I never write that book, you ask? Well, my boy, little did I know it at the time, but I had come out of the frying pan into the fire. In Quebec as in Ireland, priests threatened married folk with hellfire if they did anything to avoid reproducing. In Quebec as in Ireland, women routinely gave birth to twelve, fifteen, or even twenty children, praying that half the swarm might stumble their way to maturity and that a precious one might enter the church. Oh, I hated those preachers with a vengeance, Milo, but I loved your grandmother. Being pious, Marie-Jeanne wouldn't hear of abstinence or birth control; the minute each babe had finished suckling, she would come panting to me for more seed. Her thirteenth delivery killed her at age forty, and sorely do I miss her still . . .

TERRIFIC, MILO—THAT'S A brilliant way of filming the ocean crossing. For once you're thinking budget. No need to charter a ship or hire seven hundred actors to play the wounded, wild-eyed returning Canadian soldiers; the whole thing can be shot on set, in the studio. Brilliant. You deserve a kiss.

. . . . .

Awinita, July 1951

SOUND TRACK: IN the background, far away at first, the beating of Indian ceremonial drums. *Ta, ta-da DA, ta, ta-da DA* . . .

> *THROB-throb-throb-throb;*
> *Is this throbbing a sound*
> *Or an ache in the air?*
> *Pervasive as light,*

Measured and inevitable,
It seems to float from no distance,
But to live in the listening world—
Throb-throb-throb-throb-throbbing
The sound of Powassan's drum.

Remember you read that poem out loud to me once, Milo, as we flew from New York to Bahia? Its author, Duncan Campbell Scott, was not only a great poet, but arguably the most ruthless throttler of native culture in Canadian history. In the 1920s, even as, in Salvador, Police Chief Pedro de Azevedo Gordilho was busy repressing capoeira, candomblé and *sambistas*, Scott ran all over Canada persecuting Indians and forbidding their festivals. *Ta, ta-da DA, ta, ta-da DA, ta, ta-da DA* . . . White folks have always lived in terror of that sound. It's the sound of their own bodies, their own desires, which they throttled centuries ago to become conquerors . . . Sorry.

TA, TA-DA, DA, *ta, ta-da DA* . . . In the foreground, so close as to seem to be coming from inside our very brain: zippers, belt buckles, the swish of pants being removed, a man breathing heavily, a man swearing under his breath, another man, another, another and, between pants, swearwords in English and in French, *you little cunt, little slut, little slut bitch,* belt buckle clinking, these sounds gradually fading and the drumbeats coming closer, *ta, ta-da DA, ta, ta-da DA* . . . zipper unzipping, a shout. *You like it, don't you? You like my big fat cock bangin' into your savage little Indian pussy, don't you? Come on, tell me you like it, you little whore. You like it, don't you, eh, you fuckin' little slut? Hey, little Indian, hey, baby,* drumbeats getting louder, *I'm gonna come, lemme come in your mouth, baby, can I come on your face, lemme come in your ass, baby,* drumbeats now drowning the words out, *yes yes yes YES oh my God, oh mon Dieu, oh oui oh oui ouh ouh, oui, OUI,* the belt buckles, panting, pants, swish of pants and clink of buckle and zip of zipper ultimately rendered inaudible by the extremely loud drumbeats.

Awinita's face (our face) reflected in a pond. We're still only nineteen, but our expression is grave. As we stare at ourselves in the water's still surface, our face sprouts long brown hair and laughs at us. Our body shrinks and we turn into some small, round, furry animal, maybe an ockqutchaun *(woodchuck). Quivering, we bound away.*

Awinita is fast asleep on Declan's chest in the cruddy little bedroom above the bar. Half sitting up in bed, smoking a cigarette, Declan looks drunk and in an evil mood.

"Nita," he says (but she's breathing from the depths of sleep). "Nita!" he repeats, stubbing out his cigarette and jerking her to wakefulness.

"What?"

"What's the matter with you?"

She doesn't answer. Wouldn't know where to start.

"Ever since the baby was born, it's as if you don't wanna make out with me anymore. Come on, whassup?"

"It's only been a coupla weeks, Deck. I'm tired, dat's all."

"We used to have such good times in bed, baby. Come on . . . Make an effort, honey . . . Make me happy."

"I'm tired, Deck."

"You make your johns happy all night long, no problem there, no I'm tired there! Just suddenly when it's my turn, the tap runs dry."

"Later, sweetie."

"Don't you later-sweetie me. You know we gotta clear outta the room by noon, and I'm not allowed in your place up on the Plateau. I don't like this, baby. I'm not gettin' any and it pisses me off.

I'm a normal guy with normal needs and you're my gal, remember? Maybe you get your kicks elsewhere, but I sure as hell don't . . ."

"Lemme sleep, man. You should get some shut-eye, too. You had too much to drink."

Turning her back on him, she pulls the sheet up over her shoulder. He rips it away.

"Don't you tell me what to do, bitch. You're not my mother."

He moves onto her.

"Hang on, Deck . . . you wearin' a safe?"

Large animals—oxen?—writhing in agony. Their bulky bodies heave, they bellow.

Awinita in the apartment on the Plateau Mont-Royal, chatting with her roommates. One of them—Deena, a young Mohawk Indian from the south of the province, also a bleached blonde—always gives her beauty tips.

"Wow, Nita. You should get your hair done, you know that? Your roots are really visible."

"Yeah, I'll get around to it. Soon as I've paid off my debt."

"I'll be all paid up a month from now," says Cheryl. "Got a terrific weekend job up at that new hotel near Trois-Rivières, Le Paradis des Sports."

"Lucky you! How'd you land that?"

"Owner was in town coupla weeks ago. Guy named Cossette. Musta liked the way I went down on him."

"You're goin' up in the world, with all that goin' down. Wow! Put in a good word for us, Cher!"

They laugh.

"Sure thing. Uh . . . Actually they say they don't want native girls, to start out with . . . But at least you're working again, Nita. That's amazing. Got your figure right back, eh?"

"Yeah, nobody'd ever guess you just had a baby just three weeks ago!"

"Not even floppy around the tum."

"Hurts, dough," Awinita says.

"What hurts?"

"Work."

"Yeah, I know," says Lorraine who is older than the others, twenty-five or so. "Been through it twice."

"I never had a baby, but I can imagine."

"Your johns notice anything?"

"Nah . . . but *I* do."

"Well, tell 'em to be nice 'n' gentle with you."

"Yeah, sure," says Awinita, and the four of them laugh.

"You know what the best painkiller is, don't you?" Lorraine says.

"Uh . . . love?" says Awinita, and the four of them laugh.

"Nope. Cold as ice. Keep guessin' . . ."

"Aspirin?"

"Better'n love, but still barely lukewarm."

"Poppers?"

"Gettin' warmer . . ."

CUT to Awinita and Lorraine locked into the bathroom together. Subjective camera: we're seated on the toilet lid, our face visible in profile in the mirror above the sink. Close-up of a needle slipping into a vein in our inner arm.

"It's a gift, Nita. Won't cost you a cent, this first time. Just a gift, to make you feel better."

Close-up of our face in the mirror. Slowly its muscles relax, its tensions dissolve, its contours fill with bliss. They melt and fade to whiteness . . . Yes, the divine milky whiteness of heroin you know so well, Milo, darling, and which you've always longed to convey on film. We could put Arvo Pärt's *Litany* on the sound track. Our eyes close, our lips and mouth go slack and we sink deeper and deeper into the liquid ecstasy, floating in it as we did in our mother's womb, hearing the soft throb of our mother's heart, which is also our heart and that of Mother Earth, that Indian drumbeat we recognize from before . . . *Ta, ta-da DA, ta, ta-da DA* . . . As our flesh melts and the universe dissolves around us, we nod off, our forehead pressed against the bathroom sink, but even that chill hard edge is a pleasure as exquisite as the first spoonful of vanilla ice cream on the tip of our tongue when we were three years old. Our hand falls off our lap, our arm flops to our side and dangles there. We open our eyes long enough to see Lorraine smile down at us and move away . . . CUT.

Awinita has gone home for a visit.

Full summer sunlight glancing off the high blond waving grasses of the Waswanipi Reserve, uncultivated land as far as the eye can see. She walks past the old folks sitting on benches beneath the eaves of their miserable huts. As they gaze after her, we see their brows knit at the way she walks and the way she is dressed. Their disapproval isn't about her being a prostitute; it's about her being a city chick, a stranger. Her demeanor can't fit in here anymore. The community is losing its members one after the other, a slow hemorrhage.

In the shade behind their shack, she sits down with her mother, a hunched and wizened woman of maybe forty-five. Their conversation will be in Cree with English subtitles.

"Many moons it's been," says her mother, plaiting sweetgrass.

"Yes. Too long."

"And the envelopes stopped coming. But now you're here and it's better than many, many envelopes."

"I had debts to repay. Life will be easier now, I hope."

"Difficulties come to us all, we face them. Your body is strong?"

"My body is strong. The brothers and sisters?"

"There was hunger this year in springtime, but none of us died. Life thrives. The world follows its course. And we must all go back to the earth our mother, who patiently waits for our time to come, her arms wide to welcome and hold us."

"Yes. When there's more money, I send it to you."

"If you have extra, send it so I can buy more flour."

"Now I must go back to the city. The trip is a long one; night will be day before I arrive."

"Be joyful."

"Take advantage of life."

Gently, unsmilingly, the old woman presses the braid of sweetgrass into her daughter's palm. Awinita rises and moves off. And, as the punishing sun finally starts to set . . . CUT.

A series of toilet scenes, still and always from Awinita's point of view.

Seated on the throne of a toilet, now at Liz's place, now in the cruddy bedroom on Saint Catherine, we wipe ourselves and twist around to check the toilet paper. It comes up bloodless.

Time after time after time, we swivel to find no blood.

Close-up of our impassive face in the bathroom mirror. Our hair is now half blond, half black.

Sound track of men groaning and muttering, panting and swearing, zipping their flies up and down, unfastening and refastening their belt buckles.

A frog tries to leap out of a well. It gathers tremendous energy for each leap but never manages to reach the top. After each failure, it finds itself back where it started, only tireder. Sometimes it bangs its head on the stone wall, but it can't help leaping; its urge to reach sunlight and fresh air is irresistible. At last it weakens and sinks beneath the water's surface. There is light there, too, but of a different kind. A still, glazed-green light shrouds the frog.

. . . . .

VI

FLOREIO

In capoeira, any exercise involving dexterity or trickery; jogo floreio.

Milo, 1965–67

THE CHILD I love is turning into the man I love.

At thirteen, his body begins to explode with hormones. He can feel it in his muscles, throat and loins. His voice changes, and so does the way he looks at girls. Edith's breasts are enormous now, and she actually lets him pull up her sweater or blouse and struggle with her bra (undoing it is off-limits) until one of them flops out and he can kiss it and suck on its nipple to his heart's content. Edith isn't beautiful in any conventional sense of the word; she's freckled and dumpy and lumpy—but oh, the feeling in his balls when she smiles knowingly at him from across the classroom, or slips her tongue into his mouth as they kiss! During his nocturnal sessions of watching TV with the sound off (they have a color TV now, and, thanks to Milo's inventiveness, Cary Grant, Montgomery Clift and Lucille Ball all speak fluent, funny French), he can joy himself on the chesterfield by concentrating simultaneously on Sophia Loren's cleavage, the memory of Edith's nipples and the fantasy of another girl at school—one who has a lovely face but is too stuck-up to talk to him.

We won't necessarily use all this material, Astuto—we just need to be aware of it. It will be conveyed to our spectators by the confident way the boy now walks, the pugnacious set of his shoulders, the proud carriage of his head. Following his mother's advice, he trusts few human beings (especially not his cousins, and super especially not his aunt)—but it's evident at a glance that he trusts himself . . .

ON THIS BRILLIANT autumn Sunday afternoon, Grandpa Neil has invited him up to his study to talk. Both the wilting, faltering old man and the budding young one take pleasure in their exchanges. Neil's natural gift for the gab is reinforced by his aching, impatient hunger to speak English. He sees Milo as an unhoped-for reincarnation of his younger self, and because his own writing path has grown dark and twisty over the years, running into one wall after another, his fondest hope is to help his grandson carve out a destiny that will lead him straight to literary fame.

"So did you manage to read *Hamlet* since last week?"

"Yes."

"And?"

"There's a lot I don't get. Why can some folks see his fader's ghost and oders not? How does he tink he can venge his fader's murder by pretending to be crazy? Why's he so nasty to Ophelia?"

Neil wasn't expecting these thorny questions, so he goes ahead with the short lecture he'd prepared.

"Well, you see, Milo, generally speaking, people don't want to be told the truth, they want to be reassured. Often, if you tell them the truth, they'll get angry and punish you. They prefer dogma to science. Science tends to be depressing, because it shows us we're not as important as we think. Nowadays, everyone learns in school that our Earth is one of nine planets that revolve around the sun, right? But four hundred years ago, Copernicus shocked all of Europe by suggesting that this might be the case. People were certain that God had made the universe just for us, with the Earth at its center and the sun, moon and stars revolving around it. The Italian astronomer Giordano Bruno was burned at the stake in 1600 for confirming Copernicus's theory, and a mere two years later, Shakespeare wrote *Hamlet!* You recall that Prince Hamlet attended the University of Wittenberg? Well, a student of Copernicus's named Georg Joachim was teaching there at the time, so naturally Hamlet would have been obsessed with all these new theories. Indeed, he describes the Earth as *a sterile promontory*, the sky as *a foul and pestilent congregation of vapours*, and man . . . yes, Milo, man himself . . . as a *quintessence of dust*. Never had anyone dared express so dark a view of humankind."

"It's not dat different from what de preacher says," Milo objects. "Dat we're made of dust. *Ashes to ashes and dust to dust.*"

"Hmm."

Again unsettled by his grandson's sharpness of mind, Neil takes refuge in free association.

"You know, when I was a boy growing up in Dublin, all the church services were in Latin, and on Ash Wednesday the priest would dip his right thumb into an urn of ashes, go along the altar where we choirboys were kneeling and make the sign of the cross on our foreheads, intoning the words *Memento homo quia pulvis est.* Know what that means, Milo?"

Neil writes it down for his grandson.

"Uh . . . is it about men who like other men?"

". . . because of the word *homo?*"

Neil laughs until tears roll out of the corners of his eyes and down his cheeks, losing themselves in his long gray beard.

"You're right. In Greek *homo* means *same*, as in *homogenized milk*. But in Latin it means *man*, as in . . . er . . . *homicide*. Quite a mishmash, eh? So the priest's words mean, not *Don't forget to move your pelvis, you little queer*, but *Man, forget not that thou art dust*."

Milo nods a bit uncertainly.

"Remember that book I showed you by the great James Joyce?" Neil plunges on, forgetting to pursue his demonstration of how Hamlet's nihilism arose from Copernicus's heliocentric theory. "The one in which he inscribed my name?"

"*Dubliners*," says Milo, who forgets nothing.

"Exactly. Well, there's a funny story about that book. You'll see the connection in a minute."

Settling back in his armchair, Neil takes a minute to light his pipe, delighting in the ease of their exchange.

"You see, Jimmy Joyce had one devil of a time getting that book published; it took him all of seven years! He wrote it in 1907–1908, and it was two whole years before he found a publisher for it. Finally, in 1910, he signed with a certain Mr. Roberts. But then he went off to live in Europe, and due to all the real names of businesses and all the dirty words he used in the book, Roberts started worrying about libel suits. So he hemmed and hawed and postponed and delayed, and Joyce threatened to sue him for breach of contract. Believe it or not, Milo, the case was handled by my own father, a magistrate of the Dublin courts!"

(Did Neil really tell you lies as flagrant as that, Astuto? Or are you stretching the truth of his stretching of the truth? Anyway, let's keep it in—*se non è vero, è ben trovato* . . .)

"Court cases take time . . . But finally, when Jimmy returned to Dublin for his mother's funeral in 1912, everything was set to go: the printer, a man by the name of Falconer, had already churned out the broadsheets for a thousand copies of the book. Do you know what a broadsheet is, Milo?"

"One big page that'll later be folded and cut up into lots of smaller pages?"

"On the nose. But on the very verge of publication, getting cold feet in turn, Falconer decided to shred the broadsheets. Well, when Jimmy learned of that, Milo, he went berserk. He told everyone his book had been *burned*, not shredded. That way he could compare himself to the great Giordano Bruno. Yes! James Joyce had been burned at the stake for having told the truth, not about the rotation of heavenly bodies, but about the everyday life of ordinary Irishmen. A bit of an exaggeration, wouldn't you say? As if Rome and Dublin were the same city, Pope and publisher the same authority, Bruno and Joyce the same man."

"Homo homo," Milo says, and again Neil rewards him with a roar of laughter.

"So what did Joyce do to punish Roberts? He wrote a cruel, castigating poem called "Gas from a Burner." I have a copy of it here somewhere . . . ah, here it is. *Burner,* in the present case, refers not to your usual gas ring on a kitchen stove but to Roberts himself, because he burned Joyce's book. As for *gas,* well . . . it's like when you have gas after eating pork 'n' beans. You understand? Roberts's promises, in other words, were nothing but a lot of stenchy farts! Jimmy had the poem printed in Trieste and insisted that his younger brother Charles distribute it in Dublin. Charles did so against his better judgment, and my cousin Thom, who as you recall was a former schoolmate of Jimmy's, got his hands on a copy and brought it to my place. Ah, Milo, that's a day I'll never forget! We weren't wee lads anymore, I was twenty and Thom a decade older, but we fell to the floor in stitches when we reached the final lines of poem:

My Irish foreman from Bannockburn
Shall dip his right hand in the urn
And sign crisscross with reverent thumb
Memento homo *upon my bum.*

"Milo? *Milo?*"

Marie-Thérèse's angry voice soars up to our hero from downstairs.

"Where are you, for the luva . . . ? It's goin' on four and you haven't even started your homework yet! That's enough English! Get down here right this minute! Lickety-split!"

As he goes downstairs to do math under his aunt's maniacal supervision, Milo breathes a faint sigh of relief. He worships his grandfather, so it disturbs him when Neil talks to him as an equal . . .

I LOVE YOU, Milo. I love you. I want to make love to you here and now. I want to take off all my clothes and your hospital pajamas and gently unhook the tubes from your body and kiss you all over as you grab my hair and pull it—kiss your eyelids, your face and lips, kiss your neck as you offer it up to me, kiss your hairless chest and feel your beautiful penis rise in my hands and harden in my mouth, turn you over and kiss the smooth brown skin of your muscular back, wet you with my fingers as you moan, and enter you . . . Oh, Milo! If only we could join our bodies again, as we've done so often in the past—in New York, arriving you from Toronto and me from Buenos Aires, or in San Salvador, arriving you from Paris and me from L.A.—pleasuring each other's throbbing, searching cocks with our mouths and hands and anuses, whetting each other's appetites, whipping each other's desires, rising together to a violent frenzy, and oh, your shout when you came, Milo, unforgettable, a punch of joy that hit me right in the chest . . . *How can it be over?* How can this be *us*, you know what I mean? Two old fogies whispering a screenplay at each other through an endless November night in a public hospital in Montreal's city center . . . and you, my love, in the throes of the dreaded illness?

I don't understand how you managed to catch it in Rio, given that we'd both been fervently faithful to condoms since the late 1980s . . . Whatever happened, Astuto, darling? Maybe you shot up again—and somehow, despite the forty new needle exchange programs recently implemented by the Brazilian government, despite the millions of free needles distributed throughout the country over the preceding year, you happened to use an old, dirty one and get infected by it? Tell me, Milo . . . No, I know you can't. You're right, I'll shut up. Let's get back to work . . .

A DINNER SCENE.

"I've found you a boarding school," announces Marie-Thérèse. "Way better than any of the schools around here. You don't even have to wait till September; they'll let you start in at Easter. They made an exception for you because of your good marks."

"Wha . . . what do you . . . ?" stammers Neil, but Régis's voice drowns him out.

"Hey, good for you, little runt! You're gonna do better than your cousins, or even your uncle!"

"Eh! I should think so!" says Marie-Thérèse. "I should hope so!"

"What about Oscar?" Milo says. "Can he come to the school with me?"

"Don't be silly, Milo," says Marie-Thérèse. "You can't organize your whole life around a dog! We'll take care of him while you're gone, and you'll see him during your semester breaks."

So you go off to that boarding school and find yourself surrounded by a dozen horny Jesuit priests, a score of frigid nuns and a hundred boys in the first randy rush of puberty. Aware that *this* is one of the forms of hell on earth your mother warned you about, you cross the days off the calendar as they inch by, slow and slobbery as snails.

The other boys go home on weekends; you don't. (Why not? Was the school too far away from your home or what?) You find yourself alone in the empty building, bored and anxious, anxious and bored, left to your own resources: reading, playing billiards, fending off the perpetually wandering hands of the priests—and, especially, worrying about Oscar. You can almost hear him whimpering as he waits at the door, nose aquiver, searching for your smell that never comes.

June rolls around at last and you come home to the farm. The reunion between boy and dog: mutual relief and all-engulfing euphoria. Sure, you're glad to see your grandfather, too, and the cows, and even, in a small way, the kitchen. But there's no comparison: Oscar is king of your heart. With Oscar at your side you can handle anything . . .

(At this point in the film, every spectator will have guessed that Oscar is going to die; the only question is how. Oh, Milo . . .)

When you go back to school that fall . . . Oscar simply can't understand your having abandoned him *again*. He waits for you, refusing to budge from his post at the door. He grows depressed and thin. Though she sees perfectly well what's happening, Marie-Thérèse refrains from telling you about it; she doesn't want you to have a less-than-sterling report card at semester's end. The dog ceases eating completely. He whines and strains at his leash, thins and whines and strains and mopes and sleeps . . . and then he dies. He isn't yet thin enough to have died of hunger; he dies of a broken heart.

Régis insists that Milo be informed at once.

"Okay," says Marie-Thérèse, "but we'll tell him he got hit by a car."

"No, we won't. We're not going to lie about it."

"It's not really a lie, it's just to protect him. One way or another the dog's dead; there's no changing that."

"I'll tell him," Jean-Joseph puts in, in the deep, authoritative male voice he's been perfecting in logging camps over the past two years. Now twenty, he weighs more than both his parents put together, so neither of them dares to object.

Jean-Joseph calls the boarding school to announce his visit, only to learn that Milo is in the infirmary. Even as, unbeknownst to him, his dog was dying of his absence, the boy came down with a galloping case of scarlet fever. When Marie-Thérèse hears this, the panic on her face is so sincere that Jean-Joseph knows he'll spend the rest of his life hating the Injun bastard.

"I'll go see him," he says. "I've got a job starting the day after tomorrow, not far from where he is. Let me handle it, Ma."

He arrives bearing not only a picnic basket filled with victuals from Marie-Thérèse, but also a plan, which he immediately puts into action. Eyes sadly downcast into the pretty nurse's cleavage, he tells her in a low voice that Milo's beloved dog has died, and requests an hour alone with the boy to break the news to him gently. When the nurse respectfully leaves the room, he locks the door behind her, sets the picnic basket down with a thump and rips the bedding off Milo's body. Says he's sure Milo is getting an excellent education in this school that is costing his parents more than they've ever spent on him, Jean-Joseph, and his brother, François-Joseph, put together, but that there is one aspect of Milo's education that is no doubt being sorely neglected here and that only he can see to. So saying, he unzips his fly and starts shooting undiluted

hatred into you through his crotch gun, along with harshly muttered words about your *redskin whore of a mother*, your *primitive
blood* and your *savage bastardom*. None of this is particularly new
to you, Astuto. You've known for a long time that human penises
can be used for the best and worst of purposes, *Heaven and Hell
are man-made and here on earth*. You've heard Jean-Joseph and
François-Joseph pant and grunt as they scrabbled in the dark of
your bedroom . . . played the go-between in your aunt's passion-
ate love affair with Jacob Bernstein . . . guessed a fair amount
about your mother's profession . . . seen boys here at school
emerge from confessional boxes, tears in their eyes and cheeks
aflame . . . so you simply go elsewhere in your brain and wait
for it to be over. When at last your cousin bucks out of you, zips
himself up and leaves, you get up, cross to the sink and wash
yourself thoroughly.

A few minutes later, the nurse returns.

"You poor boy, how terrible. I had a dog that died, too, I know
just how you feel . . ."

That is when the sky collapses on your head.

The following day Milo's fever subsides. The minute the nurse
walks into his room, he tells her he needs to put through a phone
call to his aunt.

"No, Milo, you know the rules. Boarders may write letters once
a week, but they're not allowed to use the telephone."

The Jesuit priests are called in, and then the school director. All
encourage him to get over his pain at the loss of his dog by going
back to class. He sticks to his guns, will talk of nothing else. At last,
because of his dazzling school record, they acquiesce.

"Auntie, you know Jean-Joseph came to see me yesterday. Well,
he raped me."

"What are you . . . ?"

"Your son raped me. If you don't want me to tell the whole world your son's a pansy, get me out of this school. I'll tell the preacher. I'll tell Uncle Régis. I'll tell my grandfather. I'll tell Jacob Bernstein and every woman in the neighborhood . . ."

"You do that, Milo, I'll kill you."

"If you don't want me to tell, get me out of here. Right now. Today."

By nightfall he is home.

. . . . .

Neil, 1919

IF YOU DON'T mind, Milo, I think we should use only interiors for the sequence about Neil's first months in Canada. That all right with you? Trying to reconstitute post–First World War Old Montreal would put Blackout Productions into the red for a decade.

So we could find him . . . say, seated at a tiny table next to the window in a corner of a frilly, curtained, doilied, lacy, flowery-wallpapered bedroom, reading Shakespeare's *Henry V* by dim lamplight and shivering as the venomous wind snakes round the window frame and licks him with its cold tongue. It's late January; Neil has been in Montreal for two months and they've been the most miserable two months of his life. Horrendous cold—at forty below, the Celsius and Fahrenheit thermometers agree whole-heartedly. Feels like forty below, they say, staring at each other and echoing their verdict back and forth in the icy silence. Forty below! Stones would freeze in this weather; souls would freeze.

We hear Act III, Scene 4 as Neil reads it out loud to himself in two different, mock-female voices: a dialogue between Catherine, the French princess and Alice, her chambermaid. His accent in French is perfectly abominable.

"*Je m'en fais la repetition de tous les mots que vous m'avez appris des a present.*"

"*Il est trop difficile, madame, comme je pense.*"

"*Excusez-moi, Alice. Écoutez:* de hand, de fingres, de nails, de arma, de bilbow."

"D'elbow, *madame.*"

"*Ô Seigneur Dieu! Je m'en oublie;* d'elbow. *Comment appelez-vous le col?*"

"De neck, *madame.*"

"De nick. *Et le menton?*"

"De chin."

"De sin. *Le col,* de nick; *le menton,* de sin."

"*Oui. Sauf votre honneur, en vérité, vous prononcez les mots aussi droit que les natifs d'Angleterre.*"

He snorts. Who would have thought that Shakespeare could teach him French? All he has to do is work backward: elbow is *coude*, neck is *col*, nails are *ongles* . . . Now, if only he had an Alice!

CUT to dinner that evening. We're in the pseudo-Victorian Sherbrooke Street home of Judge Ross McGuire, friend and former colleague of Neil's father, who has unenthusiastically agreed to provide lodgings for the young man until he gets his bearings in the new country. Now twenty-seven and burning to be free, Neil is dismayed to find himself once again eating Irish food (roast beef, potatoes, gravy, green beans and creamed onions), served by an Irish maid to an Irish magistrate and his Irish wife. His father explicitly instructed him never, in this household, to broach the topics of James Joyce, Maud Gonne, or the Easter Rising.

"Yesterday," mutters Judge McGuire as he swallows a large slice of roast beef almost whole, including fat and gristle, "Sinn Féin went ahead and proclaimed independence. Looks like war to me."

"War, war, haven't we had enough war?" Mrs. McGuire asks rhetorically. "First the Great War in Europe, then the Bolshevik Revolution in Russia . . . and now, no sooner have our men come home than the Sinn Féiners start acting up again."

"Forgive me," Neil says. "But having arrived so recently from Dublin, I must say I understand their point of view. It would be worse than frustrating, humiliating, to come so close to independence and see it snatched away from us at the last minute."

In excitement, Mrs. McGuire's narrow rear end bobs up and down on her chair.

"But why could they not be content with what they were *given*? Every single *one* of their sixty-nine candidates was victorious in last month's elections!"

"Including twelve with death sentences on their heads," her husband interrupts, his mouth full of mashed potatoes, "and twenty-one others currently serving prison terms."

"Still," insists Mrs. McGuire, "they *did* win fully three-quarters of the seats! It would have given them a powerful voice in Parliament. They would have been able to make themselves heard!"

"Yes, but in *British* Parliament," Neil points out. "They don't want a powerful voice in *British* Parliament, Mrs. McGuire. After all the sacrifices they've made, they feel it would be an unforgivable compromise."

"Yes, they were most generous about sacrificing other people's lives, weren't they?" says the judge while chewing, gravy dribbling down his chin. "The lives of poor, ordinary, run-of-the-mill Catholics, who found themselves caught up in strikes, lockouts and riots, and corralled into a political movement about which they knew nothing."

"They want a parliament of their own," intones Neil with dignity. "The Dáil Éireann. From all I can gather, *that* is what has just been ratified."

"It means war, I tell you!" splutters McGuire. "The new chief of state will be Éamon de Valera, who *also* happens to be in jail in England! Frankly, my boy, would you not rather see Ireland run from Westminster than from Holloway?"

"Con Markiewicz wasn't above saying yes," Mrs. McGuire points out. "I must admit I'm proud of that woman. Just think: the first female member of Parliament ever, an Irishwoman! British women have voting rights now," she adds, in a bit of a non sequitur. "Canadian women, too; well, except here in Quebec . . ."

"I knew her," Neil blurts out.

"Who? Lady Constance?"

"Yes. I mean, I saw her a few times."

"And where would that have been?"

Mercifully, the maid barges in.

"Shall I warm the apple torte now, ma'am?"

"Yes, do, Maggie. We should be ready for it in three or four minutes."

CUT to Neil walking the streets of Old Montreal. At these temperatures, the wind is searing. It burns your cheeks, whips powdery snow up your trouser legs, and dives into the space between your scarf and neck, attacking your vulnerable, warm flesh. In a matter of minutes your nose can freeze; your ears can freeze; your fingers and toes can freeze.

It's a miserable city in which to pound the pavement in search of employment. Neil had thought that being a river port like Dublin, Montreal would feel familiar to him, but nowhere along the Saint

Lawrence can one hop and skip from bridge to bridge as along the Liffey, cutting capers and dreaming of one's green-as-a-meadow future (ah! that memory's nearly a decade old!). All is harsh and cold and hard and cold and gray and cold and dark and cold and hostile; and cold. The pavement beneath his feet is sharp and slippery with frozen slush. His shoes are wearing thin; even new, they could not have withstood this punishing climate. To survive in Canada, he'll need not only new shoes but a new personality, new hopes, new values.

On his first evening in Montreal, Judge McGuire had plunged him into a bottomless melancholy merely by showing him a map of the province. Half a dozen Irelands could fit into it, the judge had told him, but it is empty. Apart from the small towns and smaller villages spaced out along the river that plunges its sharp wedge diagonally through the province's southernmost section all the way to the Great Lakes, it is unpopulated. Nothing but Indian and Eskimo tribes of a few hundred members each, scattered over an inconceivably gigantic, uninhabitable, icy tundra dotted with a zillion frozen lakes.

Neil doesn't know quite *why* the thought of Quebec's immensity and emptiness so distresses him, but it does.

After about forty minutes, he literally can't stand the cold anymore; his legs have turned into sticks of ice and he fears they'll snap if he remains outdoors even one more minute. He ducks into a hotel lobby on Notre-Dame Street.

INTERIOR—DAY, if this gloom can qualify as daylight. Acutely depressed, Neil pushes through swinging wooden doors into the hotel restaurant and heads for a small table next to the window. His depression is not merely that of any lonely, unemployed person who finds himself in a crowded place where everyone else seems to know who they are and why. It's worse. It's the depression of exile.

Visible through the nasty freezing snow, painted in white letters on the side of a smoke-blackened brick building across the street, he reads the words *G. A. Holland and Son Co. House Furnishers, Carpets, Draperies*. Perhaps this firm would hire him? Perhaps he could spend the rest of his life selling draperies in Montreal? It makes him want to die. *Who are Holland and Son, anyway? Where did they come from and what the feckin' hell are they doing here? Why do people cross oceans? Why do they do anything? What were you thinking of, Willie Yeats, when you advised me to immigrate to the Americas to write? Did* you *come over to Montreal to seek inspiration? Not at all! You preferred to remain holed up in your comfortable old apartment in London and your wild, romantic thoor in County Galway. As for Jimmy Joyce, he cleverly moved from Trieste to Zurich to Paris, and can now spend the remainder of his years traipsing along the Seine, holding forth in bars and tying up whores! What, prithee, can one hope to write in forty-below weather in a port city along whose river one cannot even walk?*

Neil weeps hot tears inside.

The waitress comes up to him and, his head being bowed, the first thing he sees of her is an immaculate white apron on a black uniform. Adopting his point of view, we notice as he does that her curves (as men used to say) are in all the right places, but that she has buttoned her blouse awry. This reminds him of Yeats's cardigan, which again makes him feel a piercing nostalgia for Ireland.

"*Qu'est-ce que j'vous sers?*"[2]

He doesn't understand.

"What?

"*Qué c'est que vous allez prendre?*"[3]

2. —What c'n I get ya?
3. —Can I take your order?

He utters the first French word that comes back to him from the Shakespearean dialogue read the previous day.

"*Menton.*"

"*Quoi?*" The girl wrinkles her nose and giggles. "*Un menton?*"[4]

"*Coude*, ventures Neil. I'm trying to learn French."

"*Eh bien, avec ces mots-là, ça fonctionnerait mieux dans un cours de danse que dans un restaurant. Voulez un café?*"[5]

He decides to exploit his weakness rather than conceal it.

"Coffee?"

"*Café.*"

"*Ca-fay.*"

"*Avec du lait?*"

"*Dou-lay.*"

"*Oui, m'sieu'.*"

"*Oui, m'-siou'.*"

She smiles at him.

"Buttons," he says.

"Butter? *Du beurre?*"

"No . . ."

Gently, gesturing, smiling, he demonstrates on his own shirt that her blouse has a buttoning problem. The girl glances down then up, and laughs out loud.

"Oh, dear, I got my buttons mixed up again, I don't believe it! Thanks for telling me . . ."

CUT to Mount Royal Park on a sunny day. Several months must have elapsed, because the snow has melted and the trees are in full blossom. Sitting on a bench, Neil and the young waitress

---

4. —*What?* . . . A chin?
5. —Well, with those words you'd be better at the tailor's than in a coffee shop. Wanna coffee?

pursue their mutual exploration. Though Neil's French has improved, his accent is still god-awful.

"I'll be a great writer . . . You'll see, Marie-Jeanne. Before my thirtieth . . . uh . . . day of birth . . . I'll publish a great novel."

"Will you write a show for me?"

"What? A shoe?"

"A show, not a shoe! A show I can star in!"

"Yes. You're my star, that's for sure!"

CUT to Saint Helen's Island in the summertime. The two of them walking there.

"Nowadays there are more English than French in Montreal . . . but in the olden days it was a French city. It was founded by a Frenchman, three hundred years ago: Samuel de Champlain, his name was. And he named this place Saint Helen's Island after his wife, Hélène Boullé. Just think, she was only twelve when they got married!"

"And you . . . seventeen when you marry me. Lucky I said yes, you're already getting old."

"Hey, wait a minute! *I* haven't said yes yet! . . . I think Champlain married Hélène Boullé for *sa dot*."

"*Sa dot?* What's dat?"

"The money a family gives their daughter at her marriage."

"Ah, okay, dowry. I see. So what about you? What's your dowry?"

"Well, tell you the truth . . . I spoke to my father about it . . . and he offered to buy up a plot of land next door . . . and give it to me as a wedding present . . . But that's not what I want, Neil. I want to be an actress! My career's just getting off the ground!"

"You can't live forever in those Homes for the Protection of Young Women run by nuns! And if we try to consummate our marriage in the home of Judge McGuire, it'll make a big scandal . . .

We have to look the truth in the face, my love. I've been unable to find work as a lawyer in Montreal, and it's beneath me to do menial labor . . . I'm a graduate of Trinity College Dublin, after all! I'd rather chop down trees. I'm sure it would give me good ideas for a novel. If it's good enough for Tolstoy, it's good enough for me."

"Who's Tolstoy?"

"Uh . . . never mind. Let's accept your father's offer. Let's go live out at your place, at least at first . . . We could try it just for a year, and then see . . ."

"Yeah, only my daddy doesn't yet know what kind of a man he's making his offer to! A damned Englishman!"

"I'm not English, I'm Irish; it's not the same thing! We hate those damn Brits, too! Besides, they're Protestant and I'm Catholic . . ."

"You told me you didn't go to church."

"To marry you, I'd go all the way to Hell! Don't worry, I still know how to sing *Sancta Trinitas, unus Deus, miserere nobis. Sancta Maria, ora pro nobis.* How do you like that? And I even have a French name! Don't you like the sound of Marie-Jeanne Noirlac?"

"Yeah . . ."

"And don't you like me?"

"Yeah . . ."

"All right, then . . . So shall I pop the question to your da?"

"But you don't know the first *thing* about forestry!"

"Now, Marie-Jeanne! I know enough! Where do you think the paper comes from, on which I shall write my books?"

Sound track: organ music. The final shot of this sequence will be a long, sweeping panorama of the Mauricie region around 1920. We'll need a helicopter. Starting high in the sky—endless forests of pine, maple, birch and oak, but mostly pine—we'll go swinging slowly down into a lumber camp. All the noise absent: saws, axes, crashing trees, shouting men, crackling branches, rushing river . . . The organ music will give us a bit of distance from the macho thrill of the thing. A sort of permanent Boy Scout camp, if you will: logging is dangerous, exhausting labor that requires not only youth and strength but exceptional physical coordination. After watching the lumberjacks for a while, we move to the drivers, leaping with picks and hooks to guide the logs downstream. Close-up on their legs as they leap and slip from log to log, doing footwork that makes Fred Astaire look as if he's standing still.

Down, down, down the Saint-Maurice River to the pulp-and-paper mills at Trois-Rivières, past that to the village we already know from forty years later, the little church in which Milo and Normand will be punished for drawing dirty pictures . . . Moving slowly across the threshold of the church, we peek inside and see that it is packed, for Marie-Jeanne's father, Pierre-Joseph Chabot, is a landowner known and respected by all. Turning, we see Marie-Jeanne herself—lovely, a white veil floating over her dark hair, cheeks pink and eyes bright with excitement. Arm in arm, she and her father hover in the entrance, Neil just behind them, waiting for the priest's cue. At the last possible minute before the ceremony begins, Neil notices Marie-Jeanne has again buttoned her dress awry. And so, whereas the organ and congregation have already launched into the hymn that will bring them forward to the altar to pronounce their vows, he swiftly undoes the seventeen buttons in the back of his bride-to-be's white dress and even more swiftly does them up again. Her father's eyebrows rise but Marie-Jeanne smiles and blushes, bubbling over with love for her Irishman. She has obstinately preserved her virginity, and the prospect of its imminent loss is making her head spin. The three of them march down the aisle.

Dressed to the hilt, Marie-Jeanne's brothers, sisters, aunts, uncles and cousins entirely fill the first two rows of pews. Neil has been adopted by this family, and before long he will be engulfed by it.

Never, ever, will they release their grip on him.

．　．　．　．　．

Awinita, August 1951

WE COULD START off with a close-up of Declan's face. Before a word is uttered, his expression will say all. It's the expression of an irresponsible young man whose girlfriend has just told him she is pregnant.

The camera retreats and we discover we're again on Saint Helen's Island. Declan and Awinita are sitting at a remove from each other, staring out over the water in different directions.

"You're puttin' me on."

"．．．"

"You just *had* a baby. Even my mom had a few months' breathin' space between kids. You can't get pregnant again right off the bat."

"I didn' give suck."

"Wha?"

"Can't get knocked up again if you nurse de baby."

"So anyhow. So okay. So why you tellin' *me?*"

"It's your kid."

"Ha. Fat chance."

"Listen, Mister Cleaning-Fluid. You and me had plans, remember? Even dough I learned ages ago you should never believe a guy wid a hard-on, I let you talk to me 'bout love and livin' in the woods and stuff. You ask me what's de difference tween you and a john? Answer: no john ever got into my body widout a safe on."

Declan runs his hands through his red hair a couple of times. Glances up at the seagulls, perhaps envying them their freedom. Takes a swig from his whisky flask. Finally mutters:

"My kid . . ."

"Simple as dat."

"We gonna have a kid together, Nita?"

"*I* gonna have one, dat for damn sure."

"Well, let's get married, then . . . eh? Listen. Come up to the farm and meet my family."

Close-up on Declan as he briefly imagines bringing a pregnant Indian woman home with him. We see the scene in distorted color in his mind: Neil raising his eyebrows, turning to him and whispering, *Does she even know how to read?*; Marie-Thérèse frowning and pursing her lips; the little boys, Jean-Joseph and François-Joseph, snickering and pointing at his fiancée's parti-colored hair.

"Naw, forget about that," he says. "Jus' les get married."

He's beginning to slur his words.

"Sure, Deck. I'll marry you . . . minute you get a job."

"I'm lookin', I'm lookin' . . . It's not easy to find work, specially now I got a police record."

"You know . . ." says Awinita, "once dere was an Attikamak chief who said he'd give his daughter only to de best hunter of de clan. De girl, she was in love wit a strong young brave named Yanuchich. He had a good reputation as a hunter, but her fader want to make sure. He tell Yanuchich he can marry his daughter only if he bring back a hundred hides. So de brave, he go off into de forest . . ."

Long silence. A cargo ship glides down the river in front of them, and a moment later wavelets lap at their feet.

"Yeah?" says Declan, bored, taking another swallow of his cheap bourbon. "Then what happened?"

"Nuttin'."

"What do you mean, nothin'? Somethin' always happens in stories."

"Not dis time. The girl wait. She wait and she wait, and she wait and she wait, and Yanuchich never come back."

"That's it?"

"Dat's it. She wait so long she get old, and turn to stone, and she still waitin' today. Dey say you can see her stone head out near Shawinigan. Dat how the town of Grand-Mère got it name."

"Aw, who gives a shit. That's a boring story, Nita."

"Yeah. I don't like dat story, either, Mister Cleaning-Fluid. Just to let you know, I'm not gonna wait till I get old."

"Okay, I got the message. Listen, I'm lookin' for a job, okay? I'll find one, don't you worry. There's so many strikes these days . . . Maybe I could check out Imperial Tobacco."

"Strikebreaker not reg'lar work, Deck. An' meanwhile . . ."

"Okay, don't rub it in. Meanwhile I'm still living offa you. But somethin'll turn up, I promise you . . . Now that I'm gonna be a dad, I'll clean up my act and start earning good money."

With Doris Day's "Shanghai" on the sound track, CUT to the visiting room at Bordeaux Jail a week later: Awinita and Declan talking to each other under a glass partition.

Same music (a big hit this summer; the radio plays it constantly). Awinita shooting up in the tiny bathroom next to the cruddy bedroom above the bar. When she emerges, swaying slightly, a client is sitting on the bed waiting for her. In his mid-seventies, with scant white hair, a heavy paunch, and trembly flesh on his jowls and arms, he's already naked except for his glasses, watch and socks. Awinita glances at the Formica table—the money is there.

Hands shaking, the man takes off his watch and glasses and sets them on the bedside table. Keeps his socks on. Lies down and holds his arms out to us. We move toward him, melting, partly because his myopic blue gaze seems kind, but mostly because of the drug rush in our blood.

"What's your name, honey?"

"Nita."

"Hey. I'm Cal. How old are you, Nita?"

"Twenty-two."

"Really? You look about fourteen! Must be because *I'm* so very old . . . Let me tell you a secret, Nita. Are you listening? Nobody can believe they're really old the way their grandparents used to be old when they were young. You know what I mean?"

"Yeah."

"Deep down, you feel young your whole life long."

"What can I do for you, Cal, baby?"

"Not much, I'm afraid. Don't know when I last managed to get it up. Just come here, that's it . . . just let me look at you . . . Just let me touch you, honey . . . oh, you're so lovely . . . So beautiful. So beautiful. So beautiful. So beautiful. So beautiful. Oh . . . that is amazing . . . Oh my God . . . Oh . . . Oh . . . Oh . . ."

In shades of gray and black, swirls of paint coalesce into patterns, slide out of them again, and finally crystallize into the black remains of a fire: charred, smoking ruins with the harsh taste of death. But then . . . unexpectedly . . . time passes backward over the scene. The

burned beams and boards become whole again, climb onto each other,
fit together and slowly form the little shack in which Awinita grew up.
Moving around the shack, we come upon . . . Awinita herself, age
eleven, sitting on the front steps and watching the sun rise.

"Oh my God!" gasps the old man, who has just come in her
hands. "Oh, I don't believe it. That was astounding, Nita. Thank
you so much . . . You're a lovely, lovely girl."

Awinita doesn't answer. Engrossed in her vision, she lies on her
side and stares out the window.

"Thank you, Nita," the white-haired john says, picking up one
of her limp hands and covering it with kisses. "Thank you, thank
you, thank you." A while later he puts his clothes back on, adds an
extra bill to the one that's already on the Formica table, and leaves
the room . . .

(Don't cry, Milo. Yeah, I know you never cry, but don't cry
anyway. Let's try to think of a funny scene that might have happened as, curled up in your junkie mother's womb, you evolved
from junkie embryo to junkie fetus . . .)

That extra bill came in handy—Awinita's hair is blond again.

Neil Kerrigan walks into the bar and glances around. He catches
sight of Awinita's blondness. Magnetized by it, he comes to sit next
to her at the bar.

You're right, it wouldn't be funny for Neil to be one of Awinita's clients that summer. Not totally improbable—the erotic life
of sixty-year-old widows in rural Quebec can't have been terribly
exciting, and on some of his day trips into the city to visit book-
stores and stock up on rare editions, Neil might well have stopped
off in the red-light district for a bit of pleasure. So, not impossible,
but not funny, given that Awinita is currently pregnant with his
grandson. Too kinky for our film.

"What can I get you?" the barman asks him.

"A Molson would be lovely, thanks. And if the young lady doesn't mind, bring her another glass of whatever she's drinking. I need help to celebrate."

"Do you mind, miss?" Irwin asks Awinita, as if he hadn't seen her several hundred times before.

When she turns to Neil, some part of Awinita's brain probably registers the fact that his eyes are the same shade of green as Declan's. But the heroin muddles her thinking, and besides, she's had johns with eyes of every color in the rainbow, even a couple without eyes.

"Tank you, sir," she says. "What you celebratin'?"

"The Virgin Mary just went hydroelectric!" Neil proclaims in a loud voice, raising his glass to all and sundry.

"Somebody turn her on?" Awinita asks.

Neil shouts with laughter. At sixty, having chosen, like Yeats, to spend the final years of his life as a Mad Old Man, he no longer cares what people think of him.

"Ladies and gentlemen, our dear premier, Maurice Duplessis, made a big speech today (I'm sure you all heard it on CBC) to inaugurate a new hydroelectric installation at Beauharnois. Isn't that fantastic? Come on, sing along with Duplessis, everyone, and raise your glasses to Hydro-Québec!!"

"You got a problem with Duplessis, Irishman?" says one of the tipsier customers, lurching up to Neil.

"Not at all, except that he also made a big speech out at Notre-Dame-du-Cap the other day (I'm sure you all heard it on CBC) officially dedicating our Belle Province de Québec to the Virgin Mary. Everyone who was anyone was there! *Le clergé, les grands journaux, tout le monde.* And he made sure we found out that just a stone's throw upriver, at Le Paradis des Sports hotel on Lac des Piles, his old pal Georges Cossette would be allowed to sell liquor without a license . . . except during Sunday Mass, of course, ha-ha-ha!"

"I know dat place," murmurs Awinita. "Not far from Grand-Mère, right? I got a friend who work up dere."

"That's right. Everybody hear that? The young lady has friends who work at Le Paradis des Sports. I'm certain they're on excellent terms with Georges Cossette, Maurice Duplessis, and other gentlemen of the same circles. And I'm certain that with a little extra persuasion, they will also be on good terms with the American jazzmen who come to play in that prestigious establishment. Isn't that fantastic?"

"Fuck off, you bloody Mick!" the drunken customer blares. "Go home and screw those druids of yours if you're not happy here! Duplessis is a good man!"

"He's a man of my bleedin' age!" roars Neil, his green eyes ablaze, his salt-and-pepper beard abristle. "And having lived in the province of Quebec for thirty-three years now, I have the right to say what I think of Maurice Duplessis, for the luva Christ! I think Maurice Duplessis is one arsehole of an opportunist, who sings the praises of the Good Virgin when he needs to wangle votes from the populace, and of Hydro-Québec when he needs to attract investment from the Brits! That's what I think! It's a free country!"

"Free, my ass," says Awinita.

But no one hears her because Neil and the drunken customer have come to blows and the others are shouting and taking sides and Irwin is busy shooing the whole testosterone-drenched free-for-all out of the bar and onto the sidewalk, and this scene will hopefully give our spectators some badly needed comic relief.

CUT to a Friday morning scene in the kitchen with Liz.

"It just doesn't tally, Nita."

" . . . "

"Who do you think you're fooling? Irwin's at the bar every night, he keeps track of the number of guys each girl goes up with. His count for you this week is twenty-nine, yours is seventeen, so I wanna know what happened to the other twelve. What happened to the other twelve, Nita? You keep this up, sweetheart, and you're out of here. Now tell me the truth. Where's your money going?"

"Just . . ."

"I wasn't born yesterday, Nita. You supporting a boyfriend, a habit, or both?"

Awinita doesn't avert her gaze. Her face is impassive.

"Been doin' a bit o' H."

Liz's expression alters.

"Oh, no. Oh, no. That's a lousy idea, sweetheart. Poppers are one thing, okay. Long as you don't overdo it, they help get you through your working night. But H . . . Nah, I've lost too many girls to H, honey . . . I don't want you on that shit. It's death, man. How long you been shootin' up?"

"Not long."

"Okay, listen. I'll give you one chance, not two. I'll pay for you to get cleaned up. As I've told you before, this is not a charity operation; I'm doin' it as a favor to myself. I've invested good money in you, and I don't wanna lose my investment. That clear?"

CUT to a room in a private medical clinic. Awinita, trembling and trickling sweat, stands at a window that gives onto a white wall. We grip the windowsill, then our stomach . . .

The camera, which is our gaze, explores the room, watches objects writhe with a furtive life of their own, receives reality as sheer horror. The window is light, then dark, then light, then dark. Awinita's withdrawal lasts twenty-nine days and twenty-nine nights . . .

(Sound track: to be dealt with later. Yeah, Milo, I agree—it should be rough but not redundant, not jejunely illustrative of the pain your mother is enduring. Maybe just slip an MP3 into the vortex of a garbage incinerator—something like that?)

Calmer now, we are lying on the bed, on top of the bedspread, staring up at the ceiling.

A jack-in-the-box suddenly springs out of a colored block and starts bouncing gaily around. The floor of the room is dotted with other blocks, no doubt containing other jack-in-the-boxes. It runs slam-bang into a closed door, topples backward in a somersault, and finds itself right-side up again, joyous and unscathed. Just then the door opens and the Bad Giant appears. He raises his huge, hairy foot and brings it down on the jack-in-the-box, crushing it . . . but the spring is strong and it bounces up again, knocking the Bad Giant flat on his back.

Awinita sits up in bed and rings for the nurse.

"I'm clean," she tells her.

. . . . .

VII

Malandro

Delinquent, bandit, bad boy. In the early twentieth century, the malandro *was an individual whose way of life was based entirely on improvisation.*

Milo, 1967–70

UPON RETURNING TO the farm after Oscar's death, Milo goes into a black hole and stays there. Weeks, months maybe—he loses track of time. Goes through chores and homework, robotlike. No one can reach him.

Neil is worried—*Won't you come up and read with me, Milo?*—no, he will not, not yet. He needs to swathe his being in protective robes of silence and shadow, plunge into somber splendor, the closets of his early childhood, the blackout screen at the end of TV movies, and also, when summer finally rolls around again, the deepest, darkest water at the center of Lac des Piles . . .

(I'm seeing more and more clearly that what you love when you love somebody are that person's loves. Loving you, Milo, means loving your love for Oscar. Neil. Lac des Piles . . .)

On the far side of the lake is an *Anne of Green Gables* sort of house—Milo has swum across to it several times. A cushy green-and-white summer cottage with a glassed-in porch, property of a wealthy gay movie producer by the name of Sherman Dyson. As wealthy gay movie producers were an exotic species in rural Quebec back in the mid-1960s (and who could have guessed that you your-self would one day fall in love with just such a creature?), every aspect of Dyson's identity was an inexhaustible source of gossip in the area. His wealth aroused people's envy, his homosexuality their sarcasm, his profession their reverence . . . and no one knew what to make of the fact that, the previous spring, he'd gotten married. The bride was rumored to be a good deal younger than he, and a model, and a looker, so it may not be far-fetched to suggest that Milo's pow-erful crawl- and breast-strokes across Lac des Piles, that summer after Oscar's death, took him with perhaps unwonted frequency in the direction of this particular summer cottage.

And indeed, one day . . . there she was.

A dream scene. The young woman has her back to him when, approaching shore, he first catches sight of her. Her skin is tan, her hair blond and wavy to mid-back, and she is clad in a mere idea of a white bikini. Arriving in shallow water, Milo takes great splash-ing steps to conceal the rise of desire between his legs. Hearing the swoosh of water, the young woman turns and appraises him with a smile. She doesn't flinch or blush or flee. At fifteen he is fully formed, and what she sees coming toward her is not a tall, skinny, gangly teenager but a solid, sturdy, brown young man, water running down his chest and thighs as he advances, rilling over his shoulders from his black-auburn hair (long and thick in summertime).

"That was quite a swim," she says when he's within hearing range. "I'm Kim."

At once, to Milo's ears, *Kim* is the sexiest name in the world. Its resonance vibrates with *crème* and *chrème*[6] and *whim* and *brim* and *sperm*, all the way to his balls.

---

6. cream . . . chrism

"I'm Milo," he says.

And the dream continues, the dream continues, Kim takes his hand and leads him across the patio and into the elegant green-gabled cottage. By the time his eyes grow accustomed to the penumbra, the two of them have already floated through the kitchen into the bedroom, the young woman is already helping him remove his trunks and guiding him onto the bed and taking his astoundingly outstanding member in her hands . . . Close-up on the boy's expression, surprise then deeper delight as a woman's mouth voyages him toward a new universe of pleasure, and when, not much later, his virginity gets lost in a rush of joy manyfold richer than anything he'd concocted with the help of Sophia Loren or Edith or the cows, Kim kisses him tenderly on the lips.

"Thank you, baby," she says breathily. "You're as marvelous as you look . . . I needed that. You wanna meet my husband?"

Ever willing to deal with what life chooses to dish up to him, be it rape at the hands of a lumberjack cousin or enchantment in the arms of a blond model, Milo slips his swimming trunks back on and pads after her. Dyson's office is next to the bedroom and the man has been there all along in a big leather working chair, reading a magazine and puffing on a cigar. Kim makes the introductions with graceful arm movements.

"Sherman, Milo. Milo, Sherman."

"You speak English?" Dyson asks as he shakes hands with the strapping boy, and then, when Milo nods, "Know anything about gardening?"

"I know vegetables better dan flowers, but I learn quick."

"He learns quick," Kim confirms, repressing a giggle.

"Okay, you're hired."

CUT to a series of scenes from the remainder of that unforgettable summer of 1967 in which, day after day, Milo acquires the basics of horticulture and eroticism in languorous alternation: we see him trimming hedges, sculpting rosebushes, mowing the lawn, adding fertilizer to flower beds, and learning all about patience and perseverance in his amorous acrobatics with the older woman. Kim teaches him that there are heavens beyond the first, and that even the seventh is not the last . . .

(I must say I'm profoundly grateful to Kim Dyson. Sexually speaking, your kindergarten was pretty atrocious but your grade school was top-notch. Few men are so lucky as to have had a kind, skillful, affectionate professor to initiate them into the subtleties of physical love. After a few weeks, the professorship turned into a tandem: Sherman joined the two of you in bed. And your luck back then, Astuto darling, has been mine these three decades . . .)

Marie-Thérèse is incensed at what she divines is going on across the lake . . . but every time she opens her mouth to light into him about it, Régis stares her down and she clamps it shut again, for Milo is suddenly making a significant contribution to the household finances.

Having few outlets for her fraught feelings toward her nephew, Marie-Thérèse goes back to (*bong*) hitting him over the head with the (*bong, bong*) telephone receiver. He lets it happen. He doesn't much care. The world is rife with dangers. There are aunts who wield telephones, bears whose powerful arms and chests can crush the air from your lungs, snakes whose venom can stop your heart, wolves whose teeth can tear you limb from limb. You need to know about the world's dangers and protect yourself. Milo covers his ears to prevent Marie-Thérèse from doing further damage to his hearing.

One day, though, her words pierce through the cotton fleece of fog in his brain and hit him in the heart:

"You ungrateful brat! You evil seed, you good-for-nothing! I wish I'd never agreed to take you in! You love the gutter, it's in your blood, your grandfather should have left you there." *(Bong!)* "I was going to have a house built next door just for you, a nice place you could live in when you grow up. But if you wanna fritter your time away, all right, fine, no point my breaking my back to make some-thing out of you! Go join your slut of a mother and your delinquent of a father on Saint Catherine Street! That's where they made you! Go ahead, go back where you belong, no skin off my back!" *(Bong!)*

He carefully stores in his memory the words *Saint Catherine Street.*

Just before summer's end, Marie-Thérèse hits upon the only punishment that can really get to him: she has found him another boarding school.

"A real Catholic school, this time," she declares.

"You mean," says Neil ". . . with morning and evening prayer, catechism and confession, the whole kit and kaboodle?"

"Yes, of course! The kid needs to be taken into hand. He's the only one in his class not to have been confirmed yet. We have to straighten him up . . ."

On the eve of Milo's departure, Neil summons him to his study.

"It hurts me, my boy, to think of you struggling with the self-same soul fetters as I did at your age . . . But no matter what they do to you, don't go to confession. Tell those meddling priests that what goes on in your body and soul is none of their flaming busi-ness! Here, put these in your suitcase. These three small volumes will stand you in better stead than a thousand prying priests."

The books are Homer's *Odyssey*, Shakespeare's *Tragedies* and Cervantes's *Don Quixote.*

THE ENSUING YEAR can be compressed into a single minute:

We see Milo attending catechism classes . . . using a photo of Kim—and memories, ah memories—for his solitary pleasure . . .

hiding Homer's *Odyssey* behind his geography book when he's under supervision in the study hall . . . especially playing hockey. Reviving skating reflexes learned years ago with the Manders family, he throws himself into the game with a vengeance, passing the puck, swerving on the ice, moving strong and low and fast, skating backward, forward and sideways, scoring point after point . . . but eschewing rowdy displays of comradeship, never letting the other players, with their enormous gloves, thickly padded knees, shoulders and groins, bobbing helmets and clacking sticks, throng round to hug and pat and jostle him when he scores, preferring always, when not on the ice, to wait alone in the rafters reading *Don Quixote* . . . We see him in church, with *Othello* hidden inside his hymnbook . . . using a photo of Jane Fonda in *Barbarella* . . . kneeling at the altar to take communion with twenty other boys . . . striking up a conversation with a boy he sees reading Aeschylus and Euripides in the library—a shy, overweight, devout, bespectacled, pimpled adolescent whose nickname is Timide. Kneeing the testicles of a tall, blond, snotty student named Augustin, for having teased Timide . . . sitting across from Timide during meals in the large dining hall and making him explode with laughter, scattering crumbs in all directions . . . teaching Timide to smoke without coughing and to fend off the insinuating words and fingers of the priests . . . Stealing extra food from the kitchen so that he and Timide can snack in the dorm at midnight . . . descending deep into himself so as not to feel the pain when caught and whipped by one of the sisters . . . gluing samples of leaves and flowers into his botany album, labeling them carefully and showing them to Timide . . . stealing wine from the chalice in church and sharing it with Timide . . . being dragged to a confessions box on a Friday morning . . .

Here we can zoom in on his dialogue with the priest.

"What did you do, son?"

"None of your business."

"This is serious, Milo. I'm asking you if you've sinned in thought, word, or deed."

"And I'm telling you to mind your own business. No way I'll ever tell you what goes on inside my head."

"You shouldn't talk that way to a man of God, Milo."

"I didn't ask to talk to you."

"You're under our authority here; you can't do just anything you please."

"Neither can you!"

"If you go on talking that way, my son, I'll have no choice but to punish you, you realize that?"

"I'm not your son, for Chrissake!"

"And on top of it all you take the name of Our Lord in vain!"

Milo detests priests and finds it hard to tell them apart. They all seem to wear the same glasses, have the same phony smile, the same cruelty masquerading as virtue . . . Preferring brutality to hypocrisy, he'd rather deal with his cousins any day.

The holy sisters drag him out of bed before dawn and force him to wax the hallway or sprinkle the skating rink for two hours. But he sleeps little anyway, and would rather wax a floor or sprinkle a skating rink than have nightmares. He finds the work soothing, does it carefully and well. Loves being alone. The sisters yank him away from early Mass and send him down to the kitchen to make toast for 150 breakfasts . . . But he can dream while making toast— far better than in church, where organ music, incense smoke and priestly prattle clog his senses within minutes.

Throughout the long winter months he deals patiently with his fate. But as April begins to wane, as the snows melt and the river ice breaks up and the sluices open and the juices run, an atavistic urge rewakens in his veins . . . and, suddenly, no. No. None of this. He must be gone.

In the dorm one night at half past twelve, he sneaks over to Timide's bed.

"You awake?"

In his upper bunk, the fat boy flops over and struggles to focus.

"Here. Put on your glasses, we're hightailing it out of here. Just you and me, okay?"

"Where to?"

"Montreal. Get dressed."

"Montreal! You must be nuts! It's a hundred miles away!"

"Take your blanket and stuff a few clothes in your knapsack. I'll wait for you in the hall. It's the perfect night, there's a full moon. Everyone's asleep . . ."

"Everyone but the wolves."

"You and I are the wolves now. Come on, Timide, get your ass in gear!"

As Timide reluctantly descends from his bunk, Milo notices Augustin, the tall blond snotty boy, archest of his archenemies, feigning sleep in the bunk below. Has he overheard their plans?

Hiking Timide's pudgy, clumsy, terrified body over the high wall of the institution is no mean feat, but Milo is all-powerful to-night. *Free! Free!* his mother's voice sings softly in his brain. *Ta, ta-da DA, ta, ta-da DA* . . . By one in the morning they're on the road: full moon, springtime, owl calls, river thundering down below, good graveled road underfoot. *Ta, ta-da DA, ta, ta-da DA* . . . Milo's knapsack is packed tight with food stolen from the kitchen and his heart is high with hope.

Timide's step, however, is less buoyant.

"What are we gonna do in Montreal?"

"Find my mom."

"I thought you were an orphan!"

"No, my parents are alive, I just haven't met them yet. But I know where my mom lives, on Saint Catherine Street. We'll surprise her. You'll see, she'll be thrilled! And then she'll help us out . . . But first we'll stop off at the house of a girl I know."

(This next scene, Milo, is one of the least glorious episodes of your life . . .)

Two or three days have elapsed, and while Milo's enthusiasm is unabated, Timide is in bad shape: exhausted, sweating, smelly and scared, his feet covered with blisters. The runaways arrive at Edith's place after dark.

"Where's your friend?" whines Timide.

Milo pulls him around to the back of the darkened house and picks up a pebble. CUT to Edith at the window. At sixteen as at twelve, what she lacks in beauty she makes up for in warmth.

"Milo, wow! This is fantastic! The police are looking for you guys. My parents heard about it on the radio. They're combing the whole area. And here you are, wow! Hang on, I'll be right down!"

CUT to the woodshed half an hour later. A flashlight propped amidst the stacks of wood and kindling gives the place an eerie glow. Edith, dressed only in a nightgown, drops to her knees on the dirt floor and slowly bares her breasts. Timide's eyes pop out of his head. He backs away in terror, repeatedly making the sign of the cross and whispering, "Non, non . . ." but Milo constrains him, gently pushing him forward.

"Look, Timide . . . Look how beautiful they are . . . Come closer! See the way a girl's nipples harden when you stroke them real gently? . . . See? Come on, give it a try . . . Hey, you've seen titties before, haven't you? You sucked your mother's titties when you were little like everybody else! It's okay to like it, you know . . ."

Edith laughs. She draws the two boys toward her, then purposely falls over backward so that Timide finds himself on top of her, his face squashed between her breasts. He jerks away, beside himself with fear. Edith laughs again.

"Hey, take it easy, big boy! I won't bite!"

"N-no . . . n-no . . ."

"You getting hard down there . . . ? Nope . . . soft as chicken liver. Don't you know a thing about love, hey, Timide? Watch your friend Milo, he'll show you the ropes . . ."

And Milo, whether as a grotesque reenactment of the previous summer's antics with Kim and Sherman or an involuntary replay of his violation at the hands of Jean-Joseph, tries to include poor Timide in this his first copulation with Edith, forcing the boy despite his tears and protestations to remain not only with but virtually between the two of them as they work themselves up, Milo's boots scrabbling amidst rakes and brooms and Edith's head banging up against the logs, Milo's hips thrusting and Edith's heaving, Milo's throat emitting grunts and Edith's squeals, finally attaining orgasm (Milo's) in the sawdust.

When Milo comes to his senses, Timide is sobbing uncontrollably.

Edith helps the two of them to their feet and dusts them off, then hands them a box of cookies and a tin of sardines: "This is all I could find."

CUT.

A long, depressing shot of the two boys walking through forest in silence: "I'm sorry, Timide . . . I'm sorry. I don't know what came over me."

CUT TO: The boys' dead campfire early in the morning. They've spent the night huddled against a hillside. As chill dawn whitens the sky, Milo scrambles to his feet.

"Let's go," he says, bending over the bumpy lump that is Tim-ide's body. "Today's the big day."

"Let me sleep, you bag of shit!"

"No, let's go. Come on, Timide, let's go. This is no time to fall apart. We're almost there, I can feel it. Can't you? Can't you feel the big city right nearby? Come on, get the hell out of bed or I'll finish the trip without you!"

As there's nothing Timide dreads more than finding himself alone in the middle of nowhere, he angrily rises and gets dressed. The boys scramble up to the crest of the hill . . . And there it is, shimmering and scintillating in the pink-mauve softness of the spring dawn, white ribbons of smoke rising from its chimneys and early sun rays glancing redly off its skyscrapers, rippling down from the mountain at its heart to the river whose long arms hold it in a tight embrace, stretching beyond mountain and river as far as the eye can see: the island city of Montreal.

Awed, Timide and Milo lie flat on their stomachs and gaze down at the unfathomable cement-and-glass beast.

"There's my mother," says Milo, stretching out an arm. "See? I told you we'd make it! She's right there."

The following second, in close-up, we see his body snap into a state of unbearable alertness. Pressed against the earth, his skin and flesh have sensed the vibration of a motor vehicle. Now his rearview vision records the silent blue flash of a revolving light . . . and before Timide realizes what's going on, the two of them have been roughly cuffed and shoved into the backseat of a police van.

HOW SHOULD WE film your jail stints, Astuto?

The nice thing about prisons as compared with closets is that you get to meet other prisoners. It was within the walls of that juvenile detention home that you first met and talked with Indians.

At school you'd learned oodles of things about the British and the French and their proud, heroic, capitalist descendants in North America . . . but about the native inhabitants of this land? Nothing but colorful shreds of phony folklore. The more Indians you met, the madder you got. Never in human history, it seemed to you, had a people so utterly accepted its defeat. The problem was that in addition to having had their land stolen and their way of life destroyed, Indian men had seen their youngest and prettiest women snatched away by swarms of ugly, aggressive, bearded, foul-smelling, land-hungry, profit-seeking white men—who, moreover, having crossed the ocean womanless, were as horny as bulls—so that within a couple of decades there was a huge métis-blood population. Undone, Indian men had basically locked themselves away for the past three hundred years in a resentful, alcoholic silence. Yeah, I know, Milo, protests and petitions by native Canadians managed to make a few improvements in the second half of the twentieth century, but basically it was way too little way too late . . .

WE COME UPON our hero in his grandfather's study. Close-up on his face at age sixteen: detention has changed him.

"So they put handcuffs on you, did they?"

Milo nods.

"A surprising sensation, isn't it? Unforgettable."

"You were arrested once, Grandpa?"

"I was, yes. But I was a grown man by then, several years older than you are now. You've always been precocious, eh, whippersnapper? First you skipped two grades at school and then you skipped straight to the juvenile delinquents' home, without even stopping off at reform school along the way."

"Dey're talking of sending me to a reform school *now.*"

Neil puffs away at his pipe and rocks in his rocking chair, taking his time. Both men are happy and neither is impatient.

"What did *you* do, Grandpa?"

"We'll come round to that. I can see why you ran away from that boarding school, Milo, given the punishments they'd been inflicting on you."

"It was your fault."

"Oh, yes? How's that?"

"I talk back to de priest who ask me to confess."

"What did you tell him?"

"None o' your flamin' business!"

"Ha! Good for you!"

Another pleasant pause. Neil knocks the burned tobacco out of his pipe into an ashtray. Refills the bowl with fresh tobacco from a green leather pouch Milo has always loved, tamps it and lights it with a taper drawn from the fire in the fireplace. Sucks slowly and sensuously at his pipe, causing not only the tobacco but the light in the western sky to smolder.

"And you stuck with your young partner all the way, did you?"

". . . Yeah."

"That's the main thing, to be trustworthy. To stand by those who're counting on you. The worst crime isn't robbery, Milo. If it were, all of our political leaders would be in jail. The worst crime is treachery, for that is a crime against one's own soul."

"What did *you* do, Grandad?"

"Well, you remember I took part in the Rising in Dublin, at Easter 1916. I was a member of the Irish rebels, who'd just then begun to call themselves Sinn Féin. Now, my cousin Thom and I were posted at the entrance to Saint Stephen's Green, a lovely park in the city center. And on the Tuesday after Easter Monday, who should come striding toward us but Major John MacBride. The major was on our side, but he was also the sworn enemy of Willie Yeats, who for years had been in love with his wife, Maud Gonne. You remember my telling you about her?"

"Yes."

"Ah, Milo's Mighty Memory! Well, MacBride knew me to be a close friend of the poet's. Running into me at Saint Stephen's Green, he suddenly saw his chance of getting back at his rival . . . and he denounced me to the Brits!"

"How'd he do dat?"

"Well . . . as the son of Judge Kerrigan, you see, I'd normally have sided with the Empire. So the rebels had decided to use me to infiltrate the enemy ranks and find out what the Brits were planning. I was wearing a British uniform. Can you believe, my boy, that in April 1916, while the First World War was raging across the Channel and all their military strength was needed to fight the Germans, the British deployed *forty thousand troops* in the city of Dublin?"

"So, uh . . . was Thom a spy, too?" asks Milo.

"Oh, I didn't tell you. He was dead by then."

"What?"

"Yes, a frightful event. The Brits shot him point-blank before my very eyes. But I don't want to bore you with my veteran's tales. Suffice it to say that having been denounced by John MacBride, I was arrested, handcuffed, dragged off to Dublin Castle and held in custody there for two long weeks. Had my father not intervened, I should have met with the same sorry fate as the other heroes of the day. Yeats's famous poem would have been called 'Seventeen Men' instead of 'Sixteen Men.' A different rhythm indeed!"

"What? Dey put you in jail for two weeks and you almost got shot by a firing squad and you never told me about dis before?"

"I thought I should wait until you'd reached manhood, Milo. Now that you've been behind bars yourself, I think you can understand."

"Den I can tell you what I did when dey let me out last week," Milo grins.

"What did you do?"

"Well . . . when I first got locked up, I tought we were denounced by de blond kid, Augustin his name was, who used to bully Timide and always had it in for me. But my friend Edit', she come to visit and tell me it was Timide himself who call de cops from a phone boot', one day when my back was turned! Dat explains why he went straight back to school when we got busted, and I got locked up. So . . . first ting I do when dey let me out, I give Edit' a call . . . She borrow her mom's Volkswagen and drive me all the way to de school. When we get dere, I crawl in de back of de car and crouch down on de floor to wait . . ."

(We can do this scene in flashback, with you telling your grandfather the story in voice-over. Of course you neglected to mention what you and Edith had done to Timide in the woodshed on the way down to Montreal . . .)

"Finally Timide, he come out to smoke on de front steps with Augustin and a coupla oder guys. I'm de one taught him to smoke! . . . I can see he's de big school hero now, moved way up tanks to his week's adventure running away wit me. Edit' call out to him. *Hey, Timide, baby! Wanna go for a spin?* He hesitate. He still shy, but he want to show off in front of de oder guys. *In that jalopy?* he say, stalling. *Tought you might like a change from lookin' at priest bums!* Edit' say. So Timide say okay. He come over, get into de passenger seat, Edit' step on de gas and de car leap away from the kerb. I got my arm round Timide's troat fore he know what happening. His mout' pop open and I stuff my handkerchief inside. We drive out to de reservoir. I got a baseball bat in de trunk. We drag Timide out of de Volkswagen and I smash up bot' his knees."

"Y-you did?" gasps Neil, swallowing. "The-then what did you do?"

"We drop him at de hospital."

Milo and Edith shove the broken boy out of the car onto the sidewalk, near a sign that reads HÔPITAL SAINTE-MARIE.

"Well . . . that's fine, then," says Neil, clearing his throat. "Long as you dropped him off someplace he could be taken care of . . . You're right, traitors deserve to be punished, as Polonius tells his son Laertes when he goes off to university. You remember that soliloquy from *Hamlet*, don't you? *Be thou familiar, but by no means vulgar.*"

Milo takes over.

> *Dose friends dou hast, and deir adoption tried,*
> *Grapple dem to dy soul wit hoops o' steel*
> *But do not dull dy palm wit entertainment*
> *Of each new-hatch'd, unfledged comrade. Beware*
> *Of entrance to a quarrel, but being in,*
> *Bear't dat de opposed may beware of dee*

"Impeccable!" Neil says, enchanted with his scion. "But my most important advice to you, Milo, comes still and always from Yeats.

> *How can they know*
> *Truth flourishes where the student's lamp has shone,*
> *And there alone, that have no solitude?*

". . . Never fear solitude, Milo. In this time of political turmoil, beware of Loud Speakers. Remain ever a student."

CUT.

Ripping him out of his reverie, the guard suddenly comes and clangs on the bars with his billy club:

"Telegram."

Milo's eyes focus. "Yeah?"

"It's not mail day but we decided ta do you a favor."

"I don't need your favors."

"Okay, you can go to hell."

"Give it to me."

"Oh, so you want it now? Say please . . ."

At lightning speed both Milo's hands are through the bars and around the man's throat.

"Hand it over or you're dead."

"Bloody savage," says the man, handing him the telegram . . .

(Yes, okay, Milo. The telegram can only be from Marie-Thérèse's daughter, your cousin Marie-Gabrielle. Though she was closer to you in age, only four years older, she didn't play as important a role in your life as your male cousins, so I figured we could save a few thousand dollars by leaving her out of the story. But you're right—no one else in the family could have sent you this message, so we'll *have* to go back and put Marie-Gabrielle in everywhere . . .)

GRANDPA NEIL DIED IN HIS SLEEP ON WEDNESDAY. HIS FUNERAL TOOK PLACE YESTERDAY, IN THE SAME CHURCH WHERE HE MARRIED OUR GRANDMA FIFTY YEARS AGO. THE CHURCH WAS ALMOST EMPTY, NOBODY KNEW HIM ANYMORE. IT WAS SUCH A PITY NOT EVEN YOU WERE THERE, MILO. WHEN WILL YOU BE GETTING OUT THIS TIME? YOUR LOVING COUSIN, GABRIELLE

The prison gives Milo a day's leave. We see him heading home through the forest at nightfall. His nose catches a scent. He tenses, then breaks into an animal run. *Ta, ta-da DA, ta, ta-da DA* . . . Sound track: no panting, only his steps thudding softly on the forest floor, like the soft beating of a drum. In the distance he sees white smoke billowing above black trees. Not the house. Behind the house. He goes around. A towering bonfire. *Ta, ta-da DA, ta, ta-da DA* . . . Jean-Joseph is tossing armloads of books and papers out the window of Neil's study on the second floor. François-Joseph is deftly catching them and adding them to the high, hissing flames. Both are singing, laughing, roaring drunk.

Milo turns on his heel and vanishes.

In the morning, after walking past the smoldering, smoking, stinking mound of ashes that was once his grandfather's library, he bursts into the kitchen where his aunt is making hotcakes. As usual, her first reaction is to yell at him.

"Where have you been, Milo? The boys saw you arrive last night. You sneak up on us like that, you don't say a word to anyone and then you vanish. We looked for you everywhere!"

She catches sight of his face and her tone changes. There are now large amounts of air between her words.

"What . . . what's wrong with y . . ."

Milo goes over to the drawer and takes out the sharpest knife.

"Milo . . . you're upset about the fire, is that it?"

He approaches, wielding the knife, expressionless.

"It was just books, Milo!"

He advances on her.

"It was just books! Milo! What was I supposed to do with them? And besides, they were all in English!"

He pushes her up against the wall. Raising the knife, he looks calmly into her eyes.

"Régis! *Help!*"

The knifepoint comes to a hovering halt a quarter inch from Marie-Thérèse's chest. Then Milo turns and plants the knife with all his might in the exact center of the maple wood table. His mother wouldn't want him to spend the rest of his time on earth cooped up in lawcourts and jail cells. She'd want him to be free.

"You'll see me again when you're dead," he says.

The knife is still vibrating when he slams the door and walks off the Dubé property for the last time.

. . . . .

Neil, 1920

SEPTEMBER. SLANTED SUNLIGHT. Maple trees aflame. Breathtaking beauty of the Quebec countryside during its brief autumn. The camera pans across the Chabot property (familiar to us as the Dubé property from forty years later) to a woodshed, its door open a crack. Sliding through the crack along with the sunlight, we fall on a page of Neil's notebook. Uneasily perched on a stack of old apple crates, the writer is trying to write. We're reminded of a similar scene in his Dublin bedroom a few years ago . . . but his inner voice is even more anguished now than it was then. As Neil works on his text about exile, the camera glides through the woodshed and enters a vaster, barnlike space, lit in chiaroscuro by flashes of sunlight coming through small windows. There, it explores an enigmatic concatenation of tables and woodstoves, vats and tubes, bottles and utensils—not the laboratory of a mad scientist, but the ordinary paraphernalia required for the manufacture of maple syrup.

The thing about exile, Neil begins in voice-over, *is that it forces you back into childhood. Even the first time around, being a child was mostly unpleasant. As soon as you can think, you are painfully conscious of being smaller and weaker than the powerful, prestigious giants who surround you. They despise, dominate, manipulate and look down on you. You are impatient to grow up, break free of them, become your own man. Thus, it is confounding and humiliating, at nearly thirty years of age, to find yourself, as it were, back at square one again. If your exile includes a language change, your sense of stupidity and helplessness will be compounded . . . no, compound rhymes with confound, let's say aggravated . . . no, exacerbated . . . no, aggravated . . . by your lack of proficiency in the new tongue. You get by all right in private conversation with your loved ones, for loved ones tend to be indulgent . . . but when you are obliged to deal on a daily basis with a large group of people, well acquainted among themselves and accustomed to communicating through quirky colloquialisms, inside jokes, onomatopoeia, muttered prayers and blasphemies, you suffer not only as much as but more than a child—for, unlike the latter, you have no hope or even wish of attaining proficiency in the local idiom . . . It is most exasperating. I love Marie-Jeanne, but . . . No, cross that out. This isn't my diary, it is a personal reflection on the universal theme of exile . . . Brought up in the city, you find yourself in the country. Armed with a law degree from Ireland's finest university, you are suddenly being instructed in the fine points of making maple syrup. Formerly on intimate terms with the greatest poets and novelists of the day, you now prefer the company of cows to that of what passes, locally, for humanity . . . No, that's too nasty. After all, there were peasants in Ireland, too; I simply didn't frequent them. I fought for their rights, of course—indeed I risked my life doing so—but I did not have to eat, drink and sleep with them, put up with their pungent body odors and their primitive sense of humor. New paragraph.*

Tolstoy in no way jeopardized his literary greatness by cutting wood with his muzhiks, because he did so on his own property, in the country and the language of his birth. He was not hampered and handicapped at every step by foreignness, but remained master of the situation. The violent changes inflicted by exile plunge you back into the immaturity and dependency of childhood. They turn you into a mumbling, stumbling, stuttering nincompoop, incapable of running your own life. Bad enough for the common mortal, this state of affairs is disastrous for the writer. In the space of a mere few days—the time it takes to travel from the Old Country to the New—he very literally loses the ground beneath his feet. His pen's feverish activity is turned to ice by a series of paralyzing questions (I can correct these metaphors later): Who are my readers? Who are my characters? What is my subject?

Since crossing the Atlantic, I've met precious few people who ever heard of the Liffey, the Easter Rising, Padraic Pearse or Major John MacBride; French Canadians care not one whit about the Irish rebels, Sinn Féin, or the act recently passed by British Parliament allowing Protestant Unionists in the North to retain control of the six counties of Ulster. My country is splitting in two, Good Lord, and so is my head . . . Mrs. McGuire told me that here in Montreal in 1916, only a couple of months after the Easter Rising, there was an anticonscription demonstration at the Place des Armes. The French Canadians didn't want to be enrolled in English Canada's war—which is to say England's war—any more than the Irish did. Mrs. McGuire can see the analogy because, like me, she has a foot on either side of the ocean. But if my future reading public is made up exclusively of Irish-born residents of Quebec, what stories can I, should I, must I tell? I'm losing my stories! They're dying on my lips!

Just as Neil tearfully scribbles in his notebook *They're dying on my lips!* we hear a blood-curdling female scream. The camera rushes back to film him as he leaps to his feet and bolts from the woodshed, letting pencil and notebook tumble to the floor.

CUT to the bedroom in which Marie-Jeanne has just given birth to their first son. The mother is still flat on her back, but the child has already vanished. Several devout, efficient females—her mother, a couple of older sisters or cousins (he can never keep them straight), a nurse and a young midwife named Marie-Louise—rush to and fro, taking care of everything in French.

Neil has become a stranger in his own home. No, it is not even his own home. He has become a stranger, period.

"Is it a boy?" he asks timidly from the doorway, not quite daring to cross into the room.

"Yes, sir," says Marie-Louise as she strides down the hallway, arms piled high with bloody sheets. "Yes, it's a little boy. Mrs. Noirlac wants to name it Pierre-Joseph, after her father."

Neil winces.

CUT to that evening: At last the little family is alone together. The baby sucks fiercely at Marie-Jeanne's breast, and her face is suffused with light.

"All men are Joseph," says Neil.

"What, darling?" says Marie-Jeanne. "What are you mumbling in your beard?"

"All men are Joseph," he repeats. "Every childbirth is a Nativity, know what I mean? It's between mother and child. I sit here looking at the two of you, and you shine so brightly it makes my eyes hurt. Joseph is irrelevant. It's obvious he can't be the father."

"Neil!" says Marie-Jeanne with a laugh like the soft jingling of sleigh bells. "Don't tell me you think I cheated on you!"

"No, but our baby's the child of God. It's a miracle, every childbirth is a miracle. Joseph has nothing to do with it and he knows it.

He sits there in the stable, feeling silly and out of place . . . Uh . . . anything I can do to make you more comfortable, dear? Want me to smooth out the hay under your rear end?"

"What are you trying to tell me, sweet Neil?"

"Nothing, just that . . ."

Moving over to the window, Neil stares out into the gathering dark.

"All I'm trying to say is that . . . I'm somebody, too."

"What do you mean? Of course you're somebody!"

"I mean, I make an effort, I do my best to adapt, to learn every-thing there is to learn about maple trees, spruce trees, moose and the Battle of the Plains of Abraham . . . but I, too, come from somewhere, for the love of God! I, too, have a past, a history . . . I don't want for my whole life to be drowned here erased and re-placed by yours . . . So all I'm asking is that you take *one little step* toward my own history."

"What kind of step? Oh! Did you hear that? He burped!"

"Leave me the boys."

"Sorry?"

"We'll divide the children up between us. You'll take the girls, choose their names, talk to them in French, bring them up to be nice little Catholic women from Quebec . . . and I'll take the boys: Irish names, English language and a lay education."

Marie-Jeanne looks at her son, her husband, her son. She loves Neil with all her heart, but dreads her father's ire.

"Otherwise," says Neil, raising his voice, "if everything I've ever been and done gets wiped out, I don't know how I can ever be a man in this household, much less a writer. Please understand me, Marie-Jeanne: I can't create works literature if I feel I have no heir, no hope of passing on my lore and learning."

Marie-Jeanne is still hesitant. Neil tries another tack.

"Besides, the sad truth of the matter is that anglophones earn a better living in Quebec than francophones. They're the ones who run businesses, they're taking over the pulp-and-paper industry . . . The future is anglophone. If you want our sons to make something of themselves . . ."

"Well, okay," says Marie-Jeanne with a sigh. "I have to admit I can see your point."

"So this one won't be named Pierre-Joseph, okay? He'll be named Thom."

". . . All right."

CUT to a close-up of a tiny coffin being lowered into a tiny grave. Drawing back, we see a few dozen members of the Chabot family gathered in the town churchyard, their faces glistening with tears. Neil hugs Marie-Jeanne to his side. The camera moves back in to read the words engraved on the tombstone: THOM NOIRLAC. 3 SEPTEMBRE 1920–17 SEPTEMBRE 1920.

. . . . .

Awinita, September 1951

TOTAL DARKNESS. BLACK screen. It's four A.M. in the cruddy bedroom above the bar. Declan's speech is distinctly slurred (so to speak).

"Yeah, yeah, yeah, yeah . . . I promise you, Nita. Sumpin'll turn up."

"You already said dat."

"I know, but this time I mean it. Soon's our baby's born, I'll clean up my act."

"Dat's a whole six months from now, Deck."

"Yeah, but jobs are always scarce in September. My chances'll be better in the spring."

"Why's dat?"

"I heard tell."

"Where'd you hear tell? In jail?"

He hits her. We don't see the blow, only hear it, and Awinita's yelp of indignation.

"Hey! Shit, Deck!"

"Don't talk down to me, Nita. With seven sisters, I had enough o' women talkin' down to me since I was born."

"Yeah? Well, I had enough o' guys hittin' me."

"That's not what they do to you. They screw you. Every Tom, Dick, 'n' Harry's got the right to screw you. I'm the only who has to ask permission."

"Least it makes you special . . . You oughta be grateful to 'em for screwing me. It's deir money you live off."

"Oh, *thank* you, Tom! *Thank* you, Dick! *Thank* you, Harry! Specially Dick. *Thank* you for fuckin' my wife, you great big Dick!"

LIGHTS (Awinita has just turned on the bedside lamp).

"I not your wife, little boy."

We're in her eyes, in her body, when Declan's fist makes contact with her jaw. The blow sends us careening backward to stare at a corner of the phony oakwood headboard.

"Fuck, man. Ya broke my fuckin' jaw."

"Did I?"

Declan is sincerely shocked.

"I tink so, asshole . . . You're destroyin' your only source of income, you know dat? Who gonna come upstairs wit a girl got a twisty purple face?"

Declan breaks down. Blubbering drunkly, he kneels at the side of the bed and covers his face with his hands.

"I'm so sorry, Nita. I'm . . . so . . . sorry! Can you ever forgive me? I'm so, so sorry I hit you, Nita, you're pregnant with my baby . . . I'll never lay a finger on you again, I swear it. I solemnly swear I'll never lay a finger on you again. Oh, Nita, can you ever forgive me?"

His shoulders heave, and tears come trickling through his fingers. We put a hand on his head and, sobbing, he buries his face between our dark breasts.

"I'm out of sorts 'cause I went home over the weekend . . . hitchhiked all the way there . . . Thought everybody'd be glad to see me . . . but they didn't give a fuck . . . Didn't pay me any attention . . . I'm used to Marie-Thérèse being nasty, but this time it was especially . . . my da. He lit into me, called me weak and spineless . . . Said I had no gumption, no political convictions, nothin'. Said I was wasting my days on earth. How can a da talk that way to his son, Nita? I'll never talk that way to my son, I can tell you that . . . He called me *spineless*, Nita! My own da called me *spineless!*"

Gradually his sobs space themselves out and, with his head still weighing heavily on our chest, he begins to snore.

An X-ray image of Awinita's spine, perfectly straight and normal. But suddenly her vertebrae turn into red balloons. They swell and expand until they literally become *her, and the rest of her body is awkwardly curled up inside the colored, bobbing balls.*

Awinita's apartment on a Friday morning; Liz is staring at her.

". . . You pregnant again, Nita?"

". . ."

"Hey, Nita, don't tell me you're pregnant again. Don't tell me."

"I didn't."

"Sweetheart, that's bad news. You know that?"

"Yeah."

"You want me to give you the address of somebody who . . ."

"Nah, it's a'right . . . I like de guy."

"You're not supporting him, I hope."

"Nah . . . Well, a bit. Just till he finds work. I don't give him much."

"Listen, Nita. If I were you, I'd get rid of that baby before it's too late. Your credit's running out. If you're not careful, you're gonna find yourself in the street. And a pregnant Indian whore in the street, I don't need to tell you that spells trouble. Sweetheart, you wanna get married, settle down and have seventeen kids like those rabbity French Canadians, go right ahead! It's no skin off my back, just so long as you pay me back what you owe me. I got plenty of hot young babes just itchin' to take your place. You met Alison yet, by the way?"

"Who's Alison?"

"Moved into your room yesterday. She'll be sleepin' in Cheryl's bed, seein' as how Cheryl found herself a cushier job out at Trois-Rivières."

"I tought dat was just a weekend gig."

"Yeah, well, I don't do part-time, Nita. You're either with me or you're without me. Is that clear?"

"Sure."

"Then toe the line, I'm warning you."

CUT to the girls' bedroom.

Alison is a thin, fragile-looking Haitian girl, clearly a novice. Lorraine and Deena giggle as they teach her the ropes.

"It's nothin', man," says Lorraine. "Don't worry. I mean, what's a dick, right? To them it may be the be-all and end-all, but to you? Nothin' at all!"

"Yeah," Deena chimes in. "Dicks come and go, you know what I mean?"

The two of them cackle wildly.

"Dat ain't true," says Awinita from where she's standing in the doorway.

"Huh?" says Deena.

Awinita looks at them impassively, not moving. Speaks simply.

"I tought it was notin'," she says, "but it ain't. You take deir dick, deir pain comes along wid it. Dey leave de pain behind. Dey go off, and de pain stays behind wit you."

FADE TO GRAY.

Amidst moving shadows, a monster shakes in evil, soundless laughter. Other shapes surge and swarm before our eyes, shivering darkly. There is a shooting star.

Maybe that shooting star is you, Milo darling? Maybe it's your soul suddenly entering your body? Awinita has just passed the critical three-month point of her pregnancy.

· · · · ·

VIII
SAUDADE

*Powerful nostalgia or lack. The term
is virtually untranslatable.*

Milo, 1970–75

WE NEED TO think about what we want to keep in and keep out from now on, Milo, baby. As it stands, we've got something like, uh, ballpark estimate . . . seven hours of film. Sure, there are a coupla precedents in the history of the medium—sublime trilogies such as Satyajit Ray's *Apu* or Fritz Lang's *Doctor Mabuse* . . . But still, we have to be careful. Wouldn't want the audience's attention to wander, now, would we? Especially in this next sequence, which deals with the most chaotic period in your whole life . . .

MAYBE START OFF with news footage from the spring of 1970, during which the Front de Libération du Québec sets off one bomb after another, killing six people and inflicting considerable material damage on symbols of English domination in the province. Windsor Station in Montreal (through which Neil dragged little Milo the day they first met), monument to Queen Victoria, Dominion Bank, Queen's Printing Press, Loyola College, private mailboxes in the cushy Anglo suburb of Westmount, Bank of Nova Scotia, Royal Air Force . . . Milo can be seen gleaning these events, sometimes on TV as he chats and laughs with prostitutes in sleazy bars, more often over the transistor that keeps him company as he shoots up in the men's room of the Voyageur bus station, wanders through the dark back streets of Old Montreal, and sleeps out under bridges.

A summer's night. High on heroin, Milo sinks onto his back in the grass, looks up at the night sky and sees a shooting star. (Right, Milo, *you're* the shooting star. Yeah, I get the joke, you're the star of the film and you're shooting up. Great, very good, very funny.) Segue from the shooting star into the whiteness of his heroin heaven at age eighteen. Not a bland, colorless, boring white—no, a divine, milky, creamy white; a frothy, nourishing, tepid white, sweet as fresh cow's milk—not buttery, not fatty and stomach-turning, no, the milk and honey of the River Jordan! The drug picks him up in its soft white arms and gives him the sublime, melting, liquid sensation of being held and rocked and soothed and sung to, comforted and cuddled and kissed forever and ever, amen.

Yes, Astuto, I know how much you loved heroin.

One day in May, the whiteness in Milo's brain turns into that of a flock of Canadian geese that fills the entire sky. Pan to the young man staring up at them. Clinging to his arm is a pert and pretty, dark-haired girl by the name of Viviane, also looking up. Their mouths are open in amazement. Milo recites a few lines from "The Wild Swans at Coole."

> *De trees are in deir autumn beauty,*
> *De woodland paths are dry,*
> *Under de October twilight de water*
> *Mirrors a still sky;*
> *Upon de brimming water among de stones*
> *Are nine-and-fifty swans.*

Viviane looks at him adoringly.

"Sounds beautiful!" she says. "Who's it by?"

"Yeats."

"Never heard of him."

"A great Irish poet from the beginning of the century. Good friend of my grandfather's."

"Boy, that grandfather of yours sure made a big impression on you. You talk about him all the time. You gonna introduce me to your folks one of these days?"

"Absolutely."

Milo grins broadly . . . and, to keep her from asking more questions, plants a fierce kiss on her mouth. Just then, in a deafening beating of wings, the wild geese alight in the field next to them and the couple bursts apart. It's as if they had caused the event—as if a thousand large white birds had landed just to watch them kiss. They contemplate this living, threshing sea of whiteness at close range.

CUT to a red Chevy convertible, Viviane at the wheel, her dark hair tied back in a ponytail, speeding through the state of Nevada. As the sun beats down on his face, Milo leans back in the passenger seat with his feet on the dashboard.

CUT to the two of them making torrid love in a small hotel room in Reno, Viviane on top.

CUT to a private home in L.A., a couple of deck chairs by a swimming pool. Dressed in a skimpy bikini, Viviane is sipping a gin and tonic through a straw and letting a tall, dark, handsome stranger talk her up. Milo and their host are playing chess at a table under a pergola a few yards away. From time to time, Milo glances over to check out the scene next to the swimming pool, and the host watches him watching. When Viviane and the stranger rise and glide toward the house hand in hand, Milo moves his queen.

"Well, well," the host says. "I wonder where that lovely girl-friend of yours has wandered off to."

"Checkmate," says Milo.

CUT to Milo running alone on the beach as the sun sets over the Pacific Ocean. A long, searingly beautiful shot.

He and Viviane hug each other good-bye. She puts her suitcase into the trunk of a white Chrysler convertible and the handsome stranger drives her away.

Milo and his host at midnight, next to a campfire on the beach. After dropping a couple of tabs of psilocybin, they make sublime love in the sand. The camera politely turns upward to film more shooting stars overhead, but we gather from the sound track that Milo's sex pushing warmly into him is making the host so happy that he weeps. Milo shouts when he comes—a gorgeous shout.

(Important decision that summer: you take advantage of the hospitality and kindness of this wealthy Californian to shake your drug habit. Even in the ideal conditions your host provides for you, your withdrawal—like your mother's twenty years earlier—lasts a full month and is undiluted hell . . . but you wade through it, Astuto wonder, and come out on the other side. I love you for that, though I admit I haven't got the slightest idea how to film it.)

At summer's end, Milo drives Viviane's red car back east through Canada. Stops in Saskatchewan to pick up a female hitch-hiker with carrot-colored hair. The girl is wearing blue jean cutoffs, a bright pink shirt knotted above her midriff, dirty old sandals and a black Stetson, pulled down past her eyebrows so the wind won't blow it off. Milo chats with her as country-western music blares from the radio (Patsy Cline? yeah, let's say Patsy Cline). The girl laughs a lot, crinkling her eyes at his jokes. Her name is Roxanne.

Milo and Roxanne make love in a cheap motel room. Close-up on the bedside table: we recognize a packet of birth control pills. Times have changed.

Milo moves his things into Roxanne's dark little apartment in East Toronto.

CUT to an interview with the dean at the University of Toronto.

"Yes, Mr. Noirlac, I've grasped the fact that your girlfriend is registered in the nursing program here, but I'm afraid that does not qualify you ipso facto for our theater program. We absolutely must have access to your school record, at least some sort of proof that you graduated high school."

"I understand, sir, but alas, my school it is in ze rural Quebec, and it burn down in ze spring."

"I see. Well, it's probably just as well you left; all hell's breaking loose up in La Belle Province, as they call it. Large numbers of Quebeckers will be leaving soon, if you want my opinion. Large numbers of anglophones, especially, taking their money with them. An independent Quebec won't have an economic leg to stand on. Be that as it may, if you wish to attend this institution, you'll need to take entrance examinations."

"No problem, sir."

CUT to the dean warmly shaking Milo's hand as he winds up a short speech on Opening Day.

"Not only did Milo Noirlac pass those exams with flying colors, ladies and gentlemen, but I'm proud to announce that the university has awarded him a scholarship to cover his tuition for the next two years."

The audience applauds.

Voice-over (actually I'm not sure of this, but we can put it in now and take it out later): beyond the drone of Opening Day speeches at this institution formerly known as King's College, maybe we could hear Neil's thoughts during his commencement ceremony at Trinity half a century earlier: *Do they not know? Is it* possible *they do not know that Irish babies are dying of hunger a mere stone's throw from here? That hundreds of our country's best men are rotting in the jails of Britain for having dared to defend our dream of independence? That their world is about to go up in flames?*

Yes, Trinity College in Dublin and King's College in Toronto—founded some two and a half centuries apart but both under the auspices of a friggin' British monarch, eh? . . .

IN RAPID ALTERNATION between English and French: scenes from the year 1970–71, the Toronto scenes shot in studio, the Quebec scenes taken from press archives. Sound track: excerpts from the FLQ Manifesto, maybe mixed with rock music from the time (Charlebois or Joplin) . . . and always, faintly, in the background, the capoeira beat.

Milo sitting up late into the night, working with gusto at the kitchen table, smiling as he writes . . . *Like more and more Quebeckers, we are fed up with paying taxes that Ottawa's envoy to Quebec wants to hand over to anglophone bosses to "incite" them, if you please, to speak French and negotiate in French. Repeat after me: main-d'oeuvre à bon marché means cheap labor;* British diplomat James Richard Cross and Labour Minister Pierre Laporte are kidnapped by the Front de Libération du Québec. *Ta, ta-da DA, ta, ta-da DA . . .*

Milo and Roxanne walking in Toronto Island on a Sunday afternoon—cottages, gardens, paths, sunlight trickling through red leaves and dappling the sidewalks . . . *fed up with our obsequious government, bending over backward to seduce American millionaires, begging them to come and invest in Quebec, that Beautiful Province in which thousands of square miles of forests full of game and lakes full of fish are the exclusive property of these all-powerful lords of the twentieth century* . . . Pierre Elliott Trudeau announces the implementation of the War Measures Act. Mounted police gallop madly through the streets of Montreal . . . *Ta, ta-da DA, ta, ta-da DA* . . . Canadian army helicopters whir overhead.

Milo and Roxanne making love . . . *fed up with hypocrites like Bourassa, who use the armored cars of Brink's, that perfect symbol of foreign occupation of Quebec, to maintain the province's poor "natives" in the terror of poverty and unemployment to which they are so well accustomed* . . . Sirens, flashing lights, police searches . . . *Ta, ta-da DA, ta, ta-da DA* . . . Posted on every street corner in downtown Montreal, thousands of helmeted, camouflage-uniformed soldiers hold their machine guns at the ready . . .

Milo and Roxanne quarreling in the kitchen—Roxanne throws a cup at Milo; it grazes his forehead and smashes against the wall; he leaves the house. *Fed up with promises of employment and prosperity, whereas we'll always be the eager servants and bootlickers of the big shots* . . . Civil liberties are suspended. Huge demonstrations are held. *Ta, ta-da DA, ta, ta-da DA* . . . People are beaten, kicked and dragged by the police; blood runs down their faces. Five hundred well-known artists, writers, organizers and militants are arrested and thrown in jail.

Milo watching TV, a six-pack of Molson and a carton of Player's at his side . . . *As long as there are Westmounts, Mount Royals, Hampsteads and Outremonts, those impregnable fortresses of Saint Jacques Street and Wall Street high finance, we Quebeckers will resort to any means necessary, including dynamite and guns, to kick out the big bosses of economy and politics, knowing they will stop at nothing to screw us over* . . . Pierre Laporte's dead body is found in the trunk of a car, a chain around its neck. *Ta, ta-da DA, ta, ta-da DA* . . . Silence. CUT.

Milo in bed. The Black Hole has got him.

Roxanne (wearing different clothes, to show that days are passing) bends over him solicitously: "What's the matter, my love?" . . . "Are you going to get up today?" . . . "You haven't left the house in more than a week." . . . "What's the matter, my love?" . . . "Did something happen?" . . . "Did something happen, Milo? Are you depressed?" . . . "Do you want me to call a doctor?"

Turning away from her, Milo pulls the blankets up over his head and feigns sleep. Sleep is still and always a problem for him. (Even today, my love, even today . . .)

The telephone rings. He sits bolt upright in bed and yells.

Roxanne rushes into the bedroom: "What's the matter? Jesus Christ . . . You scared the shit out of me."

She bursts into tears. Milo holds out his arms to her in hopes that she will comfort him.

"It's okay," they whisper to each other. "We'll be all right."

"I just made some tea," says Roxanne. "Do you want a cup?"

Milo nods. Slowly gets out of bed and hobbles into the kitchen. Can't look at Roxanne. Sits down at the table. Pours salt instead of sugar into his tea.

"Milo!"

They look at each other . . . then avert their eyes, each embarrassed to see the other knows they know that it is not okay. They will not be all right. No, not at all . . .

I've seen you that way, Astuto. I've seen you sink into lots of black holes over the years and lose lots of stuff in their depths—and when I say stuff, I mean fairly important stuff. Language. Your name . . . your profession . . . your age . . . your wallet . . . your computer . . . track of time. Yeah, I've seen you vanish, man. Turn into a void before my fuckin' eyes—and a *lasting* void, at that! No way anyone can kiss you then. Nothing anyone can do but let you stare at the wall for as long as it takes you to snap out of it. It's pretty impressive. You succumb utterly to your malaise. Surrender all arms. Relinquish language and revert to pure, animal survival. Say nothing, see no one, stay home, stare at the wall. A triumph of inertia. A splendor of blackness. All your energy condensed into an invisible point in the depths of you, one that takes up no space but freezes everything around it. *It feels like turning to ice,* I remember your telling me once. Yeah, like Glacier—the white giant of Indian legend who invaded the northern lands in prehistory, shaping hills, polishing stones, slowly displacing millions of tons of rocks and gravel, covering all, paralyzing all for thousands of years. *But ice is nice,* you added. *Can't do much wit water. Ice, you can sculpt.*

I don't know how many times I saw you endure these crises of inexistence. Far from improving as you grew older, they grew worse—because you'd earned your stripes as a screenwriter; people knew you were brilliant and they expected you to perform. All of a sudden, strangled by anxiety, you'd find yourself unable to write. You'd miss deadlines and appointments, break promises and contracts, fall behind on obligations. Money would stop coming in, unpaid bills would pile up, bankers and tax inspectors would start harassing you. You would unplug your phone and stop checking your mailbox—no one could get in touch with you. And of course, the worse it got, the worse it got. The idea of their mounting resentment would make you cringe with shame, so you'd crawl further still into your hole.

At last, after weeks or even months of hibernation, something would move and it would be over. In one fell swoop, your light would be and your strength would come rushing back a hundred-fold. You'd write feverishly, day and night, pouring your innermost being onto the page . . . And people would forgive you every time, because what you wrote in those phases was just, unassailably, excellent.

I've always loved you, Milo, neither *despite* nor *because of* your black holes. *With* them . . .

SUCH, HOWEVER, WAS not the case with Roxanne. After two years of riding your soul's roller coaster with you, hanging on for dear life, she got fed up and kicked you out. Bequeathed you her black hat and left you to your black holes. You were twenty-one, with a college diploma and not a red cent to your name . . .

There was only one place in the world you could head: New York City.

Odd jobs: waiter, taxi driver, fishmonger, lighting technician, nurse's aid . . . You take up boxing for a while, discover you have a gift for the sport, start making good money at it and even consider going professional . . . but one day you're fighting this humongous black man and you knock him out. Looking at him lying motionless on the floor, you realize this sport could kill you, so you hang up your gloves: your mother wouldn't want you to meet so pointless an end.

Riffling through the *Times* one evening in a Dunkin' Donuts on Seventh Avenue (in 1974 if I'm not mistaken), you're brought up short by a headline—Seán MacBride, cofounder of Amnesty International, has just received the Nobel Peace Prize. The name rings a bell. MacBride . . . MacBride . . . You close your eyes and your grandfather's voice comes arcing back to you over the thousand miles and days: *Poor Mrs. MacBride was reduced to following Irish news from abroad . . . for fear that, were she to leave France, she'd lose legal custody of young Seagan.*

Seán and Seagan: *homo homo?* Yes, Milo. Same man. His mother, Maud Gonne, had fought her whole life long for the rights and the release of political prisoners, she'd even founded an association called Amnesty—and now, by God, her little boy had gone and won the fucking Nobel! You'll drink to that! Hightailing it out of Dunkin' Donuts, you head for an Irish pub you're partial to on Forty-Second Street—and, in loving memory of your grandpa Neil, dead these five years, down half a dozen pints of Guinness, that near-black beer topped by a stripe of creamy foam . . .

FADE TO WHITE.

. . . . .

Neil, 1920–1923

SOUND TRACK OF live music: Québécois songs accompanied by fiddle and accordion.

(We'll need to get a researcher working on this, Milo; I'll bet you've got no idea what songs would have been sung at sugaring-off parties in the 1920s, am I wrong?)

The large barn space, next to the shed in which Neil was trying to write about exile when his ephemeral son Thom was born, has been temporarily converted into a dining/dancing hall. Long tables have been set up. Squeezed together on benches, several dozen men, women and children wolf down heaping platefuls of fried potatoes, fried sausages, hotcakes, tomatoes and toast, all drenched in maple syrup. Behind them, others dance, stomp and clap in time to the tunes stirred up by the little orchestra.

As she gracefully lifts her skirts to twirl beneath her cavalier's raised arm, we see that Marie-Jeanne's stomach is rounded by the beginnings of a new child. Close-up on their feet, Neil's now heavily booted and Marie-Jeanne's sensibly shoed, moving not too clumsily round and round, toeing in and toeing out. Close-up on their faces: Neil's red-bearded; Marie-Jeanne's rosy-cheeked and sparkly-eyed.

"*T'es pas vertigineuse?*"

"*On dit pas t'es pas vertigineuse, on dit t'as pas le vertige!*"

"*T'as pas la faim?*"

"*On dit pas t'as pas la faim, on dit t'as pas faim!*"

"*T'as pas fatigue?*"

"*On dit pas t'as pas fatigue, on dit t'es fatiguée!*"

"Oh! I give up. *Elle est trop perverse, votre langue.*"

"Anyway, I'm neither dizzy nor hungry nor tired . . . Just immensely happy. What about you?"

"I'm all right."

"You worried about Ireland?"

"Yes."

"Quebec is your country now, Neil. Even if he speaks English, the boy I'm carrying won't be an Irishman, he'll be a French Canadian. Are you sure it's a good idea to read the Irish press all the time? It keeps you from sleeping at night, and in the daytime it keeps you from being where you are, sharing our joys and miseries. *We're* your family now!"

"You don't understand what's happening over there," says Neil in a low voice. "My comrades-in-arms are in the front lines. How am I to think of anything else? The IRA shoots eleven master spies from Britain who were following them everywhere, and how do the police respond? By shooting into the crowd at a rugby match! Twelve dead and seventy-two wounded! It's insane, Marie-Jeanne!"

"I agree completely, it's an unforgivable sin. The British will have to answer to God for Bloody Sunday . . . But as for you,

Neil Noirlac, you should stop worrying your head about all that. You've been here two years already . . . It's time you cut the umbilical cord between you and your native country!"

NEIL'S MEMORIES OF Bloody Sunday would come back to you, Milo darling, when a similar massacre took place in Brazil in August 1993. On pretext that four cops had been murdered by young drug lords, the Rio police stormed into cafés and private homes in the favela of Vigário Geral, opening fire at random. Twenty-one people were killed, none of whom was connected to the drug world in any way. History repeats itself, horrors rhyme and you, Astuto, were so porous, so sensitive to the tales of others, and yourself so unrooted in a particular time and place that the bloody rebellions and repressions that haunted your bad dreams and black holes could have been unfolding in Dublin, Montreal, or Rio . . .

CUT TO A sumptuous panoramic shot of the Mauricie region from on high. The camera will move simultaneously through space and time. Trees sprout leaves that change color, fall off, sprout green again (we're reminded of one of Awinita's cartoon fantasies) . . . Snow falls and melts, animals materialize and vanish . . . And in each season we will see Neil— dressed now in heavy winter gear, now in a T-shirt and light trousers, now in a red-and-black- or green-and-black-checkered wool shirt—working with other men, lopping branches off trees, inserting taps into trunks, pouring golden syrup from barrels into bottles, making maple taffy . . .
Voice-over: Neil as an old man, talking to his grandson.
It wasn't easy for me to get used to living here, Milo. It felt uncanny, not to say immoral, to be dealing with moose and maple syrup as my country sank into hell. A month after Bloody Sunday, in

December 1920, Westminster passed Lloyd George's Government of Ireland Act, effectively separating Northern from Southern Ireland. The North said yea, the South said nay, and they've never changed their minds since. All through the spring I could think of nothing else. I was desperate to join the Irish Republican Army, now run by Michael Collins and the brilliant, ebullient young Seán MacBride. Remember I told you about Maud Gonne and John MacBride? Well, this was their son. Like myself a few years earlier, he was taking a law degree when politics claimed his soul. At sixteen, he became the youngest lieutenant in the Irish Republican Army. In May, they took over the Customhouse and laid waste to it. Milo, it took my breath away! The Customhouse—the most conspicuous and detested symbol of British power in Ireland, after Dublin Castle—a heap of smoking ruins! The whole British administration paralyzed! Meanwhile Yeats, in London, went on churning out Irish plays and poetry; Joyce, in Paris, went on serially publishing his masterpiece Ulysses; *and I, I, Milo— who had played such an important role in Ireland as lawyer, poet and rebel—what was I doing? Sitting here in Mauricie eating pork 'n' beans with Marie-Jeanne's family. From the outside, an ordinary man among ordinary men. But from the inside: raging, suffering, crippled by my brain in a world of brawn.*

Your aunt Marie-Thérèse was born in June. She was a sweet, healthy wee thing; Marie-Jeanne sang and spoke to her in French. In Ireland, North and South were at each other's throat. My mother wrote to say that she and my father were considering having their assets transferred to banks in Belfast. Yes, even Catholics, now—if they were wealthy and pro-British—were being targeted, terrorized, forced to flee.

Southern Ireland won its independence on Christmas Day, putting an end to seven centuries of British presence. But the minute the terms of the treaty were made public, the Dáil, the Sinn Féin and the IRA split apart and madness set in—that special form of madness known as civil war. Backs were stabbed and guts ripped open as South killed South, son killed father and brother killed brother, not only in Dublin but in the provinces, down to the tiniest of villages. As time went by, people forgot what the issues were; caught up in an unending concatenation of revenge and bitterness and misery, a festival of gore, an orgy of hatred, they simply fought to fight and killed to kill. The army got pushed up into the hills; thousands of men were jailed. Maud Gonne MacBride begged that the prisoners be treated with leniency, instead of which they were summarily shot. Executions are terrible, said the Minister for Home Affairs, but the murder of a nation is more terrible. Yeats, now deeply immersed in a phase of automatic writing with his wife, Georgie, saw symbols everywhere. Convinced that the Christian era was drawing to a close and that we had twenty centuries of undiluted horror in store for us, he wrote "The Second Coming":

> *And what rough beast, its hour come round at last*
> *Slouches towards Bethlehem to be born?*

Meanwhile the leaves changed color, dropped and sprouted anew, the Saint-Maurice River and Lac des Piles froze and thawed, the sap in the maple trees rose and overflowed, my sweet wife's breasts and tummy swelled and shrank, our children mewled and spewed and grew. One day I received a letter from my mother. I'm sorry to have to share this with you, Milo, but my history is part of yours and I feel you should know even the worst of it . . . Judge Kerrigan being known for his pro-British legal decisions over the years . . . our home had been broken into, our china smashed, our paintings slashed, our pillows eviscerated, our garden trampled . . . and my younger sister, Dorothy, who happened to be at home alone playing the piano that day, savagely beaten and raped by IRA revolutionaries or whatever they claimed to be. She was lucky to escape with her life . . . My family promptly fled to Belfast, a city in which I'd never once set foot.

After reading that letter, Milo, I spent the rest of the day vomiting —just as I had on the boat coming over. I now had no place to go home to.

In May 1923, sickened by the inanity of the fighting, Éamon de Valera surrendered and the civil war ground to a halt. It had lasted two years and caused several thousand deaths . . . That fall, Willie Yeats was awarded the Nobel Prize in Literature.

I could not go on.

END OF PANORAMIC LANDSCAPE SHOT.

CLOSE-UP ON NEIL in December 1923, thirty-one and miserable, on his knees at Marie-Jeanne's bedside as she nurses Marie-Thérèse.

"I can't go on like this, Marie-Jeanne. I'm sorry . . . I adore you, but I have to make some changes . . . If I can't write, I'll go crazy. Listen . . . I'm going to look for employment as a journalist in Montreal. I'm sure I'll find something . . . I promise to come back. You can trust me . . ."

"Listen, Neil! I have something to tell you! It's a secret, you're not supposed to know yet. My father wanted it to be a surprise, for your Christmas present, but as of next spring he's going to add a floor to the house, just for you. Isn't that fantastic, Neil? He's going to build you an office, and you'll be able to write!"

Neil's head sinks until his brow touches Marie-Jeanne's smooth-skinned hand. Night falls over the endless winter forest of Mauricie.

FADE TO BLACK.

. . . . .

Awinita, October 1951 . . .

THIS WILL BE the roughest of the Awinita sections, Milo, darling, as your mother starts shooting up again and you grow inside her womb, your tiny heart guzzling heroin and pulsing it through your bloodstream into your just-forming brain, numbing all your nascent senses. A section with no dialogue, just fragmented images melting one into the next as your mother fades in and out of consciousness . . . sits at the bar and drinks phony drinks with her johns and real ones with Declan . . . smiles at the johns and frowns at Declan . . . takes the johns' money and gives it to Declan . . . climbs up and down the stairs between bar and bedroom, bedroom and bar . . . takes off her boots, stockings, blouse, bra and panties and puts them on again, all her clothes getting tighter and more uncomfortable on her body as you grow but of course she can't afford a pregnancy wardrobe . . . closing her eyes so as not to see the faceless needy men pushing into her, asking her to love and care about them, until they come and leave.

This time, if you agree, we could go all the way inside her mind and simply knit together a series of fantasies and nightmares, using a sound track now familiar to us—that endless series of belt-buckle and zipper noises, panting, swearwords and racist insults, moans and groans. Yes, I know, Milo—you're worried that not only the MPAA but the audience itself might tire of hearing these sounds, but if they think about it they'll realize that what seems annoyingly repetitious to us after five minutes must be soul-death to those who, for whatever reason or combination of reasons, devote months or years of their lives to helping strangers ejaculate. Okay, these sounds could be drowned out every now and then by the beating of native drums, how's that? (In October 1951, the laws that for over half a century had forbidden African Brazilians from doing capoeira, and Indian Canadians from holding potlatches, powwows, and sun dances, had just been abolished . . .)

A train rushes toward a tunnel at top speed—but it turns out that the black arch is only painted *onto the concrete, and the train smashes into it headlong. Somehow all the passengers are squish-bounced out of the windows. They land gaily on their feet and run around laughing and shaking each other's hands, congratulating each other on their good fortune.*

A city plunged in darkness. No streetlamps or neon signs. Even the cars have no headlights, but their blindness neither increases their caution nor decreases their speed. They keep smashing into each other— this time the passengers get killed, and it is their ghosts who nimbly leap away from the wreckage. They are small, amorphous gray creatures who dart about, gesticulating helplessly, eyes widened in shock. They weep silently on each other's shoulders and console one another.

A narrow, glossy black snake's head emerges from a hole in the ground. The snake twists its neck around to make sure that no one is watching, then hoists the rest of its body out of the hole. It is shockingly fat and clumsy, like an obese woman dressed in a black leotard, with a couple of extra limbs and bulges. The snake clumps around in a meaningless, ugly shuffle-dance, then rolls disgustingly on the ground.

A baseball goes soaring through the air in slow motion. The stitching comes apart while the ball is still in flight, and hundreds of tiny white parachutes drop gracefully from its insides.

A man shouts in anger. Suddenly his voice undergoes all its metamorphoses in reverse, and within seconds he is a howling baby.

Bodies plummet, human bodies hurtle downward through the air with groans of fear that sound like droning airplanes. A white flower opens with searing grace and purity.

The flame of a candle—now steady, now flickering, but always

*burning—reflects the sundry images with which it comes into contact.
There is a vague procession of people, animals, buildings . . .*

    *A green shoot comes up from the dark earth. It sprouts two tiny
bright leaves, then stops growing.*

    *A milk bottle cap shoots off; the milk spews upward and falls in a
thick white curve of milk.*

That thick white curve of milk showers gently and felicitously
down upon you both, Awinita and Milo, covering your bodies in
a fountain of warmth, the mellow marrow-ecstasy of heroin. Eyes
close gently, breathing slows, lips relax, hands open—oh, abandonment, oh, utter abandonment—woman and womb, skin and
membrane, the mother a child to her child, the child a mother to its
mother, adult and infant curled up around and inside of each other,
outside of Time.

. . . . .

IX

NEGAÇA

Deception, provocation. Pretending to do one thing (a movement, an attack) and in fact doing another to surprise one's adversary.

Milo, 1975–90

A NIGHT SCENE, lit by torches, on Terreiro de Jesus in Salvador de Bahia's upper city—a large and beautiful square surrounded by old churches and cafés. Young black men in white pants have formed a street *roda* and passersby are being drawn into it. Radiating from the central berimbau, energy circulates from one body, voice and soul to the other; by turn, the capoeiristas sing and kick and spin and wheel and cartwheel, beat drums and shake tambourines—*ta, ta-da DA, ta, ta-da DA, ta, ta-da DA*—smiling always, even when they miss a beat and fall or accidentally strike an adversary. The rhythm is hypnotic and insistent, monotonous and precise. It's not by virtue of making an effort that they play together; rather they are part of a single body, the pulsating joyful body of the fight-dance. Raising your foot in a kick-spin, you all but graze your adversary's face, the beauty is to miss him but just barely, if he dances well he'll feel the blow coming and be ready to second-guess you and avoid it, knock you off balance and gracefully threaten you in turn, as the two of you watch and duck, swing and smile and wheel and dive and lollop, the beat carries you forward, then your turn is over and, moving to watch the next pair bow to salute each other in front of the central berimbau, you encourage them with our singing, drumming, clapping and your smiles. *Ta, ta-da DA, ta, ta-da DA, ta, ta-da DA* . . . There's no winning or losing in this game, only playing, endless playing, you want your adversary to be strong not weak, smart not dumb, you're delighted to trick him and delighted to be tricked by him, boy learns from girl, white learns from black, old learns from young, the teaching is the doing is the beauty is the grace is the humor, endlessly you go on learning, smiling, moving, feinting, never missing a beat. *Gingare*, the dance of life: the controlled, prolonged, sustained, ineffable excitement of capoeira is like an endless climax.

Receding from the vortex of the event, our camera turns and finds itself nose to nose with . . . another camera. Shooting the *roda* in black and white is a film crew from New York, Milo among them . . . Moment of mutual embarrassment. Like dogs, the two cameras sniff each other out, moving around to see what's going on in the back.

Because Milo's body has begun to move of its own volition, he is being gradually but imperiously included in the performance. The Bahians watch him, approving with nods and gestures the precise élan of his limbs . . .

OH, MILO, WHAT wouldn't I give to have witnessed that scene! Your other forms of physical training were all reactivated at once: hockey for clever swerves, swivels, pivots, and feints; boxing for swiftness, lightness of footwork and accuracy of arm thrusts; sex with Paul Schwarz for sensual, graceful interaction with other male bodies. This was what you'd been looking for all your life. The Bahians saw it, too. No room for doubt—buoyed up by the solid, attentive warmth and approval of the crowd, your head went down, your legs went up, the speed increased, and your body, like that of the other young men, became a pure, moving cipher. Eyes wide open, you gave yourself up to the capoeira rhythm as it irrigated your flesh. *Ta, ta-da DA, ta, ta-da DA, ta, ta-da DA* . . . You knew this beat from before, long before, from your mother's heart that gently, rhythmically played her ancestors' tales into your ears when you lived inside of her, Milo, yes, you had this beat in your blood and could feel it now, coming up from the ground of Terreiro de Jesus, zinging through the sacred berimbau and galvanizing your whole being. Unexpectedly, at age twenty-three, you felt at home for the first time in your life.

Sorry. Yes, of course we'll go back to the third person. And yes, of course we'll change the name, don't worry. What's in a name? (To call your mother *Nita* is to destroy the meaning of her name, which is *fawn* . . .)

CUT TO THE following day: a gathering in a tiny open-air café at São Joaquim, Salvador's outdoor market. Seated with several of the capoeira initiates, you're smoking cigarettes, drinking weak beer and chewing the rag. Your friend Homer, the African American director of the candomblé film you've come to work on, translates for you from the Portuguese.

". . . They wanna know where you learned capoeira."

Milo shrugs and grins.

"Dey taught me."

". . . They say you're one of them."

"I feel it, too. An honor. Ask dem if I may pay for de next round."

That evening, the New York crew is invited to the home of a local capoeira *mestre*. Smiles follow plates of fejoada and glasses of caipirinha around the table. Several shots from different angles, to show hours passing, elation rising. Late in the evening, a corpulent woman of sixty or so, sexily swathed in a green cotton print dress, comes to sit next to Milo. Her skin is copper-colored, her teeth bright white, her English halting but clear.

"I saw you dance last night. The fire was in you."

"Oh, so dat's what it was!" Milo laughs. "I wondered."

"You're Milo Noirlac, a French person from Quebec. I asked around. My name's Manoela."

"Trilled to meet you, Manoela."

"I'm Indian. I come from the south of Bahia, near Porto Seguro. My people are the Pataxo Hahahae."

"Hahahae, a fine laughing name."

"My husband was *madingueiro*, too . . . He worked many years with Mestre Pastinha."

"You say *was* . . . ?"

"Two years ago in a fishing expedition, he . . . drown. Our children big already, live far . . ."

"I'm sorry. Life must be lonely for you sometimes."

Other people pull him back into the conversation. It goes on and on. Later, Manoela comes back to Milo and says,

"Your skin is talking to mine."

"Your skin is answering mine."

CUT to the two of them making love that night, in Manoela's more than modest bedroom. Afterward they lie in bed, holding each other.

"You're Indian, just like me . . . aren't you, child?" she murmurs.

"How you know dat?"

"'Cause of your silence."

"What do you mean? I spent de whole evening talkin' my head off."

"Can't fool me with that, baby."

They laugh and kiss and laugh and kiss. The next morning, as they drink strong coffee together on the doorstep, he tells her in a few words the tale of his birth, even adding (in a rare élan of total trust) that when he was three or four Awinita revealed his middle name to him, a Cree word meaning *resistant*.

"So she don't leave you completely."

"She did, Manoela."

"No, child. You're a little baby, she live with you a few days, look at you closely and see you going to make it. You understand? If she give you this name, it mean she got confidence in your fate."

Several shots of Homer filming other capoeira performances in and around Salvador, Milo achieving a higher degree of integration each time. Learning as he goes, laughing, feinting and radiant, talking with people, making love now with women, now with men. Just before his departure, he undergoes a *batizado* ceremony and is given a new name, one that suits him to a T: *Astuto*.

On the flight back to New York, Milo and Homer go over their notes, talking about what's in the reels and how to edit it, occasionally rocking with laughter.

CUT to Milo working alone in his Lower Manhattan apartment. The phone rings (in 1975, still one of those jangly, heavy black Bakelite contraptions) and he jumps out of his skin.

"What?" he yells at the phone before picking it up.

"Milo?" says a soft, high, wavering female voice at the other end: a French voice, but whose?

"Yeah. Who's calling?"

"It's your cousin. It's Gabrielle."

Through Milo's eyes, we look out the window at a bric-a-brac of brick walls, fire exits, garbage cans and broken bottles.

"Milo, Mommy is dying. She wants to see you."

"How did you find me?"

"Your friend Edith told me you were in New York, so I called information. Daddy asked me to get in touch with you, Milo, he's all het up . . . Mommy has womb cancer. I don't want to bother you, I know you've got another life and you don't think about us anymore . . . but Mommy's only got a few days left to live and she's been asking to see you. She wants to apologize to you . . . you know . . . for the bonfire."

"I got noting against you and Régis, Gabrielle . . . " says Milo, interrupting softly. "I got noting at all against de two of you . . ."

Very gently, he hangs up . . . CUT.

THOSE YEARS, MILO says yes to any project, whether documentary or feature film, that will take him back to African soul dancing on American soil.

You see, Astuto? We were fated to meet. When I returned to the NYU Film School as an alumnus and gave a presentation of my new film on Haitian voodoo, it was inevitable that you'd come to the projection and I'd fall for you the minute I set eyes on you. I don't know what *you* saw in *me*, apart from a supremely hand-some, intelligent, gifted, almost-successful genius of a film di-rector; anyway, we made love at your place that very night . . . You amazed me in bed. No hang-ups, no shyness, no apologies or kinks . . . Just eagerness, inventiveness and stupendous generosity.

We talked the next morning over breakfast, and the more I got to know you the more I wanted to work with you . . . By the time we separated later that same day, I'd signed you up as cowriter on my next film.

A riffle through Milo's travels, travails, trails and trials over the next few years. We see him attending film festivals, meeting direc-tors, making a name for himself as a screenwriter. He's not a writer in any usual sense of the word—avoids writing in his own name, even letters; doesn't want people to know how to reach him, find him; often refrains from answering even phone calls (his telephone phobia will never leave him). Time shadows him always, hard on his heels, and he moves on, never stops moving, *gingare*, like a capoeirista in Bahia or an Indian in the forest, effacing his tracks as he goes along so as to leave no evidence behind . . . He has no style of his own but has hit upon the perfect compromise between Neil's ultraliterary tradition and Awinita's oral one—*writing orality*. In his dark bedroom in Manhattan as in the closets of his childhood in Montreal or in front of the silent TV set in Mauricie, he listens intently to the voices in his head, then transcribes their words with confounding accuracy. Being half deaf in one ear has impaired his inner hearing not at all . . .

JUNE 1980, MONTREAL World Film Festival. Close-up on Milo, not quite thirty, at a fancy dinner party. He glances around the table— white tablecloth, champagne, oysters, women in sparkling jewelry making long, careful curls bounce when they toss their heads back to laugh, men holding forth in loud proud voices—and thinks it is fine. Whatever. (He thinks his Lower Manhattan hole-in-the-wall is fine, too.)

A young actress, bleached blond, wearing a slinky, strapless black dress and teetering on stiletto heels, comes over and sits down next to him. At once they dive deeply into mutual seduction . . . CUT.

In Milo's room at the Ritz-Carlton on Sherbrooke (a mile or so west of the gray stone house in which Neil was once uncomfortably lodged by Judge and Mrs. McGuire), he and the blonde are making love. It turns out that this woman, whose name is Yolande or Yolaine, he's not sure which, is even more beautiful without than with her makeup and fancy clothes.

"Hey, Milo Noirlac," she whispers into his ear when they wake up in the morning, "I adore you, you know that? I'm not sure it's wise of me but I can't help it, I love the hell out of you."

Milo smiles, presses her to him and, in the brilliant sunlight of a Sunday morning in Montreal, makes love to her again. They chat afterward, tapping silver knives through the shells of their soft-boiled, room-service eggs.

"Dis is incredible."

"What's incredible, Milo, love?"

"Dis whole thing. Being back in my hometown after all dese years . . . Winning a festival prize . . . Meeting *you*, Yolaine, de best actress in Quebec and de most beautiful woman in de world."

"*Especially* meeting me."

"Dat's for sure!"

"Will you write a role for me one day?"

"Ha! You know de Belgian joke!"

"No?"

"How do you recognize an up-and-coming Belgian actress?"

". . . Well?"

"She's de one who sleeps with de screenwriter."

They let their chairs tip backward onto the bed and go at each other again, Yolande taking the initiative this time and Milo giving himself up rapturously to her caresses.

CUT to the bathroom: Yolaine murmuring sweet nothings into Milo's ear as they shower together.

"I love your hair . . . And I love the way you write . . . And I love how gentle you are . . . And I love how you're going to take me with you on your trips . . ."

CUT to Milo and Yolande walking on Saint Helen's Island together.

"Why are you always so passive, Milo?"

"I tought you loved me."

"Yeah, I love you, but . . . I mean, a person's gotta know what they want. I say let's get married, you say fine, and then you don't do anything about it!"

"Well . . . what is dere to be done? Is it as complicated as all dat? I don't know, I never married anybody before."

"Neither did I, you idiot, but we should throw a party, send out invitations to our families, I know that much . . ."

" . . ."

"Okay, okay, I know you never met your parents . . . But you must have been raised by *some*body, Milo. You didn't grow up with wolves in the forest!"

"Dat woulda been nice."

"Come on . . . You said you had a wonderful grandfather."

"He's dead."

"And . . . don't you have a whole houseful of aunts and uncles and cousins up in Mauricie?"

"Dere's nobody left."

"You want us to get married just like that, in city hall?"

"Dat's fine wit me."

"Okay, well . . ."

Close-up of Milo's right hand, signing his name with a flourish at the bottom of an official paper. We read the end of the text: *united in wedlock on this day* . . . Signed: *Milo Noirlac*. He hands the pen to Yolaine . . . CUT.

OVER THE NEXT half minute or so: flashes from the next few years as Milo and Yolaine begin the life of a fairly happy, rather successful, moderately artistic Québécois couple of the late 1970s.

Milo running up the short flight of steps onstage to be

congratulated at an awards ceremony, Yolande clapping from the audience . . . The same situation the other way around . . . Milo making wild love with Paul Schwarz on their first scoping-out trip to Rio . . . Yolaine memorizing lines in the living room, with Milo cuing her . . . Milo chain-smoking as he writes at the kitchen table in the middle of the night . . . Yolande coming home at three A.M. and the two of them making love amidst his papers on the table . . . Yolaine jealous because Paul Schwarz is on the phone and she suspects there might be something between them . . . Milo in a black hole, in bed, his head turned to the wall, Yolande hovering at his side and worrying about him just as Roxanne used to . . . Yolaine and Milo vacationing on the Côte d'Azur after the Cannes International Film Festival . . . Sitting side by side on the beach . . . Making love in the sand after nightfall, when everyone has gone home . . .

A conversation over dinner that night. Yolande smiles at him as they raise their glasses in a toast.

"What shall we drink to?"

"To us, my beauty!"

"Yeah, but to us what?"

"To us, I dunno . . . Do we have to add someting?"

They sip their drinks.

"That's just the question, Milo."

"What?"

"Yeah, should we add something or shouldn't we? I mean . . . should I stop taking the pill or shouldn't I?"

"Ah!"

"You said it. Ah."

"I don't know . . . D'you want a kid?"

"I don't know. But it's time I did, with my thirtieth birthday looming on the horizon. What about you?"

"Me?"

"Yeah, you! Do *you* want a kid?"

"I don't know."

"That makes two of us."

"Hmm."

"We're pretty weird, aren't we?"

"You tink so?"

"Okay, well, we can think about it awhile longer."

"Let's do dat."

"Yeah, right, we're not in that much of a hurry, eh? We can give it some more thought."

"Right."

(Remember how warmly I encouraged you to have a baby with Yolande, Milo darling? I quoted Shakespeare's sonnet to you: *You had a father: let your son say so* . . . I wanted you to live forever! But in Quebec in those days, too many adults had been unwanted, illegitimate, orphaned, lost, or abandoned children . . . Now that people could avoid having kids, no one seemed to know quite how they felt about parenthood.)

EXTERIOR, SAINT DENIS STREET—NIGHT. Paul Schwarz is in Montreal to work with Milo on *Science and Sorcery*, their project about AIDS in Brazil. Sauntering into a bar together, the first thing they see is Yolaine's back, with the arm of a male stranger draped ostentatiously around it. Not missing a beat, Milo steers Paul over to a corner table and goes on talking about how to do smooth camera work in the steep, unevenly cobbled streets of the favelas.

When she gets up to leave a few minutes later, the strange man's arm still possessively glued to her body, Yolande catches sight of her husband and freezes in her tracks. The man releases her, but Milo smiles and looks away.

She slips her arm back through the man's arm and they go out the door together.

CUT to Milo working at the kitchen table the next morning, cigarette in hand. When Yolaine comes home, he pours her a cup of coffee and brings it to her with a kiss. She clatteringly drops the cup into the sink.

"I just don't get it, Milo! I don't come home all night and you don't give a damn!"

" . . ."

"You see me with another man, I don't come home all night and that's fine with you!"

"What do you want me to say?"

"Listen, it's just not normal to be that unjealous! I'm jealous, and I find it only normal to be jealous!"

"So we each tink we're normal. Dat's normal . . ."

"For God's sake, Milo! You're just too passive! You have no will of your own! I've been telling you so for years! It is impossible to know what you really want, because you don't want to tell me! I want to make love, you say fine; I want to marry you, you say fine; the great Paul Schwarz wants to make a film with you, you say fine; and what if he wants to sleep with you? Do you say fine then, too? Maybe you do! I spend the night in the arms of another man and you say fine. Are you missing a cog or what, Milo? You should get help!"

Before answering, Milo stubs out his cigarette, carefully washes and dries his coffee cup, and puts it away in the cupboard.

"You don't belong to me and I don't belong to you. People can't belong to each oder. They can't even know each oder . . . Dey don't even know demselves! I don't feel de need to know everyting you do. I trust you. Everybody does what dey need to do, don't dey?"

"But if I *leave* you, Milo?"

"Well . . . if you leave me, you leave me. You won't be dere, so you won't have to tell me, I'll see it all by myself."

"Jesus, I don't believe it. You're *incredible!*"

CUT to the two of them in bed, writhing in each other's arms. But Yolaine's mind is elsewhere . . .

Then comes a depressing scene most of us have probably lived through at least once: on a rainy, desperately gray November afternoon, surrounded by boxes and suitcases, the couple divvies up their kitchen utensils . . . record collection . . . library books . . . all the possessions they've accumulated in five years of marriage.

CUT to Milo's right hand, signing his name with a flourish at the bottom of an official paper. Close-up on the end of the text: *divorce by mutual consent. As no children issued from this union, no legal dispositions need be made on the subject.* Signed: *Milo Noirlac.* He hands the pen to Yolande.

(And then, Astuto . . . It was just a few weeks after your divorce, wasn't it, that . . .)

One evening, in his new and much smaller apartment out in the Mile End section of Montreal, Milo is completely engrossed in the *Science and Sorcery* screenplay . . . so when the phone rings (jump, shout, *What?*), he picks up the receiver angrily. Listens. We hear a man's voice but can't make out the words. After a few seconds, Milo sits down again.

"I don't believe you . . . Who de hell is dis? . . . Okay. No, to-morrow I go to New York. Next week I come. Tell me your address. Okay. Six o'clock next Wednesday. Okay."

CUT to Milo walking down the dimly lit hallway of a shabby rooming house. The odor of poverty fairly leaps at us from the screen: a gut-rippling mixture of urine, beer and cabbage. So thick is the layer of filth on the walls and floor that Milo's hand hesitates before touching the door knocker. The door opens a crack; a bleary eye peers out; a chain is removed; Milo steps into the room.

Smaller than he, the man reeks of whisky, decayed teeth and ancient sweat. His apartment seems to have seen neither daylight nor a duster in decades . . . Thank God for images, Astuto; thank God we don't need to cast about for words to describe the place. The stench and strangeness are so overpowering that Milo has to consciously will his body to stay nailed to the spot.

"Sit down," the old man says. "Make yourself at home."

Milo lowers himself into a faux-leather armchair whose springs whine in protest at his weight.

"So explain to me what you're talking about."

"It's true. I swear it's true. Cross my heart and hope to die, I'm your da."

"My fader's dead."

"No," says Declan, ridiculously flexing his biceps. "Look: There is still a bit of life left in these old bones! If I was dead I'd know about it, seems to me!"

"Who de fuck are you?"

"I'm not kiddin', I'm your da. Look! I've got your birth certificate and all."

Hobbling over to a chest of drawers, Declan pulls out a sheet of paper and waves it under Milo's nose, then points triumphantly at words on the paper: "See? See?"

But whether because of the dim light in the room or the hubbub in his brain, Milo can decipher nothing; all he sees is the black line of dirt under the old man's fingernail.

"Noirlac, Milo. Son of Noirlac, Declan and Johnson, Awinita. I'm Noirlac, Declan. I'm your da, see? Neil's son, seventh of thirteen, right smack in the middle! Didn't Neil ever tell you about me?"

Milo is thunderstruck.

"I'm the one who named you Milo! I chose your name, I did! In March '51, Miles Davis's *Birdland* songs were on the radio all the time and I was crazy about them. So I called you Milo, which is Irish for Myles. Given that we're Irish."

Silence. Then: "How did you find me?"

"Saw in the newspaper you were livin' in Montreal again. Called up information on the off chance."

"In de *newspaper*?"

"Yeah, look . . ."

Declan opens a folder containing a sprawl of newspaper clippings. Torn from the culture section of a recent *Gazette*, the one on the top includes a photo of Milo and Paul grinning from ear to ear, their arms around each other's waist. *Local Screenwriter Swings Contract with Major U.S. Producer,* the headline reads.

"So?"

"So! You're doin' good, eh? You're doin' fine. Glad to know it, Milo."

"So?"

"So I thought . . . you know . . . Me being your very own da and all, and you havin' come up in the world, so to speak . . . doin' even better than your own da . . ."

"I don't believe it . . . Is *dat* why you got in touch wit me?"

"Well, I admit I thought you might see clear to givin' your old man a hand. Makin' him a loan, like."

Silence. Declan offers Milo a glass of whisky. Getting no response, he sits down and takes a swig directly from the bottle.

"I told your ma I'd maybe ask you for a little help, and she said it was a good idea."

An electroshock.

"My moder's *alive?*"

"Sure . . . Why should everybody be dead? We ain't even old yet. We keep in touch. When you were born, I promised her I'd take care of you and I did."

"You took *care* of me? I'm tirty years old, I meet you for de first time in my life, and you sit dere and look me in de eye and say you took *care* of me?"

"Yeah, you know . . . I stayed in touch with the agency . . . I always kept track of the foster homes they put you in . . . And if I heard your foster parents were beatin' you too bad, I made sure they moved you somewhere else . . . None of that for me! Strangers, hitting my own son! No, sirree! I kept my promise to your mom . . ."

"My Indian name."

"Yeah, Nita gave you a Cree name, too. That's right."

"What was it?"

"Huh . . . it's been ages . . . Got it written down somewhere. Prob'ly find it in that chest of drawers, if you wanna take a look. Or you can call her up and ask her for yourself. She's back on the res now, up north. Happy to give you her number, if you can afford long distance calls. *I* sure as hell can't!"

"I don't believe you."

"She wrote to me last week. Go see for yourself, if you don't believe me. Letter's right there in the bedroom."

Milo rises. As he crosses toward the bedroom in slow motion, Awinita's voice moves into our ears in crescendo: *What ya doin' in de dark, little one? Come wit me! Come wit your mom! . . . Fear noting, son. The sacred is neider above nor below you . . . Don worry 'bout God or de Devil . . . Everyting you do is a prayer . . . Your Cree name means* resistance. *You gonna have to resist, little one. You gonna need to be strong . . . What ya doin' in de dark, little one?*

In the bedroom: subjective camera, swinging down in a capoeira *ginga* from ceiling (cracks and cobwebs) to floor (overflowing ashtrays, discarded clothing stiff with filth). The bed hasn't been made in ages. An upended orange crate serves as a bedside table. On the crate: an envelope.

Milo crosses the room (lightfooted, Indian, his mother's son). Picks up the envelope. Camera close-up on the clumsy, childish handwriting. Declan's name and address . . . *Montreal* spelled *Muntreal* . . . Her hand traced these words a mere few days ago . . . he's virtually touching his mother . . . Gently, he turns the envelope over. Withdraws the single sheet it contains. Unfolds it. Starts to read. Again we hear Awinita's voice . . . but strange and low and echo-filled, as if from far away.

Hi Mister Clening — Fluid
glad to hear you found your son

Milo refolds the sheet of paper. Slides it back into the envelope. Sets the envelope on the orange crate. Crosses to the door. Turns off the light. Leaves the room. Leaves the building.

IT'S OKAY, ASTUTO. There would have been no point in your actually, physically traveling to an isolated Cree reserve way the hell up north in Waswanipi and meeting Awinita. She was pushing fifty by then, and probably alcoholic and obese . . . What would you have said to each other? I mean . . . your mother had been talking to you your whole life long. She couldn't ever leave you.

. . . . .

Neil, 1927

SEVERAL YEARS HAVE passed. We come upon Neil at age thirty-five, sitting at his desk in his new den on the second floor, reading glasses perched on his nose, his red beard now streaked with gray. The bookshelves on the walls around him are empty; at their foot, bearing shipping stickers from Ireland, several crates of books have been opened but not as yet unpacked. Distracted by family noises from downstairs, he is trying desperately to concentrate but getting nowhere.

CUT to the dinner table, later that evening. Present are Marie-Jeanne, hugely pregnant, Neil, hugely despondent, and half a dozen snotty, squirmy little children, up to and including a thin, dark-haired six-year-old girl whose already-bossy attitude designates her as Marie-Thérèse.

"You're holding your fork the wrong way, Sam," she says.

"You're not my mother."

"Do what she says, Sam."

"She gets on my nerves."

"Did you hear what he said, Mommy?"

"Calm down, darling, it's not that important."

"Pass the butter."

"You didn't say please."

"Please."

"Please who?"

"The butter, goddamm it."

"Watch your tongue!"

"I'm full, Mommy."

"Mommy, can I leave the table?"

"What do you think, Neil?"

"Far as I'm concerned, they can leave the house."

"That's not funny."

"No, it's not funny."

"You can't be serious."

"No, I'm not serious. It's just a line from this new poem I'm trying to write. Some people write *Slouches towards Bethlehem to be born*, others write *Far as I'm concerned they can leave the* . . ."

"Ouch! Mommy, Antony pinched me!"

"Ask your son if he pinched his sister!"

"Did you pinch your sister, Antony?"

"Not very hard. She kicked me yesterday."

"That's too long ago. You can't pinch her today because she kicked you yesterday; otherwise it's civil war."

"What's civil war, Daddy?"

"Well, you know, back in Ireland . . ."

"Oh, no! Not Ireland again!"

"Boo, boo . . . not Ireland again!"

"Anyway, you're not supposed to talk with your mouth full."

"Marie-Thérèse, it's not your job to correct your father's table manners."

"Why should grown-ups be allowed and not children?"

"Because that's the way it is. I count on you to set a good example!"

"Yes, Mother."

"Goody-goody."

"Now, William . . ."

"What's the matter?"

"Don't insult your older sister."

"It's not an insult, it's the truth."

"Well, as your namesake Willie Yeats told me long ago, you've got to be careful of the time you choose for truth-telling."

"Oh, no, not Willie Yeats again! Mommy, I'm tired of Daddy's old stories about Willie Yeats!"

Seeing red, Neil gets to his feet.

"Oh, yeah? Well . . . if I can no longer talk to me own feckin' family about me own feckin' friends . . ."

And with a great roar of virile rage he overturns the dinner table, sending children squealing like piglets and scattering in all directions. Suddenly a different scream arcs high above the general clamor—Marie-Jeanne's water has just broken. Close-up on her face, contorted in panic . . . and on Neil's, scowling with shame.

CUT to exterior night, at the icy heart of darkness, two or three in the morning. Marie-Louise, visibly older than when we last saw her, comes out the front door. Neil staggers a bit, exhausted from pacing up and down in front of the house. Bangs his pipe against the porch steps to empty it, then scuffs out the embers in the dirt.

"Well?" he asks the midwife.

"He's got nice red hair."

"Ah! A boy!"

"Yes. Gonna make another Anglo outta him?"

"And that's not all! That's not all! I plan to make this one my *heir*."

"Oh, really? I thought the house and grounds still belonged to your brothers-in-law."

"No, Marie-Louise, I mean a *spiritual* heir. That boy in there will inherit my *books*. He'll inherit my *ideas*. He'll inherit my *dreams*."

"And have you found a name for this heir of yours?"

"Declan."

"Funny name."

"It means *full of goodness*."

"Okay, well anyway, in the meantime you can go make his acquaintance."

And Marie-Louise—white-haired, white-uniformed, white-capped—moves off into the shadows of the night.

. . . . .

Awinita, January 1952

NOW SIX MONTHS pregnant with Declan's baby and pumping heroin daily through the bloodstream she shares with it, Awinita hovers and wavers downstairs in the wake of a client. (As always, we are in her body.) The latter—a short, fat, balding sexagenarian who might be a traveling vacuum cleaner salesman on the verge of retirement—does not turn to thank us or wish us a good day but walks straight through the bar and out into the dawn, his step springy with *Good riddance* (though one would be hard put to say whether the phrase applied to his sperm or to the woman he's just paid to help relieve him of it).

We hike ourselves up onto a stool and more or less collapse onto the bar, head slumped on folded arms, vaguely expecting Irwin the barman to bring us a coffee as he sometimes does when we've been up all night. Today, however, Irwin doesn't bring coffee. He brings news.

Close-up on his belt buckle as it moves toward us along the bar and comes to a halt a few inches from our nose.

"Deena got hers."

We sit up straight. As in the first scene, we see our face in the mirror behind the bar. Surrounded by blond-and-black hair, its features are frozen; no question marks light up our eyes.

"I just told Liz and she's mad as hell. Serves the little bitch right, though. You girls *know* you're not s'posed to see your johns on the side. You *know* it. It's for your own sake, Jesus Christ. But she couldn't resist the idea of makin' some extra dough, so she followed this guy up to his place. After rapin' her with a broken bottle or somethin', he strangled her and tossed her out the window. Strokaluck, the cop who found her (he's a regular here), came and told me, quiet-like, while she was bein' hauled off to the morgue. *Native Female, Unidentified* we decided to call her. I can't be*lieve* you guys. You, too, Nita. I know you been forkin' out to that Irish lush o' yours. Those guys can be dangerous, man. That's what I'm here for, to protect you, not just to spy on you or take my cut . . . You're not careful, you'll end up like Deena, a naked corpse in the gutter."

Our motionless face in the mirror gradually turns into a black mask with huge eyeholes and a grinning, gaping mouth hole.

CUT to later that morning, a coffee shop a couple of doors down Saint Catherine Street. Sitting in front of a cup of untouched coffee, Awinita stares at a fleck of gold in the Formica table. Declan squeezes both her hands in his.

"Jesus Christ, Nita. Holy Moses. Oh, shit. Deena's dead? Holy shit, I can't believe it. Baby, we gotta get you *outta* that dump. And I mean *now*, before you have our child. We just can't take the risk, Nita. Deena strangled, Jesus, I can't believe it. Dja know her family?"

"How could I? I'm Cree, she Mohawk. Our reserves are days apart."

"Okay, okay! Don't look at me like I'm an idiot! I got enough women in my life look at me that way . . . You listening to me, Nita?"

". . . Yeah."

Declan checks to make sure no waitresses are in sight before releasing her hands and taking a swig from the flask in his jacket pocket.

"Well, you better be listening. Once we're married, I want this talkin' back to stop, that clear?"

Silence.

"You should get off the game, Nita, find some other line o' work. I mean, look what happened to poor Deena, Jesus."

Close-up on our limp, still hands and, next to them, the gold fleck in the Formica table. Hold this image for a few long seconds.

CUT to the cruddy little bedroom above the bar, that same evening. After setting ten dollars on the table under the window, our new client starts to undress. He's a tall, flint-haired, business-suited anglophone in his midfifties. Gold watch, gold tiepin (the kind of elegance you and I, Milo, have always heartily despised).

"My name's Don," he announces, approaching us with a bobbing erection. "What's yours, my lovely?"

CUT to a few minutes later: the man's face in the throes of orgasm.

Silence.

Still later, lying next to us in bed, Don strokes our large round tummy.

"So has this baby got a dad, Nita?"

"Not mucha one."

"When are you due?"

"Coupla monts, I tink."

"Pregnancy going all right?"

"Wha? Yeah, sure. No problem."

"What will you do with the child once it's born? Will you raise it yourself?"

"Nah . . . I give it up for adoption."

"And then?"

"Den what?"

"Yes, then what?"

". . ."

"What will you do next, my lovely?"

"Keep on workin', I guess."

"Wouldn't you like to earn more money than you do here?"

"Sure."

"Wouldn't you like to buy yourself some pretty clothes? Be able to go to the hairdresser's every now and then?"

". . ."

"Look at me, Nita."

We look into his eyes.

"Can you kiss me, Nita?"

"Nah . . . I don't do kisses."

"Look at me, sweetheart. Can you kiss me on the lips? Can you?"

Very slowly, we move toward the well-shaven face of the gray-haired asshole stranger of a white American businessman. Extreme close-up on the crow's feet at the corner of his left eye.

"Ah . . . that was marvelous. Know what I think, Nita? I think you should be working in a classier place than this one. Don't you agree? . . . Do you trust me, Nita? Just say the word and I'll give you a room of your own in my penthouse. You'll earn much better money and be able to buy everything your heart desires."

Awinita reaches out her hands to herself in a gesture of complete trust.

"Tell me, my lovely, will you come to me as soon as you've had your baby?"

"Okay."

"Oh, Nita! You make me so happy! Give me another kiss, my darling, to seal the agreement between us."

Giving in to the fatigue, the heroin, the hope, and the sense of being a little girl again, we sink into the man's arms and allow him to smother our face, neck, swollen breasts and stomach with kisses.

Trees, waving conspiratorially. Each leaf clear-cut and brightly beautiful. The form of a face appears in their midst. At first it frowns. Then it smiles.

"Yes," we say. "Yes. Yes. Yes. Yes. Yes. Get me out of here, Don. Yes."

HOW YOU DOING, Astuto? The machine grinds on to the best of its ability, *ʒingʒing kerplunk*. Cogs spin and whir, the projector projects, the connector connects, generations criss and cross, and we begin to sense that before long the whole kit and caboodle will be over. I've always been impressed by the fact that human beings are hardwired to respond emotionally to stories. Unless you bore them stiff with stuff like *Last Year at Marienbad*, they'll start feeling moved about two-thirds of the way through any book or movie. We're well past the two-thirds point now; I'd say we're at about nine-tenths.

Hey, babe. We've been working all night. Look! Sky's changing from dark gray to light gray. What else is new? It's November in the city of Montreal. Sun's coming up. So to speak. Sun's not moving; Earth is moving. Before you know it, the nurses will be barging in with breakfast. Jesus, Milo, you must be starving! Me? No, no, I don't get hungry. Except for sex, of course. Here . . . gimme a kiss . . . *Oh*, as Don would say . . . *that was marvelous!*

Astuto, I'm very tired all of a sudden. Think I'll lie down myself, if you don't mind. Nah, no need to move over, I don't take up any room . . . just need to rest for a while.

· · · · ·

X

BICHO FALSO

Literally, false animal. Synonymous with cunning or crafty—always a compliment for a capoeirista.

Milo, 1990–2005

EUGÉNIO BECAME YOUR son, Astuto. I mean, what could be more logical than for an Irish-Quebecker-Cree bastard like yourself to have an Afro-Caribbean son? He was your child even if you couldn't adopt him legally, and you took far better care of him than you did of yourself.

Your inquiries had brought you precious little information about his mother. However, the thumbnail sketch reluctantly provided by the police—teenager, prostitute, dead—was more than enough. You loved the boy with a vengeance. Sought and found pretexts to travel to Brazil as often as possible, accepting any and every job that could take you there, including scripting tourist trash on the beaches of Arraial d'Ajuda or Porto Seguro. The rest of the time you learned Portuguese, kept up with Eugénio's school reports, sent money to his foster mother, and regularly requested photos of the child in exchange.

Strange as it may seem, Eugénio sewed your ragtag life together. You'd soon be fifty, Milo, darling. Your wild and gorgeous energy had begun to wane, but you could feel it rising in your son.

What your muscles lost, his gained. And your black holes were fewer and farther between, because the thought of Eugénio kept you going.

Flash scenes from those years: Milo and Eugénio, both wearing white pants, walking and talking together in the favela of Saens Peña. Laughing. Practicing capoeira together at the Senzala Academy. Classes were held way up at the top of the small and shabby Olympico Club in Copacabana, with its rehearsal room built around the naked rock of a tiny mountain. The boy's eyes shine as he watches his Canadian protector kick-spin and feint.

For me, those were the halcyon years. Our film *Science and Sorcery* won a prize, and my career skyrocketed—suddenly I was being solicited and feted left and right. I admit I enjoyed that brief stint as a celebrity; never would this misfit Jewish kid from Buenos Aires have imagined he'd one day be jetting business class from Sundance to Berlin and from Venice to Locarno, drinking champagne, smoking Cuban cigars and watching his bank account grow fat. Though our paths crossed less often, whenever we did meet our love was there at once, as rich as on day one. We still fucked like gods (not Yahweh, not Allah, not Our Father Almighty—God forbid!—but the horniest pagan deities of ancient Greece).

Slow down the flashing. Halt in the year 2005.

A SCENE WITH Milo and Paul in the shower together (sorry, I can't resist doing this just once). Paul, having been wined and dined at a dozen film festivals in the past year, may perhaps have acquired a tiny bit of a potbelly, but we don't need to insist on that. After three decades of loving, their bodies are still in full trust and lust. They soap each other's cock and crack, kiss beneath the hot sprinkle, mix saliva and water on their lips and tongues, turn to massage each other's shoulders and lower back.

"Been too long since we worked together, baby," murmurs Paul.

As they fuck, the camera will take an acute interest in patterns of steam and droplets on the shower stall's glass wall.

"I got an idea," says Milo a few moments later, turning off the taps. "We should do a film about capoeira in de favelas. Eugénio could star in it; he's almost fifteen now, you know. De kid's incredible."

"Nah . . . Capoeira's everywhere these days. Video games, cartoons, you name it. Even Catwoman does capoeira, for Christ's sake! You know? I mean, it's a complete cliché."

The two men towel each other down in the spacious marble bathroom of Paul's hotel suite. (We don't need to know what city the hotel is in. Could be Miami, L.A . . .)

"No, not dat," says Milo. "A political document, you know? Capoeiristas used to be black kids who picked fights. It was always about delinquency and disorder, rebellion and resistance. De film could start out wit de black slaves in Brazil, how dey revived de music from all over de African continent and mixed it up wit Indian rhydms. For dem de dance was a *weapon*, man, for dem it was a *language*. Dose slaveowners scattered families and mixed different tribes togeder to keep people from talkin' to each oder, but deir bodies still could talk. Deir bodies still could understand each oder."

"Like ours."

"Eugénio could be de young hero. He's taller dan me now! You wouldn't recognize him, man!"

"Actually, Milo, it's not unusual for children to grow between the ages of four and fourteen. And, uh . . . I hate to point out the obvious, but height is not my sole criterion for hiring actors."

"Okay, I know you tink I'm biased cause I'm his godfader . . . but come see for yourself, it'll take you tree seconds to see I'm right. He's got his green belt already, he's a phenomenon! I swear he could do it. If you're not sure, do a screen test. We'd write de script togeder. Tree monts workin' on location in Rio. Hey, man, it'd be a ball."

"Three months? Sure, I think I can easily fit that into the spring of . . . say, 2020."

Having donned identical beige bathrobes, the two men are now seated at a low glass table in the suite's drawing room, sipping Irish whisky neat.

"Do a screen test," Milo insists. "You can find time for dat, can't you, you stingy Jew?"

I shouldn't have laughed, shouldn't have listened to you, should never have gone back to Rio with you, Astuto. Big mistake.

CUT to the practice room at Copa's Olympico Club. We'll set up the camera in the same corner as the musicians. *Toque* is established. *Roda* forms. *Gingas* get going. Under the direction of their *mestre*, dark-skinned teenagers in white pants go through a formal series of kicks, twists, leaps and swivels, jiving constantly to the rhythm, constantly to the song, their left arms regularly moving up to protect their faces. Eugénio stands out among them; so swift and supple that he seems weightless. Paul and Milo watch from the far end of the room, Milo taking notes, Paul doing nothing, stunned by the kid's grace.

CUT to early the next morning: Eugénio performing alone on the beach at Copacabana, Paul recording his spectacular whirls and leaps and somersaults in the air. (I like the fact that we're ending the film as we began it— with a man cutting capers at water's edge.) Close-up on Milo's face as he plays atabaque to accompany his son. For the first time since he was a baby in the hospital half a century ago, his eyes are moist with tears.

A studio in Gloria. Paul simultaneously shooting Eugénio and giving him instructions that Milo, when necessary, translates into Portuguese: *Terrific . . . Could you just, like, walk across the room? Good, great . . . Now, turn around . . . Smile at someone beyond my left shoulder . . . Yes. Terrific smile, thank you . . . Now if I give you something to read for a sound test—anything at all, here, take this newspaper—would you mind reading me the beginning of an article, any article? Do you understand? Can you ask him to read something for us, Milo?*

Eugénio kept glancing over at you uncertainly, and because you kept warmly nodding your encouragement, he continued to obey me despite his growing discomfort. I was uncomfortable, too. I don't know why I didn't listen to my instinct and put an end to the situation as soon as I grasped its overtones (i.e., within about two minutes), but I didn't. For your sake, Milo, both Eugénio and I forced ourselves to go on with the screen test, which therefore lasted the usual three-quarters of an hour.

Eugénio obeyed, but I could tell that he hated taking orders from a well-dressed, balding (and, okay, slightly potbellied) white man. The scene must have reminded him of etchings on the theme of slavery from his history books at school. You, the boy adored—no problem there. He'd known you forever, your skin was brownish if not black, and like him you'd grown up poor. Moreover, you were an authority not only on capoeira, but on every other important subject under the sun . . . Rap! Crack! Soccer!

I, on the other hand, was white and wealthy. Unlike you, who had to keep forcing jobs in Brazil to materialize, I could come and go as I pleased, fly into Rio and fly out again, choose the young man I wanted to elevate and leave the others behind in their muck and misery. In other words, Milo, I was the enemy.

But that's not all . . . I think Eugénio's favela friends must have seen you and me in Centro together, holding hands or . . . touching. You know . . . the way we can't help touching when we're together. They must have told him you were queer . . . made fun of you, done a grotesque imitation of the two of us . . . taunted him for having a fairy godfather. Yeah, the more I think about it, the more certain I am that Eugénio was already tense and angry when he arrived at the studio that afternoon. Furious with me for having devirilized you in his eyes—and, worse, in the eyes of his buddies . . . CUT.

CUT, goddamn it.

THAT EVENING AFTER the screen test, you went up to Saens Peña. You warned me you'd be back late, Eugénio's mother having invited you over for dinner . . . And as for me . . . Hmm, I've never told you what happened, have I?

The Café do Forte, part of the military fort built on the promontory between Ipanema and Copacabana, is a chic, blue-and-white-tiled joint with marble tables. All but one of the sandwiches on the menu are named after famous Brazilian writers and statesmen. Paul Schwarz orders the one called the "Statue of Drummond," because he finds it hilarious for a sandwich to be named after a statue. Pink-suited and preoccupied, a frown digging deep furrows into the broad, golden expanse of his forehead (okay, we'll rewrite that later), he eats his solitary supper, wipes his lips with a linen napkin, and lights a cigar. The café is about to close, waiters are pressing him to leave, so he swallows the last of his brandy, pays for his meal with a credit card and heads back along the promontory. It's the month of November, the sky is already pitch-black at eight P.M. (well, maybe there was a moon; tell you the truth I don't remember) and Copacabana's long, gorgeous curve of beach

is invisible. The walkway is studded at regular intervals with can-
nons, which Paul can't help seeing as black, metallic cocks jutting
out from between two black, metallic testicles for the purpose of
ejecting black, metallic projectiles that will sow death and destruction . . . He's always been depressed by the way men (not just
straight men) deny their vulnerability by hardening their bodies
and turning them into weapons.

No, scrap that. Can't use the Forte de Copacabana scene. It
would be our first departure from this film's guiding principle—
always follow one of the three main protagonists.

Hmm.

You don't know what happened, do you, Astuto? Eh, my love?
And if you don't know, I'm afraid I can't help you, because whatever happened it killed me and we haven't been able to give each
other new information since.

Was Eugénio among them? He told the police he wasn't, but
you'll never know for sure. Did his pals claim to be selling sex
or drugs? I handed them my wallet at once. Did Eugénio offer
to sleep with me, to sell me his body? Did his friends ask for my
credit card numbers or did they ask how much I'd pay them to sod-
omize me? I handed them my wallet at once. Was I called names,
mocked, humiliated, slapped, jostled and raped before I died, or
did they kill me right off the bat? Did Eugénio sneak up on me
from behind and stick a gun in my back the way the British soldier
did to your grandpa Neil on Saint Stephen's Green in 1916? Did
he pull the trigger, or did one of the other kids? Did anyone hear
the gunshot? I doubt it. Remember how we used to tense up every
time we'd hear loud retorts coming from the favelas? And someone told us it was fireworks. In Rio, loud explosions mean fun and
games; M16 assault rifles are quick and quiet. Did I put up a fight,
instantly collapse in a heap like Neil's cousin Thom, a scarlet stain

gradually spreading on the back of my pink suit? I handed them my wallet at once.

It doesn't much matter, Milo marvel. It's up to you. All the words are yours, anyhow. All the voices have been yours since the beginning. They've always been your consolation and your salvation. Whispering tales in your ear as you waited in the closets of your childhood. Making up dialogue as you watched TV movies in the living room at night. Whistling in the dark . . .

. . . . .

Neil, 1939

What shall I do with this absurdity—
O heart, O troubled heart—this caricature,
Decrepit age that has been tied to me
As to a dog's tail?

A dark, late-December afternoon, up in Neil's study. Forehead propped on left hand, baby finger holding in place the spectacles, which, if left to themselves, tend to slide down his nose, Neil is committing to memory what he considers to be William Butler Yeats's greatest poem, "The Tower." The bard died nearly a year ago, and Neil is still in mourning for him. He peruses his poems and plays, relives their momentous encounter at Ballylee, and tries to believe, appearances notwithstanding, that he, Neil Kerrigan *alias* Neil Noirlac, will one day make his literary mark.

The poem conveys both Yeats's despair at being no longer young and raunchy, and his resolve never to espouse the easy

virtues championed by society. He says that despite the encroach-
ments of old age, he'll remain true to his wild, poetic visions . . .
until they, too, are dissolved by time and death. When he wrote
"The Tower" in 1926, Willie had barely crested sixty. Neil himself is only forty-seven, but having just learned that he is to become a father for the twelfth time and a grandfather for the first
(Marie-Thérèse, who married Régis at age seventeen last summer,
informed her parents this morning, if not joyfully at least firmly,
that they were expecting a baby next June), he feels decrepit age
tied to him, too, as to a dog's tail. *When will my life begin?* he moans
in petto. *Is it worse to have known grandeur and lost it, like Willie
Yeats, or, like me, never to have known it at all?*

Marie-Jeanne's voice comes lilting up the stairs: "Neil! Are you
coming down, my love? It's going on five o'clock, Christmas dinner is almost ready and you haven't yet chopped the firewood!"

CUT to Neil entering the woodshed in which he used to experience excruciating literary frustration, before he was given a room
of his own in which to experience it. He chops. And chops. And
chops. He now has the chopping-wood part of being Tolstoy down
to a fine art.

CUT to the Noirlac dining room, early evening. Fire crackling
in the fireplace, candlesticks, mistletoe, etc. Assembled around the
table is the family *au complet*: children of all ages (we won't waste
time giving them names the spectators would instantly forget) and
four adults (including young Régis, who has brought a bottle of
wine to celebrate their pregnancy announcement), to say nothing
of the two *new* humans in the making, as yet invisible . . . To contemplate the amount of life he has engendered even as he was busy
writing no books makes Neil faintly nauseated. (And he can't even
blame the former for the latter, Tolstoy having fathered thirteen
children.)

When all are silent, Marie-Jeanne lights the central candle of the Advent wreath.

"It's your turn to say grace, Neil, darling."

"*God is good and God is great, grub is ready, time we ate . . .* Sorry, just joking. We are gathered together this evening to . . . to celebrate . . . the birth of . . . of . . ."

The image of yet *another* baby coming into the world, even if it is the Son of God, all but makes him gag.

"Santa Claus," pipes up Declan, already a mischief-maker at twelve.

"Declan!" says Marie-Thérèse. "Hold your tongue, that's blasphemy! You'll go straight to Hell!"

"Go on, darling . . ." Marie-Jeanne urges Neil.

"I'd like for everyone to close their eyes, and observe one minute of silence for the European continent, again in the throes of a terrible war."

"Bang, bang!" says a younger boy.

"*Boom!*" says an older one.

"It's not the right moment, Neil," Marie-Jeanne admonishes him gently. "Please. Christmas dinner with your children is not a good time to talk about war."

Neil raises his voice: "You're right, Marie-Jeanne. There are plenty of other things I could talk about. Like how come *Finnegans Wake* is deemed a masterpiece whereas my own opus of mixed languages, written twenty-five years earlier, bit the dust. Or how come the Unionists won by an overwhelming majority in Ulster, obliterating all hope of a merger between Northern Ireland and the Irish Free State. Or how come . . ."

"Amen," says Marie-Jeanne, cutting him off.

Echoed by Marie-Thérèse and Régis in quick succession, her *Amen* goes hop-skipping around the table until all mouths have

uttered it, either in French or in English, except for the very small-est mouth, which has learned no language yet.

"Would you like to cut the turkey?" says Marie-Jeanne, holding her annoyance in.

And the dinner commences as best it can. Bowls of vegetables circulate, but Christmas cheer does not.

CUT to an hour or so later. Close-up on the nearly empty bottle of wine. Only the two men have been drinking, and, neither being accustomed to alcohol, both are feeling its effects: Régis is more outspoken than usual and Neil has grown downright boorish.

"If we're not careful, the foreigners will take over all our land, and I mean all of it! You're a big reader, Mr. Noirlac, but I bet you haven't read *Menaud Maître-Draveur*, by Félix-Antoine Savard? That's exactly what's gonna happen around here! Those Englishmen, they do as they please! They decide what they want and they take what they want and they do exactly what they want!"

"That's right," mutters Neil. "The Brits are foreigners here, whereas the French go *way* back, don't they? There was *no one* here before they came, was there? Yes, I skimmed through that racist, colonialist, repetitive piece of shite by Savard, and could not help remarking that the word *Indian* was mentioned nowhere in it, not even once . . . whereas the word *Quebec* is itself an In-dian word! Oh, Régis, I'm so tired of this cant! I've been through it before! Pearse and Connolly were using the self-same patriotic drivel back in 1914, before you were so much as a glimmer in your daddy's eye! *Hey, we stole this land first!*: a one-sentence summary of the French Canadian nationalist movement. Same thing in Ire-land, go back far enough."

"Please don't talk to my husband in that tone of voice," says Marie-Thérèse. "The difference is that the Indians didn't do any *work* on the land! We took wild forestland and tamed it by the sweat of our brow, and we're not gonna let a bunch of damned Englishmen come and steal the fruits of our hard labor!"

"Be careful, Marie-Thérèse," says Marie-Jeanne. "When you say damned Englishmen, you're also talking about your own brothers. Don't forget that! Who knows? Maybe someday they'll be head of the Hudson's Bay Company!"

"My brothers, run an enterprise? With the education our father gave them? Don't make me laugh! . . . They're fully qualified for . . . nothing at all! And I mean nothing! Even here on the property they never lift a finger to help. I don't know what they'll be when they grow up, Mommy, but they won't be big bosses, that's for sure. You can burn me at the stake if I'm wrong."

"Yeah, let's burn her at the stake!" says Declan. "That used to be a witch's test: if you're a witch you won't burn. Come on, tie yourself to the stake, you ol' witch, you got nothin' to fear!"

"Declan, that's enough out of you," says Marie-Jeanne. "I'll ask you not to open your mouth between now and the end of the meal."

"If I can't open my mouth I can't eat," Declan says, shoving back his chair. "You guys have spoiled my appetite with all your quarreling. I'm sick of this family."

"Why don't you run away?" suggests an older brother.

"Best idea I heard in weeks."

"Mommy! Mommy!" a younger sister pipes up. "Declan's gonna run away from home!"

Régis gets to his feet, raises his wineglass, and loudly recites the opening paragraph of Father Savard's novel: "*Having drawn a map of the new continent, from Gaspé to Montreal and from Saint-Jean-d'Iberville to Ungava, we declared: here, everything we have brought with us . . .*"

Rising in turn, Neil drowns out his son-in-law's schoolboy recitation with his Irish roar, booming out a verse from "The Tower":

I leave both faith and pride
To young upstanding men
Climbing up the mountain-side,
That under bursting dawn
They may drop a fly . . .

Under pressure to prove to his young wife that her father's virility won't cause his own to falter, Régis raises his voice. Unfortunately, it gets higher instead of louder, and he succeeds only in squeaking: "*. . . our religion, our language, our virtues and even our defects will henceforth be considered sacred and intangible, and must remain so to the end of time.*"

Simultaneously, Neil concludes:

> *"Being of that metal made*
> *Till it was broken by*
> *This sedentary trade.*

. . . Broken!" he adds. "D'ye hear that, all of ye? The sedentary trade of poetry can *break* the metal of which young men are made. Smash it to *pieces!*"

"Merry Christmas, everybody!" pleads one of the younger girls, trying to fix the fiasco.

At this Marie-Jeanne, both arms clutched round her belly, collapses sobbing on the table.

CUT to the smoldering embers of the fire. The house is still; everyone has gone off to bed except Neil and Régis, the two men whose wives are expecting babies. If only subliminally, both are aware that this fact was not for nothing in the flare-up between them over dinner. Another bottle has been found, and they are well into it. Throughout the following dialogue, the camera will stay on the fire grate.

"Félix-Antoine Savard does have a certain flair, I grant you that," says Neil, puffing on his pipe.

"It sound quite nice," reciprocates Régis, "zis poem de . . . *comment* . . . how you say his name ees? Keats?"

"No, not Keats. Keats is a British poet. Yeats, William Butler Yeats. An Irishman. The greatest poet since Shakespeare. He died last year. It kills me that he died."

"I'm sorry. He was your friend?"

"Yes. Yes, he was my friend . . . in another life. He's the one who told me to come to Canada."

"Really. To break metal with poetry, zat is quite strong."

"He desperately wanted to believe that because he felt his poetic gift waning as he aged and it scared him horribly. Not only his gift but . . . the rest as well. The other kinds of . . . potency."

"Wid women?"

"Yes, with women. He'd always felt that physical love and poetic inspiration were connected in him. To lose one was to lose the other . . ."

"Estonishing!"

Neil begins to laugh:

"In 1933, a few years after he wrote that poem, he underwent an operation at the hands of a famous London specialist."

Trying to repress a giggle, Régis winds up snorting.

"No! Operate on . . . down dere?"

"A surgeon by the name of Haire, himself a homosexual, incidentally, who offered men what he called the Steinach rejuvenation operation, to restore all their powers."

Now very drunk, the two men sit there laughing helplessly together.

"And did it work?" pants Régis.

"Halfway," answers Neil when he can speak. "Yes, he was delighted with the result for half of his problems, and claimed he'd been given a second puberty."

"Which half?" shrieks Régis.

"Well," says Neil, struggling to sober up and speak his answer straight, "in the five years that remained to him to live, he managed to . . . write a few more good poems!"

The fire's last ember fades and dies.

BLACKOUT.

. . . . .

Awinita, March 1952

WELL, ASTUTO, WE'VE got a fair amount of whittling down to do, but on the whole I'm proud of us. The Noirlac-Schwarz team is still going strong. Structure's there, solid, I can feel it. Just one more little piece to fit into the puzzle.

Yeah, sure, I told you we'd change the name. No problem. Maybe we could use your real name. Your Cree name, which no one in the world would recognize. Has it come back to you in the meantime? . . .

IN HER RARE moments of lucidity between fixes, Awinita plans her getaway down to the last detail. She'll pay Liz back what she owes her. Overall, the woman has been kind to her, and Awinita is loath to give whites the least justification for bad-mouthing Indians.

In the cruddy little bedroom above the bar, Don hands her an advance of two hundred dollars and flashes his white-toothed smile at her.

"Don't spend it all in one place! You'll see, baby. You'll be dealing with important people from now on. Wealthy businessmen, members of Parliament, police chiefs and the like. No more of this riffraff you've been putting up with. You're of age, aren't you, Nita? Tell me the truth. How old are you?"

"Soon twenny."

"Ouch! Nineteen going on twenty-one, eh?"

"But I los' my papers."

"Well, that's no sweat, we'll make you new ones. We should change your name, too, while we're at it. Find you a nice, sexy, new one. Nita's a bit too . . . *neat*, know what I mean? How 'bout . . . er . . . Zsa Zsa, like Zsa Zsa Gabor? Zsa Zsa! You like that?"

"Okay wit me."

"Kiss me, gorgeous. Ahhhh . . . with a new hairdo, a bit of lipstick, a slinky gold lamé dress and spike-heeled sandals, you'll knock 'em out, believe you me!"

"Need some time to get back into shape, after de baby."

"Sure you'll need time. 'Course you'll need time. Er . . . how long do you think? Coupla days?"

"Coupla weeks, more like it."

"Ha! Acting the princess already, are we? Well, we'll cross that bridge when we come to it. Main thing is to have your suitcase all ready and packed when you leave for the hospital, so my chauffeur can pick you up when you're done. An express delivery, let's hope! You started packing yet?"

"Yeah. Got a bag ready. Not much stuff."

"Good. Best to forget your old life anyhow, start the new one from scratch. From now on, you're twenty-one and your name is Zsa Zsa. Right, Zsa Zsa?"

"I guess."

Don undoes his belt buckle. "Okay, glad we see eye to eye on that. Now, let me give you another little course of instruction in what men like most.

Little rippling colored curves, the petals of a pink flower. Mouths opening and closing, either in pain or exhaustion. Eyes blinking very rapidly. This up-and-down motion throughout, this vacillation . . .

Weighed down by our enormous stomach, we walk slowly up Saint Laurent Boulevard from Saint Catherine Street. About half-way home, we turn into a little five-and-ten. Using one of the crisp new twenty-dollar bills we just received from Don, we purchase a dozen small bottles of nail polish in different hues.

CUT to the sleazy apartment on the Plateau Mont-Royal: the other girls crow with delight as Awinita distributes her tiny gifts.

"Just sumpin' to remember me by."

"Wow!" Xandra, the new girl, kisses her. "You're the one who's getting married, baby! *We* should be giving *you* presents!"

"Thanks, Nita." Lorraine grins at her. "You know where to reach me if you need me, eh?"

Alison, the young Haitian girl, weighing twenty pounds less than when we last saw her and sporting purple rings beneath her eyes, weaves her cokey way down the corridor, brandishing her new bottle of nail polish and singing a Creole lullaby.

Liz, again in her yellow pantsuit, takes the envelope of money from our hands and slips it into her belt. Then, stubbing out her cigarette, she comes around the table to give us a hug.

"Congratulations, Nita. I hear you and the Irishman are getting hitched! I just hope you're not makin' a mistake, leavin' here."

"Nah."

"I mean, at least this place is safe, right? At least you've got some understanding here."

". . ."

"You sure about this guy? 'Cause once you're out, you're out, eh? Your bed'll be gone in a jiff. You know that, don't you?"

"Sure, Liz."

"Well, it's your funeral!"

Sitting down again, Liz carefully counts the money into her cashbox. Then she nods and Awinita leaves the room.

CUT to Awinita lying on her back on the floor, hands on ballooning belly. Sound track: Billie Holiday's "God Bless the Child."

We're at the bottom of a gully. A rope is tossed down to us from a cliff top, and people yell, Just pull! You can make it! We'll hold you! *We use all our strength to hoist ourselves up, but then*—Sorry, we weren't able to!—*they let go of the rope and we go tumbling backward . . . A moment later, though, our fall turns into flight. We float. We soar.*

Getting clumsily to her feet, Awinita returns to the kitchen and looks straight at Liz.

"Do me a favor?"

"All depends!"

"Can ya write sumpin' down for me?"

"Sure, I guess so. Long as it's not the Bible!" Liz reaches across the table for pen and paper.

"Shoot."

"I, Declan Noirlac . . ."

"Whoa, whoa! How do you spell that?"

"You have to help me wit the words. Make 'em sound strong, you know?"

CUT to the coffee shop on Saint Catherine. Declan and Awinita are in the same booth as on the day of Deena's murder. As Declan reads the pact out loud, the camera slides from one to the other, filming the fear in their faces.

"I the undersigned, Declan Noirlac, father of the child soon to be born to Miss Awinita Johnson, do hereby solemnly swear to take care of said child, see to its physical and emotional needs, and pay for its education, until such a time as its mother finds herself in a position to return and take up her share of these responsibilities. Montreal, on this the twenty-eighth day of March, in the year of Our Lord, 1952. Signed, et cetera. Wow!"

"Can you sign it, Mister Cleaning-Fluid?"

"Sure, Nita. Sure, I'll sign it. I told you I'd pull my weight as a da, now, didn't I?"

"Told me lotsa stuff."

"What I don't get is *why*. What's it for? You goin' somewhere?"

"I dunno. Just . . . you know, case I die havin' de kid, or whatever."

Declan glances at the page: "Well, if you die you won't be able to . . . return and take up your share of these responsibilities, now, will ya?"

"Or if I get sick or sumpin'. Ya never know. Just so's I don't lose sight of dis baby like I did de oder one."

"Yeah, yeah, okay, I understand. There."

Though rather green about the gills, Declan signs.

"Dere's two copies. One for you an' one for me."

"There you go!"

Close-up on his hands, shaking badly as they sign . . . (we recognize the hands that left little Milo at the hospital, near the beginning of the film). Suddenly Declan rises and bolts for the men's room.

Awinita folds up her copy of the contract and slips it into her purse. She sits there, nine months pregnant, not moving, her expression as inscrutable as always.

She is ready.

There was
a word
in the darkness.
Tiny. Unknown.

It hammered in the darkness.
It hammered
on the water's plinth.

From the depths of time
it hammered.
On the wall.

A word.
In the darkness.
Calling me.

—Eugénio de Andrade

· · · · ·

Author's Note

THE CAPOEIRA DEFINITIONS used in chapter openings are taken from Cécile Bennegent, *Capoeira: ou l'art de lutter en dansant* (Budo Éditions, 2006) and Nestor Capoeira, *Le petit manuel de capoeira* (Budo Éditions, 2003). The title *Black Dance*, originally that of a work by Swiss painter Guy Oberson, was borrowed with the artist's kind permission.